RAYMOND BAILEY

THE CHRONICLES OF
SIMON

DEDICATION

To My Mother who spent many hours reading to me and taught me education was decisive in life's survival.

QUOTE

Faith consists in believing when it is beyond the power of reason to believe and people live their lives in an unreal manor, like a fantasy, called religion.

Voltaire, writer and satirist

CONTENTS

BOOK 1

BOOK 2

BOOK 3

BOOK 4

PROLOGUE

Around 30AD by consequence of fate and a miracle, a young Samarian healer traveling in pursuit of knowledge emerges through time without aging. In search for answers, traveling in various guises, he encounters life's tumultuous struggles to survive.

BOOK 1

CHAPTER 1

Melbourne to Buzios, Part One

The flight left Melbourne, Australia, around 6 p.m. local time and landed in Auckland, New Zealand, just under three hours later and re-fueled. Shortly after take-off, cheese and a fresh fruit plate were served along with a newly discovered California Chardonnay from the Joseph Phelps Vineyard. Observing the world clocks above the electronic route map, it was noon the following day in Santiago, Chile, where a stay was planned for approximately twelve hours. A pre-arranged meeting with two gentlemen from Valparaiso was established at a hotel nearby.

Drinking my last mouthful of the crisp white wine Simon hastened to the bathroom to relieve himself and brush his teeth. Putting on blue silk pajamas he slid into the oversized bed. As he closed his eyes one word was spoken, "lights," and then there was darkness, making himself comfortable and gradually falling into a deep sleep, visualized the very distant past.

CHAPTER 2

The Beginning

Born in Gitta, a small town in Samaria, I was raised by my mother. Her name was Sahba. My father, a stonemason, suffered injuries from a fall and subsequently died when I was of the age of two. My given name is Simon and my father's family name is Magus.

The exact time of my birth was during the flowering of the cyclamen plant around the third full moon, at the end of winter and the start of spring. Every year the first flower always magically appeared lying at the foot of my bed, and since passing the age of four, I have been able to count my years finding the first flower myself. Although for many years my mother continued this ritual, I managed to grow this plant in large clay pots by the time I had reached ten.

My childhood was not unlike any other child from a poor family with limited teachings; however, my mother had healing skills and knowledge of roots, plants, berries, and other foliage. The local villagers came to her for healing ointments and potions for which she was rewarded with the town's main diet of fish, seed crop, some fruit, vegetables, materials, and labor to upkeep our home as coin was rarely seen. Throughout my youth I watched and learned her art with incredible ease whilst experimenting with other flora to develop my own potions using witch hazel, aloe vera, frankincense, ginger and turmeric.

I had passed my seventeenth year when a woman and child came by our home. Her little boy of no more than a year old was wrapped in a coarse blanket. Upon uncovering the child, we discovered he was covered in rashes, in obvious discomfort, and crying profusely. My mother was in town on an errand, so I was at home alone. Offering my sympathies, I proposed some attention until my mother returned. The woman immediately declined but at that moment the child wailed so loudly it made us both jump nervously.

"What can you do?" the woman asked in desperation.

"Firstly," I responded, "Let us remove the blanket and clothing so there is no irritation to the skin."

I produced a piece of flax linen from the built-in stone storage and laid it out flat on the wooden table. My mother had acquired this cloth in lieu of coin from a merchant for whom she had provided a service. I then fetched my iron wood extract in a clay pot from the room in which we produced our various potions and ointments. The very first lesson my mother taught me was in any treatment given by a healer that our hands must be scrubbed clean, which is what I proceeded to do.

Requesting the woman place the child on the linen cloth, I thought of applying the gel from the aloe vera leaf that my mother kept wrapped in leaves, but then thought it might be too strong for such a young child. I had experimented with a local iron wood plant that originated from Persia, as I later learnt a form of witch hazel. Boiling leaves and bark produced a mildly slimy liquid which I used from time to time for my scrapes and boils with some success. Using a ladle, I generously poured the substance over his body, then used my clean and oiled hands to gently rub it into his skin from head to toe. During this time, we endured the screaming from the child. After I was done, I informed the woman that we needed to wait. She stayed with her child whilst I walked outside, if nothing else but to relieve my ears. My mind wandered whilst I observed a goatherder and his flock of goats. Soom after, I espied my mother returning from the town.

Grasping my hand, my mother greeted me with her usual fondness. Upon hearing the crying coming from inside, she frowned and looked at me. I quickly explained the circumstances. Her smile turned to annoyance and she commenced to chastise me for experimenting with my solution on such a young child. We entered the house, noticing the screaming had subdued to sobbing. I stood back whilst my mother introduced herself before she examined the child. She turned her head requesting my presence, asking me to look at the rash and tell her if I noticed any visual change compared to my first observation. I noticed the rash had lost its deep redness and the sores had reduced in size. My mother smiled as did the woman, who proceeded to thank us profusely as she offered us coin—Roman coin!

My mother requested the woman to bring her child back in the morning for another bath in the solution and to put her finest cloth on the child overnight, though preferably none at all. After she departed, we stared at the five coins not knowing its full value at all, then looking at each other and suddenly bursting into laughter.

The treatment continued, and after thirty days the child's skin was smooth and normal. The woman, whose name was Sapphira, could not thank us enough and declared that she would find a way to repay our kindness.

Summer turned to a cold winter when one evening we heard a loud knock from our front door. Upon opening, there stood a Roman soldier in all his glory. He spoke to me in my language and requested entrance.

"My name is Cassius Quintus Gallus, centurion in the northern army of Tiberius Caesar, Emperor of Rome, and I have come to pay my gratitude for healing my child," he announced. Standing motionless for a moment stunned by his appearance, I gestured for him to enter.

My mother appeared from our work room. Cleaning her hands on her work cloth, she smiled and offered the soldier a chair. "What can we do for you, Sir?" she asked.

"I have come to give thanks to this young man," he said, "And offer you meat, fruit, wine and my gratitude. These things will be brought to your home in the morning," he continued.

At that point, he stood up to take his leave, looked me in the eye with a faint smile, opened the door, and was gone.

The next morning, as promised, two young men—probably in the service of the Roman soldier—arrived with a half carcass of lamb, two full sacks of food, and a flagon of red wine. We emptied the sacks on the table, my mother and I marveling at the feast of breads, goat cheese, pomegranates, figs, olives, dates, carrots, and a cloth filled with salt.

It was in my mother's nature to share, so she asked me to call on our neighbor Jacob and bid him to visit. As I departed, I took several dates from the table and my mother smiled. I soon returned with Jacob and he too was in awe of the wealth bequeathed to us. Jacob was a potter, and a good family friend, who had helped us in the past. He was also the only one we knew who had the skills of preparing meat and pit cooking, having held previous employment in the kitchen of a wealthy merchant. He also had a large family—four children from his deceased first wife and five children with his existing companion.

After much discussion, it was agreed that Jacob would prepare a pit and season the lamb to celebrate our good fortune. The following day before dusk our two families would consume a fine dinner and count our blessings. We never had, nor did we ever again, have such a sumptuous meal of this quality together in my mother's house.

All through my youth I continued learning the craft whilst experimenting with potions and ointments of my own. Sometimes my mother would review my creations and give advice, but I mainly used to test on myself—sometimes with unpleasant results.

CHAPTER 3

Road to Jerusalem

By the time I was twenty-two years of age, through word of mouth, I had patients of my own. I treated local villagers and travelers from far distances for all manner of ailments. It was in the summer of that same year that a severe disease ravaged our town and no matter what we tried, our healing powers had no effect. Jacob, our neighbor, lost his partner and two of his children. When my mother caught the sickness, she spent nights coughing, her face red and her skin, hot. It was not long before she died, even though I tried every potion—including some with which I was still experimenting. I was stricken with such sadness.

It was during this time that a traveler came by with an infection on his arm and I immediately recognized it as a minor wound that was inflamed due to being kept unclean. During my treatment, he told me stories of a magical healer going from town to town in and around Jerusalem. I knew there must be more knowledge and remedies beyond my own and the more I thought about it, the more sense it made. My mother had passed and nothing was holding me in Gitta, even though my leaving would disappoint many of the townspeople. I finally made a decision to seek out this healer and discussed this adventure with my neighbor Jacob. Although he had little coin, he offered what he had if he could expand his pottery production using my home. If he prospered, he would put aside some of the profit to be given to me upon my return. I agreed. However, I declined his little wealth as I still had the Roman coin. I don't know if his business thrived—this remained unknown to me as I never returned.

I had made a mental note from the advice of the traveler that he had been walking for twenty-five risings of the sun. I chose set off on my journey at the beginning of the cooling season, and packed as much dried fish, bread, and raw vegetables that I could comfortably carry, along with a large water pouch and the five-silver coinage. I bid farewell to Jacob and his family and marched on my way with the sun to my left in the morning, expecting it on my right in the evening. I was surprised to see many travelers on the well-trodden carved out road, most of whom seemed to be going in the same direction as I.

The sun was setting on the 21st day when I came upon a small group of pilgrims quietly conversing amongst themselves and they looked at me with apprehension as I approached. Greetings were shared and although names were exchanged, it was a man named Peter who seemingly spoke on behalf of his companions. After some discussion and confessing my purpose for this pilgrimage Peter interrupted, grasping his staff firmly and with raised voice passionately stated his master would not entertain such vain notions. He moved quickly towards me, looked me sternly in the eyes whilst proclaiming he and those about him were his disciples, preaching the word of one God. I would do well, he continued, to be humble, listen to the teachings on the morrow, be a follower and discontinue this folly I was pursuing. They re-grouped and ignored me further as I discreetly walked away.

The next day from a distance I watched him on the hill, the man they called Jesus. Though I was too far to hear, word was passed from person to person of his preaching. I confess I did not understand much of what was related to me by various people but understood how change in the words occur from mouth to mouth. Suddenly it was all over and the crowd disbursed with bustling conversation.

It was fast becoming night on the twenty-second day. While I was sitting alone, I constructed a circle from loose stones, collected dry birchwood and some wild sage and started a small fire. As far as the eye could see there were many such fires that I assumed were fellow enquiring minds and travelers. Feeling discouraged, sorry for myself, and hungry, I stirred the wood twigs and sage, giving off a pleasant aroma. With silent movement a man had approached me and I was startled for a moment as he sat beside me.

"May I join you?" the man asked.

I looked at his kind, gentle tanned face, well-kept facial hair, and large brown eyes.

"Yes, please do, I could use the company," I said.

From under his head covered tunic he produced a half-moon shaped piece of bread, a fist size piece of goat cheese, and a pouch which I assumed was water, but soon learned it was red wine. The man broke both the bread and cheese and offered them to me with a smile. I accepted them with eagerness, offering my water in return when he spoke again. He smiled and said he could hear my stomach rumbling from far away and took pity on my situation.

"Truly?" I inquired, whilst eating the moist cheese.

He laughed softly and said in jest, "Something like that but what really drew him to me was the delightful scent of the burning sage. What is your name, where are you from, and why are you here?"

I gave what I believed to be a short version of my young life. I was aged twenty-three when my mother had passed and I continued her work as a healer. Shortly after, I heard stories from travelers of an academic appearing to the masses in and around Jerusalem so I ventured to this land to seek and learn more from a master in the art of healing.

I then realized how much I was talking, stopped immediately, and apologized. Again, he just smiled. "And what is your name," I asked.

"I have had many names, in many lands but you can call me Yeshua," he said.

From then on, and for much of the night, we spoke of many subjects—my healing experiences and research, my eagerness to travel, adventure, and desire to learn.

He spoke of people who influenced him, ancient places, history of wars, and pestilence. He also had command of many languages and although at a guess I would have said he was no older than forty, his tales and stories would have covered many lifetimes. Although I thought this, I did not question his honesty. In fact, I'm not sure why I believed every word he spoke.

After a while I put more wood and sage on the fire and we sat in silence taking in the pleasant fragrance and observing the stars in the heavens. Momentarily, he turned his head observing me, then moved closer to me. Frowning, he asked, "May I look at your hands?"

I offered them palms up and he spent the next moments caressing them, then moving closer them to the fire to study them further. I shuddered.

He came even closer and still speaking in a low tone, told me, "I do not have much time and I have been searching for a soul to bequeath my legacy. Who would have thought—you found me."

"I do not understand. I know not of what you speak," I said when I noticed he still had a firm grip of my hands.

It was then I heard distant voices calling out a name, but they were not loud enough to understand. I momentarily turned my head in the direction of the calls. I was quickly raised from the sitting position to standing whilst he continued to hold a firm grip on my hands. Our faces were barely a breath apart and he stared me in the eyes.

"Will you trust me, Simon of Gitta, will you trust me?"

I gazed at his full face absolutely motionless and murmured, "Yes." He shook me and I shouted, "Yes, and yes," even louder, though I knew not why.

Firmly interlocking his fingers with mine and telling me to do likewise, he pressed his brow to my brow.

"Remember this and my words."

Then, speaking loudly and clearly, he chanted, "As I was touched, I touch thee" repeating this over and over again in what seemed an eternity.

"As I was touched, I touch thee", repeating and screaming at the top of his voice.

I could feel the hair on my arms rise and a cold shudder down my spine when suddenly I felt a dizzy sensation. Gradually I started to release my grip, fell to the ground, when I heard him say

"I am saved, I am free"

Then I lost consciousness.

When I awoke, the sun was already high in the sky, the fire no longer aflame, and there were no signs of life. I slowly stood, moving my aching limbs whilst trying to gather my thoughts regarding the events of last evening. It made no sense and the more I thought, the more confused I became. I cleaned myself as best I could and decided to return to the village I had passed several days before.

After walking the rest of the day, taking a rest, and walking another day, it was just after dusk when I crossed a small bridge entering Capernaum and noticed an encampment of Roman soldiers that was not there when I passed several days before. Considerable activity was going on in the camp. As I continued walking, I came across a small male child who was bleeding from both knees. I approached him and asked how he came to hurt himself. He confessed he was climbing the adjacent tree when he fell to the ground. I looked around and saw a well and proceeded to draw water to moisten some dry linen produced from my satchel. Returning to the boy, I treated his grazed wounds by firstly removing the blood and then applying the aloe vera I carried.

Within moments, two soldiers appeared by my side and observed my activity with the boy. "Are you a healer?" one asked.

Annoyed when I did not immediately respond, the soldier lost patience and repeated the question in a louder, firmer tone. "Are you a healer?"

"I have knowledge of healing," I responded nervously.

"You seem juvenile, but we have need of someone to attend our centurion Primus Pilus."

Without further ado, the second soldier grabbed my arm, pulled me back up to a standing position, and forced me to walk as I looked back at the open-mouthed child. With my feet barely touching the ground, the two soldiers held my arms tightly as we approached a large tent. Once inside, I was released from their grip and saw a burly man, seated, holding a course cloth over his naked torso. It was then that I noticed much blood about him, and suspected the cloth covered a wound.

Words were exchanged between the soldiers and the centurion that I could not hear nor understood. I was gestured to approach when the centurion removed the cloth to expose a mess of tissue and blood. "You look young for a healer," he said, "And you had better know what you are doing or likely lose your head."

Nervously, I requested the soldiers to bring fresh water from the well, start a small fire, and boil half of the water. They looked at the centurion and he waved them to proceed.

From my flaxen bag I produced some yarrow flower and a bag of cloves, then looking around, I espied a small wooden table. Requesting it's use, the centurion nodded in approval. Reaching again into the bag, I grasped a smooth flat rock the size of my fist and commenced pounding the flower and cloves. During this procedure another soldier entered the tent. Looking up, I recognized this impressive figure and realized as the centurion stood immediately to attention this was his superior.

"Getting attention, Romero?" the officer asked. Then looking at me he grinned and I immediately recognized him as the soldier from my village with the sick child.

13

"Yes Sir," the centurion responded, looking at me nervously. "My men brought a healer yet I am not convinced he has the knowledge to treat us."

Once again, the officer smiled. "Don't let his youth confuse you," he said. Asking me to stand, he introduced himself. "I am General Commander Legates Legion known as Cassius Quintas Gallus and I remember you."

Almost immediately I responded, "And I you, Sir."

Before any further conversation could continue, the two low ranking soldiers returned with boiling water and a larger pot of cold water. Quickly placing the receptacles on the ground, they smartly stood to attention, clenching their right fist over their hearts. The commander instructed them to continue their tasks and obey my requests. He then abruptly left.

Placing the herbs in the pot of boiling water, I requested that one of the soldiers pour some cold water over the wound and wipe away the dirt and congealed blood with the cloth I gave them. My next request was to find the largest pot they could, fill, and boil the water whilst collecting as much clean cloth as possible. I took quite some time to clean the wound with my herb solution, which I then let dry. Meanwhile, I concentrated on boiling the cloth, rinsed, then boiled again. I added aloe vera until the plant turned mushy and I stirred vigorously. Applying some of the treated cloths to the centurion's chest. He was no longer showing the irritation he displayed when we first met. I informed him to rest and that I would return at daybreak to clean and replace the cloths. Completing my task, I requested some calm time and was shown to a cot near the entrance of the marquee.

It was not too long into my sleep when I was awoken by another low-ranking soldier and bid to follow. After one hundred paces or so we approached a very large ornate pavilion. Upon entering, I found myself in very affluent surroundings. General Cassius Quintas Gallus was seated and eating from a bowl of fruit. He addressed me. "My gratitude for the attention given to my centurion, he is feeling a lot better this morning. Please, sit, have some fruit and tell me how you found your way to my army?"

After much time, and whilst enjoying a variety of fruits and listening to my eagerness as I told of my adventures, the General sighed and continued, "On behalf of my Emperor, we are embarking on a campaign to the Asian lands and expect to return in three years, or maybe more. Under the powers bestowed upon me I am recruiting you to serve me and my senior officers in the position of healer. Three slaves will be appointed to you for whatever needs and you have until two daylights from now to prepare."

I was in shock but also knew I was unable to say or do anything to oppose him. A bivouac would be provided for me and the soldier outside would escort me to it and present the slaves to be assigned, he commanded. Prior to leaving, I enquired after the well-being of his child and wife. "They both died in the great sickness," he responded. Feeling sad, I departed and thus, began my journey of journeys.

CHAPTER 4

Return to Rome

Throughout the campaign I saw many a gruesome death, saved a few lives, improved my skills, and developed new potions. Along the way, I was introduced to unique plants such as opium poppies and used them to reduce pain, deaden the flesh, and limit movement. Henbane induces sleep and mandragora also deadens pain and controls bleeding by slowing the heartbeat.

In Assyria, I was introduced to cannabis or as the Hindu Kush Mountain people referred it as, "food of the gods" and used in their local festivals to induce trances, release curses and evil spirits. Some said it had healing powers but as yet I had not discovered it. In the recovery tents I burned the leaves that enabled the wounded a sense of calm and peace. I had obtained large quantities of the dried leaves stored in containers made from the fiber of the same plant called hemp. I also possessed much of the root and anticipated growing it at some point. I heard many stories of travelers to China, a country beyond the mountains, protected by a huge wall and a dangerous journey from which many did not return.

As the years passed and with more practice, it became clear to me that timing was always of the essence. The quicker you attended the wounded, the percentage to survive increased. Keeping the wounds clean was the biggest problem. All in all, my knowledge kept evolving and my brain was absorbing it all like a sponge. Cassius had his advisers teach me to read and write, and at the same time I developed an aptitude for other languages, which I learned from traders and captured slaves. It was the strangest thing. I would easily remember everything and seemingly had no bounds. Although reluctant at first, I also trained to defend myself, how to use weapons, and the art of warfare strategy. I never intended to be in battle, but Cassius insisted I became proficient, especially with the sword and close quarter dagger combat.

This proved to be advantageous as one day a soldier with a high fever charged through the tent for the serious wounded. He was wielding a knife in one hand and a sword in the other. With two or three good strides I was upon him, piercing his throat with a surgical knife in my left hand whilst thrusting my personal blade with my right hand into his side through the liver and heart. He was dead before he hit the ground. It was my first physical killing and despite my swift action, I felt a sickness in the pit of my stomach for taking a life. The feeling quickly passed as I felt a sharp pain. Looking down, I saw that his knife had pierced my upper body between my lower right ribs close to the outer skin.

My medical slaves under my supervision cleaned my wound internally then fused the outside with a heated blade. Feeling sore and uncomfortable, I returned to my tent, ingested a potion, and I laid down to rest. As instructed my slave returned the next morning at first light to clean and change my dressing, adding a poultice and ensuring the wound was compressed tightly. Miraculously, I was healed within ten days.

We had not seen battle for some months and dispatches from Rome carried no good news. One morning, a centurion arrived with his one hundred troops. They then spent many hours in conference in the marquee of Cassius Quintas Gallus. When Cassius emerged from his accommodations, he gave instructions to his personal guards who hastily departed. He saw me from a distance and bid me to enter his quarters. I duly obeyed. As

I passed through the entrance, I could see a concerned look on his face and after a period of silence he requested I draw near.

"We have been instructed to return to Rome by the senate and the new emperor Tiberius Claudius Caesar Augustus Germanicus," he said. "Caligula (Gaius Julius Caesar Augustus Germanicus), has been assassinated." Then, in a milder voice he bade me to sit. "You have been of great service to me, but now we return to Rome. I am bequeathing you my family name of Gallus and I will draw papers making it so. It is necessary to meet social standards, Simon Magus Gallus." And then he smiled.

Almost immediately, senior tribunes and legates appeared in time for the General's announcement. Cassius spoke loud and clearly. "We are to meet with the Western Empire army under Galius Julius Caesar Octavianus in the northern province of Pisa some eighty days rapid march from here. Start dismantling the camp and be ready to leave before sunlight in the morning."

Cassius dismissed all but his two closest two legates and me. My heart missed a beat knowing what was to come next. A close discussion between the three ensued, but I could not make out clearly the conversation.

As they broke ranks, Cassius gave me the final order.

"We have many wagons to haul, feedstocks, weapons, forges, clothing, and footwear amongst many other things needed by a large mobile force. However, there were not enough wagons to spare for the seriously wounded soldiers".

Six wagons were assigned to me for the not so badly wounded. I would need to identify those who could travel and those who could not?

Cassius continued, "As they are fellow soldiers, we would prefer not to kill those to be left behind by the sword, so it is up to you to prepare a deadly solution to be administered immediately. A burial detail had been already been assigned to start digging a mass grave."

As it turned out, only two wagons were necessary as most of the wounded were in serious condition. The potion was quick to make and easy to administer as there was little resistance. Death quickly followed. All in all, the exercise took but a full day, but this execution haunted me for some considerable time.

Before the sun rose, the march was under way and by the eighty-eighth day, the city of Pisa was in view and we could see the Western army Encampment. I lost a further seven wounded en-route, but gained another fifteen through accidental wounds and illness. Purposely, our camp was set up approximately one thousand paces from the other military camp.

My physique matured and muscles formed as I continued the advancement in the art of the sword, spear, and knife. I was able to study under Cassius's most experienced personal guard. I learned battle formation, attack techniques, defense structure, and most of all leadership and individual skills.

CHAPTER 5

Dreams and Nightmares

I t had only been one passing of the full moon when I had my first vivid nightmare—a crucifixion was taking place. I did not see his face at first as there were two others being crucified at the same time. Once he turned his head—even though the face was bloody and bruised—I recognized him as the campfire companion, Yeshua. There was a great storm but I could clearly hear him screaming out loud in a Hebrew dialect translated to "father or Creator, You made me what I am yet I knew not who I became. Forgive them for they know not what they do." He screamed again but in a language unknown to me. I awoke abruptly, shivering and sweating profusely.

It would not be the only time I had this vision, though there were some slight differences each time. I would also see Yeshua in different places—the building of pyramids, a conversation with a king known as Ramses, reviewing monument designs, and with other striking and educated people speaking languages not of my understanding. Some will become known to me in time. I also saw in my dreams others referring to him as Jesus and some who called him the Messiah and son of God. This really terrified me. Other dreams were of events and individuals that were premonitions of my future experiences, battles, disasters, plots, and assassinations. As time passed, some of my dreams became visions and more realistic. I decided to document, date them, note the number of times the vision was repeated, when it stopped, and if/when it happened. In doing so, it saved my life and fortunes many times. I accepted this curse as part of my life. Although there were the occasional times when I had relief, they never ceased. I often wondered if Yeshua or Jesus was hindered by the same condition.

Seven years had passed since my recruitment into the Roman Legion. The bloody and bitter Asian campaign had taken its toll mentally and physically. I learnt to deal with the dying, though the art of amputation took me many years of practice to perfect the process. Studying anatomy, muscle function, and bone placement provided knowledge and I had plenty of repetition. Unfortunately, many of those were wounded beyond repair and loss of blood took many lives. In plentiful cases and in secret, I poisoned their water to help them on their way, so to speak, with the minimum of suffering. I had seen much of this in my nightmares and did my best to be understanding and compassionate. In countless ways it prepared me for events to come, or at least I thought it did.

As each year passed, the dreams increased and many scared me more than life itself for I saw much pain, death, tragedies, devastation, and disasters, some of which I would experience.

CHAPTER 6

New Home

Within a day, both armies received instructions to send a token force of the commanders, their senior ranking officers, and two hundred soldiers. Collectively, they would march into Rome without an organized parade, camp at the Emperor's Legions Barracks, and all officers were to report to the palace.

After all the pomp and ceremonies, I accompanied the senior officers to the palace, however I was segregated by the Pretoria guard and showed to an adjoining room where numerous well-dressed and affluent people were obviously waiting. All eyes were seemingly on me as everyone else knew each other and I was the unknown curiosity. A short, rather burly middle-aged man approached me with two taller vivacious women following him. With a wry grin, introduced himself as Canidia Albinus, who with Martina and Locusta were in the service of the previous Emperor Caligula as healers and social medicine advisers.

After I introduced myself, Canidia was quite talkative, knew my name from Cassius, showed extreme interest in my travels and discoveries, but asked how was I related to Cassius Gallus. I let the question pass without a response as I still felt uneasy accepting this prestigious family name.

After considerable discussion he extended an invitation to his home, to show me his own garden collection, herbs, various potions, and his unique research. Shortly thereafter soldiers arrived and the centurion started calling out names with instructions to follow. When the group assembled, the rest of us were told to wait until further notice. Food and refreshments arrived and I made myself comfortable.

"What's happening?" I whispered to Canidia.

"I am not sure," he replied. "But if I had to guess, some form of retribution is going on."

I was hungry, so I busily helped myself to goat cheese and fruits with a goblet of red wine. Seemingly, nobody else showed an interest until Locusta and Martina slowly eyed the various food plates, then carefully took a few grapes which made Canidia smile. There was something strange about these two ladies, something masculine.

As time passed, small talk and whispers increased. I had fulfilled my hunger needs and made myself comfortable amongst some large cushions, drifting into sleep. I was rudely awakened by the entrance of a herald and the same centurion from earlier. It was announced in a firm voice the proclamation of the newly appointed Emperor Tiberius Claudius Caesar Augustus and celebrations were to be announced in a few days, meanwhile we were all free to leave for our homes. It was my intention to return to the camp when Canidia offered me his guest quarters and would not take no for an answer.

"Are you aware of the Poet Lucretius? "Canidia asked.

"No," I responded.

"He passed onto the next life some fifty years ago and although I was not fond of his works, there was one very profound line he wrote that I am very fond of," he said with a very wry smile. "'One man's meat is another man's poison,'" he said in a very loud and clear voice. "Rather appropriate, don't you think," he continued. "Come, let's continue our discussions in more pleasant surroundings."

Lavish to the point of being flamboyant, even tasteless, would I call his home and wondered if it reflected his hollow and exaggerated character. It was alive with the strangeness of gaudy people and all kinds of animals roaming amongst them, many of which were copulating, even between humans and beast. Obviously, it was his intention to have a feast in more ways than one. I did not indulge, but became a spectator watching in awe, suspecting some form of induced potion in the wine that eliminated their inhibitions. This went on through the night until the early dawn before the army located-or should I say—saved me.

From the spoils of war, I found myself wealthy beyond my dreams thanks to my commander Cassius Quintas Gallus. As time passed, I settled into a large elegant house once owned by a wealthy senator, who along with his family were put to death after the demise of Caligula. Cassius also convinced me that marriage to the right family would improve my chances to succeed further, when I was introduced to his niece, Herminia. She was an attractive, very voluptuous young woman of fifteen years—well-proportioned and sexually appealing. The problem was, she knew it and made everyone else aware of it. Her immaturity was unfortunately very obvious through her mannerisms and conversation. Nevertheless, I thought in time that would change.

Unbeknown to me, her uncle Cassius was charming her and patronizing me as a suitable husband and informed her that I was not only wealthy but influential, and likely to succeed in this administration. My appearance was pleasing to her so she accepted her uncle's guidance and flirted with me, implying she would be interested if I would call upon her again. Thus, our courtship commenced.

Over the next few months, I was introduced to members of the family, including Herminia's mother, Olivia who was without husband. He had died in the Armenian Wars. I was well accepted as a suitable suitor and before long a date was set for our wedding. For a few months after the honeymoon, Hermina pleased me most of the time, but Herminia's interest diminished with one excuse after another when her social life and status became more important.

Verona

T wice a year I journeyed north to Verona to meet merchants to purchase spices, silk cloth, and other goods brought in by caravan from the east. I was accompanied by six to eight servants and four elite Roman guards. It was on one of these visits that I acquired a house from one of the merchants, modest in size compared to my home in Rome. This house was of particular interest due to the design and secret rooms. This would prove to be advantageous in the future, for protecting my fortune and my life.

The merchant had it purposely built and designed by an Egyptian architect and boasted to me after a heavy night of drinking that after the complex was complete, he had all those involved eliminated. Now, he needed to leave Verona due to his health. He nonchalantly explained he had deceived another merchant on a business trade and the latter threatened his life. After I took possession, the seller, his family and his servants were found slain on the road to Florence some fifth miles from Verona. I cannot deny I may have mentioned his departure in certain circles and my reward was the return of the gold I paid for the house.

The house was just outside the city center in a neighborhood where most of the dwellings were surrounded by high walls. Within the fortifications the main dwelling had six sleeping rooms on the second floor, the largest being mine overlooking the gardens at the rear. My bedroom was the only entry to the two secret rooms. The lower floor had a large auditorium for entertainment with access to a large kitchen, storehouses, and eight small servant/personal guard rooms. A separate adjacent building was made up of stables, carriages, and four other rooms for the barn staff.

CHAPTER 8

Herminia

I managed to avoid the gossip, rumor mongering, and quest for power that seemed to engulf most everyone that I came in contact with and gave no opinions or favored one family over another. I could not say the same for my wife Herminia, who relished any opportunity to involve herself. Fortunately, she often stated that I had little or no opinion on any person or subject which eliminated me from being the focus in any conversation. In fact, she became a vain, self-centered bore to me, but remained popular with both men and women, and she frequented the often-popular orgies. It was due to this reputation and increasing dislike of Herminia that I declined to share the same bed with her. I had often seen during the Asian campaign the terrible diseases that afflicted many a soldier who practiced sex with many partners, both male and female. I had experimented with many oral and bathing solutions with some effect, but never discovered a cure. I had witnessed many diseases which caused extremely painful and horrible deaths on numerous occasions.

I had not really paid attention to my appearance but one morning after returning from my trip north, Herminia made a statement regarding my looks not seemingly aging. Sure enough, it did seem strange that my facial characteristics didn't appear any different even though many years passed. The moment passed and I didn't give it another thought. I found myself satisfied with life and through introduction and word of mouth, my following grew along with the rewards.

The seven gram gold coins were introduced by Julius Caesar and minting of such coins were controlled by the senate. One such mint in Pompei would also produce coin from gold, silver, and bronze bullion for discrete list of clienteles for a percentage in return. The weight of the coins would be regulated, but choices of design, portrait, image, or ancestral icon were numerous. Personally, I preferred to stay with the original Caesar design. The gold coins were valued at 2000 sestertii, the common silver coin of everyday trade in 100 and 500 sestertii. Much of my fortune was well hidden, as most traveled north to Verona.

I still spent considerable professional time with Canidia experimenting, sharing remedies, potions, and even women although Canidia had a preference for younger petite girls and the occasional young, preferably, small boys. He, however, was more interested in experimenting with poisons and their effects, spending considerable time in the dungeons with endless available albeit unwilling recipients. Out of curiosity, I ventured a few times to the vaults of despair to witness the depravity of torture. I learned that subsequent pain and deterioration of the flesh combined with the effect of one's mind quickly led to confession, whether true or false. Canidia had no emotions in this arena and was calculated and effective. He conducted his art with a pleasurable skill.

His strange-looking outdoor garden contained a serious collection of clearly named signs of ant farms. Siafu ants sting, but their fierce shearing jaws are their main weapons. Green Tree ants don't sting, but they have powerful and painful bites that pierced the skin. Fire ant stings are terribly painful and can be dangerous due to the alkaloids in their venom. One Fire ant can sting multiple times, and that is why these are dangerous ants. Canidia's trees, bushes, and plants were many, varied, and signed with a name and a number which as I learned depicted the strength of the poison it contained. The strychnine tree was his favorite. The fruit had highly toxic seeds filled with strychnine and brucine. Wolfsbane, a type of buttercup, is far deadlier than the pleasurable flower. They're full of alkaloid pseud aconitine and commonly used for hunting. If ingested, even a small dose will cause you to die within two to six hours. Belladonna, also known as deadly nightshade contains one of the world's most poisonous toxins —tropane alkaloids. Once consumed, mouth dryness, loss of voice, headaches, and eventually difficulty breathing occur. Away from all the rest and in a very shadowed part of the garden was a large variety of mushrooms, some I immediately recognized, but many I did not.

Despite this, Canidia was totally unpretentious and over time I learned from his skills of the art of persuasion and assassination, and death by poisoning by a mere scratch. Aside from his devious characteristics, I liked him. Besides, it was safer to be a friend than an enemy.

As years passed, my reputation grew amongst the powerful and wealthy that allowed me a very prosperous living and a highly respected position in the community. It was also a time of concern in politics with in-fighting among the senate, the army, and Caesars' large eccentric family ego.

One evening and unannounced, Cassius paid me a visit, which he had never done before. After sharing a glass of wine, he came to the point of discussing my wife–his niece—with considerable concern. He was aware of Herminia's activities and asked of my marital status. It not only took me by surprise, but I was not in the habit of discussing my private affairs. I had come to respect Cassius over the years and knew only too well it would be useless to lie to him. He listened patiently before he spoke again. It has always been my business to follow events happening in Rome and keep watch on all the political players, especially those close to me.

"So," he continued, "You do not share the same bed anymore?"

"no, "I replied. "But I did give her a powder formula to douche after her sexual activities in order to alleviate possible disease. However I am not sure she remembered to take the precaution all the time."

In parting he exclaimed, "I am sorry my friend. You did not deserve this and I will not bother you again on this subject." Then Cassius departed, leaving me wondering why he took the time to discuss this matter at all? I suspected Cassius was concerned with the political activity and the meeting went without my saying, but I also had my circle of informants. There had been a growing number of incidents of wealthy and political figures dying mysteriously. I suspected they were poisoned while Canidia and his ladies were offering their professional services to, whoever will pay. His half-brother, Britannicus, was one victim in question. I had been required to visit numerous families, and on many concerning fatalities I noticed a swelling around a scratch on one of their limbs and remembered being told by Canidia this was an easy way to administer such poisons. I chose to avoid citing this reason for the cause of death, knowing it could have serious consequences for me.

CHAPTER 9

Torture

Unexpectedly, I received a surprise visit from Lucius Junius Silanus Torquatus, an advisor to Caesar. He was escorted by the largest protectors I had ever seen, and was immediately intimidated by their presence. From my sources, I learned that Lucius was also one of Herminia's lovers. He didn't waste any time coming to the point. It had come to his notice that I didn't seem to age and he wanted my formula in maintaining my youth. As much as I denied any such existence, he became angry and instructed his guards to restrain me, then knocked me senseless.

I awoke slowly and took a few moments to realize I was naked and bound to a wooden support with my arms elevated and legs outstretched, tied to upright building pillars, dangling just a short distance above the floor. My eyes gradually focused and I was in a dark, damp room without windows and suspected it was some kind of cellar. Before me and to my slight right was a grinning, fairly toothless, skinny elderly man with a thick scar on his face from the top of his right ear down to his top lip. He had no hair on his face, including, noticeably no eyebrows, and the dim torch light shining on his bald head showed further scarring and a large growth covering both his face and brows. The chamber was smokey with a foul odor of rotting meat and I was guessing this wasn't a slaughter house.

Then I noticed from the corner of my left eye the figure of Lucius leaning on another pillar holding what looked like a long rope with multiple knots along its length. Within moments he approached me, stopped abruptly, bent over slightly, and stared me directly into my eyes. He repeated what he had asked earlier—what was my secret to maintaining my youth? To which I replied again that no such formular existed. With a deep frown and the sound of his grinding teeth, he whipped his rope at my face drawing blood from my nose and mouth. I felt pain and a numbness as he screamed out the same question, but all I could do was shake my head as I felt the warm blood trickling down my chin. If I thought I was in pain then, what came next was pure agony.

Lucius stepped back slightly, releasing the rope to the floor but holding one end with his left hand. "One way or another," he said loudly and clearly, "You will tell me your secret." Pausing for a moment, he continued. "I have a man in my employ who met you almost twenty years ago and he says you have not changed your appearance and look no older." Grinning again he blurted out the same question and his spittle settled on my face. I remained speechless.

Lucius beckoned his ghoulish looking slave and handed him the rope. On his knees, he threaded the rope beneath my body from toe to head, flicking my balls with his thumb in the process whilst crawling and chuckling at the same time. I heard the rustling of a chain and then my sniggering tormentor crawled back beneath me, flickering my balls once again, laughing even louder. Standing, he handed the same rope end to Lucius who preceded to sit on a small wooden stool just a short distance from my feet. I could see he was now holding both ends of the rope, one in each hand.

Pulling the rope taut and with a flick of the right hand, he whipped the rope beneath me, hitting my genitals with a swift whack causing excruciating pain and a scream from the top of my lungs when another sudden blow made me yell even louder. "Am I getting your attention now?" screamed Lucius. "That was just the smallest knot." Maneuvering the rope, two more strikes were dealt but harder. "I have become proficient over the years with many a subject and now you have felt knot number two. Only eight to go," squealed Lucius. There were four more strikes and two more knot sizes before I passed out.

Awoken by the shock of warm urine in my face, the grinning face of Lucius was the first thing I saw as he faced the withered man and giving him a slight nod. "Your testes are numb and bruised, so we will give them a short rest before we begin again," said Lucius. "Meanwhile, you shall be entertained in a different fashion."

My head was pounding and I felt the throbbing and pain in my loins when the old man approached me, sat on the same stool, and placed a small arrowhead under my big toenail. With precision, he drove it into my flesh causing an eruption of blood to spill onto his hand. Without stopping, he placed two other arrowheads in adjacent toes, driving them in place as I screamed in insufferable pain. The question was repeated and I mumbled the same response. The torture continued on both feet and I continued screeching until I passed out once again. I was abruptly awakened by the feel of scalding hot water over my face and body and immediately cried out at the top of my voice. As my whimpering started to diminish, I heard Lucius say, "Leave him whilst I get some refreshments so he can consider giving me what I want when I return." At that moment he departed and I passed out, yet again.

I awoke in a daze to a commotion as I was being released from my bonds. I was then hoisted by a pair of strong arms. I closed my eyes in despair. I raised my eyelids to blazing sunlight and focused on my surroundings. I lifted my head, feeling my skin peeled face hot to the touch, then immediately felt a stab of pain in my scrotum and feet. My lower body was completely wrapped in a gauze soaked with a fragrant oil and my feet were bound separately in some form of toweling. I could feel a sticky substance when wiggling my toes, although it was painful when I tried to move them further. A maiden approached with a bowl and started to apply a substance to my face. I wanted to speak but she pressed a cup to my mouth and asked me to drink. Once the cup was removed, she placed a finger to my lips and requested I rest. I closed my eyes once more and drifted into sleep.

The light was flickering from the oil dish as I once again opened my eyes. The maiden who was seated next to me arose and moments later returned with a vessel of warm milk. As I drank, a figure passed through an open door and a beautiful woman with long black hair approached me. She gracefully sat in the chair when, without realizing it, I was staring into the most beautiful face I had ever seen. In a soft but clear voice she introduced herself as Agrippina, a friend of my wife Herminia and wife to Caesar. I gasped. "Fortunately, your servant Primus witnessed your abduction and recognized your captors. I was made aware of your dilemma from Cassius Quintus Gallus," she said and smiled. "Silanus and I are somewhat adversaries, so it pays to keep an eye on his activities and keep him in his place," she continued. "I issued the order to rescue you with the support of Cassius's guard. I am so sorry for the pain he caused and I will find a way for him to pay," she said angrily. With that, she promptly left.

I was treated for many days and nights and those who nursed me was surprised how quickly my wounds were healing. Herminia did not visit me during this time, but as I learned later, she was told I was visiting Pompei so my healing process could be kept secret. My trusted servant Primus was informed of my progress and when it would be possible to take me to my home. He arrived with a litter and bearers within a week and carried me to my dwelling. On the way, Primus told me what he knew of the event and that several servants of the household and my torturer were slaughtered, but Silanus was spared per the instructions of Agrippina. Unable to walk, I was carried by servants when needed, and my feet were bathed every few hours in a combination of oils and aloe vera. My main concerns were if I would become a cripple, my swollen testicles would be deformed, and/ or my feet permanently distorted. None of these maladies transpired. The wounds healed leaving small scars and my bones reset back in place without any physical attention.

The whole episode gave me time to reflect on my situation and that employing personal guards should be a plan for the future. Most of all I would need to keep a constant watch on Lucius Junius Silanus Torquatus, his associates, and their activities. I had the bad feeling he intended to continue his pursuit to find eternal youth and somehow, he was convinced I possessed the knowledge. I was positive our paths would cross again and I would dream so time and again. At home and healing, I could not help but wonder why Agrippina had intervened even though she was a friend of Herminia. No doubt I would learn why in time.

Primus spread the word I had an accident falling from my horse and even Herminia showed some, but little, concern on her few visits. It was during the last visit that I noticed her weight loss and that she was looking gaunt and pale. I asked how she was feeling and that I noticed she looked unwell, to which she responded it was just a minor ailment and that she had lost some appetite. It became clear to me Herminia was showing physical symptoms of a sickness that I recognized from my Asian campaign. Although we had drifted apart, I still had a strong sense of support and did everything in my power to heal her, but she threw caution to the wind, continuing with her lifestyle and spreading the germs that were ravaging her mind and body. It was difficult to know when she was not on pain remedies, stimulating dangerous medications, and pungent ointments, some of which I provided.

Over the next few months, I watched Herminia slowly get worse. I could see her in pain and I made the decision, when the time was right, to end her life with a potion. It didn't take too long before the opportunity arrived. Early one evening I heard her screaming and shouting and as I entered her quarters, she was being held by her maidens who were trying to give her a remedy. After calming her somewhat, she screamed out she just wanted to die and continued sobbing.

"Keep her calm," I said, "whilst I get a sedative." I returned quickly and requested her to drink in small doses from the goblet. Within a short period of time, Herminia started to relax and with a wry smile said she felt much better and maybe a bath would help her to get some sleep. Both maidens hastily departed to prepare the bath whilst I assisted Herminia, first lifting her to a standing position, then with small steps escorted he to the large oval bath tub. Without a murmur from her, I undressed her and raised her first leg into the lavender and herb infused water, followed by the other leg whilst giving her weighted support until her body was submerged.

The maidens were fussing around when Herminia rudely dismissed them as they were being annoying. She looked at me with an expression-less face and with a deep sigh she said, "I haven't exactly been a good or faithful wife but you bore me with your strict ethics and you fuck like a bull where all I feel is pain not pleasure." She looked shocked that she was being outspoken and I suspected part of my potion made her totally relaxed and relieved her of any inhibitions.

Suddenly, she closed her eyes and drifted into unconsciousness. I made haste to her bedroom and retrieved a gift from an admirer—a small jeweled dagger she kept on her dresser, amongst other favors. How apt, I thought. Returning to the bathroom and making sure no one else was around I lifted her wrists one after the other making small sliced incisions over the veins before returning them into the water. Herminia was already dead from the potion but now it would look like suicide. Her maidens would concur having heard from her own lips she wanted to die. I left, dropping the knife in the water.

CHAPTER 10

The Funeral

Herminia's body was discovered early the next morning and I was summoned by her maidens who were in disarray and sobbing. I sent word to her family and closest friends but I was not prepared to receive later that afternoon a large entourage from the palace led by the wife of Claudius Caesar, Agrippina. I had met her briefly after my captive torture and knew she had moved in the same circles as Herminia and Canidia, and should be regarded as a woman of dominance and influence.

With her head held high, she approached me slowly and with grace until she was several paces in front of me. A fine figure of a woman and attractive indeed. She stood still before speaking. "I am aware," she said, "that you are unaccustomed to the ritual of Roman nobility passing from life to the underworld, being Samarian and all. I am here to be your guide and arrange such customary ceremonies." She had barely ceased speaking when Cassius arrived with a troop of the guard. Greetings were exchanged then Agrippina ushered Cassius away from me and out of the range of hearing. I waited impatiently and when they finished Agrippina and a large part of their entourage started to leave.

Cassius approached me and spoke in a tone. "I have accepted on behalf of you and the family that Agrippina will organize the rites and services for Herminia. To deny her will be regarded as an offense for which there would be a harsh punishment."

I agreed without resistance—in fact it would be a relief. Little did I know the extent Agrippina would go and the huge expense it would cost.

I spent the first day washing Herminia's body, placing herbs and spices in all her orifices—ears, mouth, vagina, and anus—before stitching them all up. On the second day, a group of women covered from head to toe collected her body by horses and enclosed carriage to a resting place where she would be painted and adorned. Incense would burn continually for another day prior to the procession.

The procession took place three days later with one hundred of Cassius's foot soldiers in the lead followed by at least two score professional mourners, most of which were women. It was reputed some fifty or more musicians were behind the mourners and many more actors with masks and ritual dancers behind them. A smaller group dressed as ancestors walked in front of Herminia's body that laid on a wooden bed, specially made and draped with all kinds of refined materials and flowers, carried shoulder high by six men within a cluster of thirty others that would change places two by two along the route. Immediate family that included Cassius and I were at the end with close friends, and last but not least was Agrippina and her entourage.

Many people watched as we paraded down the pre-arranged one thousand pace route to Necropolis and placed upon a funeral pyre where she was burned whilst another assembly of twenty dancers paraded around until the fire came to an end. During this time various eulogies were given from family and many friends. I personally would not and many there knew I would have very little positive testimonies to give. Cassius presented in his eulogy an apology on my behalf stating grievance was a heavy burden. It was my saving grace.

Agrippina hosted a feast by invitation only at The villa Borghese and I attended, if but briefly. The villa was once the place of perverse wanton lust and sexual fantasies practiced by Messalina, Caesar's ex-wife who was put to death. I could tell by most guests attire that Herminia's departure to the underworld would be in her style and accounts of the uncontrolled depravity were abound all over the city for many days to come. If there was a commemoration that followed, I was not going to lower myself to be party to, however I learned much later that Canidia organized such an event.

In view of my agonizing experience with Silanius, my increased number and repetitious visions, it was time to make change in my life.

CHAPTER 11

Claudius and Agrippina

The whole affair left me with a disgusted emotion but kept my opinion to myself. In the many days that followed I had but few visitors, Cassius, Canidia with his Priestesses and some of the senior Pretorian guard who befriended me on the Eastern Campaign. During this time, an invitation to a palace celebration of Caesar's fifth anniversary as Emperor was delivered by messenger. In ten days, a chariot would be sent at midafternoon and I should be fully prepared upon its arrival. The festivities would last all day and guests would arrive at all hours and leave after a respectable time or cast out if overstayed their welcome.

I made sure I was well and truly ready when the chariot arrived, which by my calculation was more like early afternoon. Upon enquiring my question was ignored or he had no tongue. Nevertheless, I told myself I had to be very wary of this dangerous cunning woman. Through one of my informants in the employ of Caesar's stables, I was made aware that Claudius enjoyed his horses and spent much time in their company. As my anniversary gift, I commissioned a metal craftsman to make a pair of Silver Spurs with a Caesar gold image plate on the side.

With my gift wrapped in silk and in a designed decorative box I entered the palace and to the receiving hall. There was a lengthy line of influential and privileged citizens waiting to be received by Caesar and I took my place when I espied Agrippina making a direct advance towards me.

Despite being passed her youth with a fourteen-year-old son, she was still strikingly beautiful. Smiling, she grasped my arm and guided me past all the waiting guests and directly towards Caesar. Taken completely by surprise, I found myself staring at Tiberius Claudius Caesar Augustus Germanicus sitting on his throne. Agrippina spoke with authority and dominance, my Caesar, this is Simon Magus Gallus a healer of high reputation. It took but a bare moment when Caesar spoke boldly to tell me that there has been much spoken of me in court, but he had never seen me there. I was unable to give any response when he asked, "What is that in your hand?"

"A gift Caesar, for your anniversary achievement," I responded. An official took the box from me and handed it to Caesar and he immediately opened the offering. Removing the spurs, he showed great delight and moved them around in his hands with admiration.

"You have chosen well, Simon Magus Gallus; it pleases me and you must grace us with your presence in the future."

With that I bowed in respect and was once more guided away by Agrippina. A servant approached with ornate goblets and a flask of wine on a platter. After pouring, he offered the raised salver to Agrippina first but she paused looking at me when I realized she expected me to take the wineglass from the tray and submit to her. This I did whilst taking my own. Then she spoke. "Tell me, how are you able to keep your youth like appearance?"

"I have never given it much thought," I responded. "I keep my hair short and I have no facial growth, I bathe daily, sometime twice, and use the oil from aloe vera nightly."

"Are you sure you don't have a secret element?" she again asked.

I shuddered remembering the same inquisition from Lucius. "You know that was the exact line of questioning that Lucius Junius Silanus Torquatus took during my capture and subsequent torture?"

"Yes," she sighed in response. "I cannot help but wonder if there was not some truth in the rumor."

"Rumor," I said "What rumor?" I asked.

"It is said you have may possess a formula, a fountain of youth potion," said Agrippina.

"I may have some healing powers but I do not possess the ability of maintaining youth," I replied with a quick chuckle. There appeared a sparkle in her eyes as she approached and pressed her body to mine and without a change of expression reached down with her spare hand and grasped my penis through my garment.

"Escort me to the gardens," she said softly.

I did like a sheep led to slaughter; her compelling nature was impossible to resist. We walked for some time passing decorative trees, bushes, plants, flowers and ponds interrupting the various wildlife until we came to a trellis overgrown with ivy. She reached through the growth and in an instant an opening appeared like a door. She gestured me to enter, immediately followed, and closed the entrance behind us. Inside was a well-lit marble room, no windows and painted walls showing explicit depictions of sexual positions, multiple penetrations, climaxing males, a donkey, and several trained talented dogs.

In the center of the room was an extraordinarily large divan and Agrippina sat on the edge. "Have you never been in a play room?" she asked looking at me with an inquisitive expression. "This used to be Messalina's, Caesar's ex-wife," she proclaimed. Looking up there was no roof except crisscrossing vines from wall to wall so plenty of light but I could see candles displayed here and there for after dusk illumination I presumed.

Still mesmerized by the scenes on the walls I mumbled that I had not. This pleased her. A moment of guilt overwhelmed me and I so stated to Agrippina to which she laughed in response. "You must be the only man in the whole of Rome with ethics but you must relax and play the pastime everyone participates in. Besides, consider yourself blessed as I do not give myself lightly. I spend most of my time watching others and when Claudius isn't pleasing me in his way or for the most part, I am pleasing him, then I pleasure myself. Now, come sit by me I wish to taste your lips."

When I first married Herminia, she was not only a virgin, but had little knowledge of the ways of the flesh. I spent much time kissing her in many forms to relax her and build emotional response, arousing her senses with foreplay before finally having her first sexual intercourse. She had cried in pain saying I was too big for her so I took my time until such point she refused further penetration and finished me with her hand.

As we lay together, fully dressed I was overwhelmed by Agrippina's hypnotic perfume and her full lips pleading mine closer until we lightly touched again and again, then licking, gently biting, before penetrating my tongue into her mouth with sensual slow movement. This continued for some time before we both took long breaths. We both stood and Agrippina removed my clothing where I displayed a prominent erection, then silence and no movement. Abruptly she murmured to herself something about Herminia that I did not catch then she repeated, "Herminia spoke of her husband making coitus uncomfortable and often painful hence her preference for smaller cocks." Then she smiled. "Now I understood somewhat." I slowly undressed Agrippina and admired her body, medium pear sized breasts with protruding stiff nipples and astonished when I saw no genital hair. She giggled and said it gave Caesar the impression of a young maiden. I giggled in return, laid her down, and rekindled our lip and mouth teasing. Our bodies intertwined, our heads between our legs with tongues tantalizing to ecstatic pleasure. We separated momentarily to adjust position and my hard member was teasing her wet vagina. Slowly I entered her and she closed her eyes and gasped. I increased the rhythm and she started to moan loudly which continued for some time and even though I felt close to an explosion I held back until she came to an enormous climax. I kept

43

my body movement gradually slowing down, my mouth found hers once more, exchanging saliva. I turned her body over, pressed flat to the covers and entered her from behind and once again increased my thrust and gradually moved her till she was on her knees allowing me to penetrate even deeper causing her to scream out loudly until I felt the warm gushing of her juices which ignited my loins and I could hold it no more. The throbbing of my penis gushing my sperm deep into Agrippa's womb sent a shiver down my spine and I relaxed onto her body with my reduced manhood still inside.

After a while she turned over, but holding onto me and kissing my neck. "You please me greatly Simon, and I shall have you again." With that she raised herself up and moved to a table where an urn and bowl lay. Pouring water in the bowl she took a small pouch and added a solution then commenced to compulsively clean herself. Looking at me, she smiled and said, "This is your teaching Simon and I am a believer in bodily cleanliness and eluding the possibility of being with child. Clean yourself, and immediately go home. I shall relax for a while but you will see me again and soon."

CHAPTER 12

The villa of Pleasure

I t was a somber ride in the chariot, the servant was waiting for me like I was expected and no word was spoken. As I discovered earlier that would be difficult for him, not having a tongue.

Over the next few days, I was in a dilemma and not sleeping well. Imagining a visit from Caesar's pretorian guard and anticipating word from Agrippina, but neither happened. I was also plagued with visions and nightmares some of which I had before and rekindled the notion of finding a solution to my problem.

Many days later, a courier on foot arrived with an invitation to a feast at the home of Cassius. I bade the courier to wait while I wrote my acceptance, gave him coin and sent him on his way. I re-read the invite and realized it was in two days which under normal social circumstances was very short notice.

I arrived early with the intention to have private words with Cassius only to discover quite a gathering had already appeared. For the most part, it was senior officers from various sectors of the legions and as I made my way into Cassius's home I was greeted by various members of his family. As we conversed, I observed Cassius from the corner of my eye speaking with several senators. I excused myself and headed towards Cassius and his group and he noticed my approach. Greeting me with affection, the senators took their leave and the two of us were alone.

"What's the occasion?" I asked. Cassius took a deep breath then explained he had received orders to march on Gaul. It would take five days to complete the caravan supply convoy, meanwhile ten legions will commence their advance two days ahead of sixty legions and full column, camp outside Verona and assemble further supplies for the campaign.

Taking my arm, he moved me several more paces away from everyone, then with a serious tone said, "I have from a reliable source Agrippina is seeking a way to dispose of Claudius. First, she wants her own son Nero to be the next Caesar, not Britannicus, son of Messalina. Second, nearly all the Generals loyal to Claudius just happen to be on this expedition to Gaul so it would be opportune to arrange an assassination. Thirdly my friend, I believe you may be in danger for several reasons and strongly suggest you ride with me, at least to a safe destination. Now, let's get a glass of wine and toast to both our successes. With that we had the first of many toasts and revived memories."

Arriving home, six soldiers on horseback and a chariot with driver awaited me with instruction to take me to the palace. I shivered, begging my leave in order to dress more appropriately but was denied. Stepping on the chariot floor I held on tight as we made haste to what I believed to be my demise. It was not long before I realized we were not heading in the direction of Caesar's palace and my head was reeling with all kinds of notions as to my fate. We arrived at an armed gate and promptly allowed entrance. We continued through an olive grove to another armed gate and like before passed through with haste. Within moments I could see a large villa on an elevated plateau and came to a halt by another gate. The tall gate opened and a maiden appeared beckoning me to approach. I stepped from the chariot and my escort made an immediate departure.

Following the maiden inside the villa, I saw no manservants—only females moving here and there. I continued to follow from the main hall through various rooms until we reached a series of pools and there in the middle was Agrippina bathing in a milky substance surrounded by naked young women who were caressing her skin with aromatic cloths. As I stared at the scene in front of me, the fragrance was intoxicating and they barely took notice I was there. One by one they left the pool and I couldn't help but notice not one of them had any body hair. Agrippina glided from the waters and her maidens were waiting with fine cloth to cover her body. Once shrouded, she moved gracefully to a large circular plush couch, sat, and smiled.

Without a word she reached out her hand and motioned me to join her. As I secured myself next to her, she spoke. "Did I surprise you?" she purred.

"Yes, greatly," I responded. "My escorts did not inform me of my destination and my immediate thoughts were more of a serious nature," I continued. She laughed, then within with a gliding movement she was upon my lips, pressing gently, advancing her tongue into my mouth. I felt warm gentle hands lifting me to a stand position as they unclasped my robes. I watched the two young naked maidens, allowing them to undress me and felt a throbbing growth starting to erect its head. Whilst my body and buttocks were being caressed, I felt the breath then warm mouth of Agrippina sliding down my shaft until it was enveloped totally in her throat and her tongue was stroking my scrotum. Slithering, wet sensations started to engulf me as one maiden suckled on my left nipple and the other placing her oiled finger on my anal entrance, proceeded to stroke in circular motion and slight probing. The tempo gradually increased almost in rhythm until I could feel my loins ready to explode, then with a slight bite on my nipple, the injection of finger into my rectum and fondling of my testicles, I shot my load down Agrippina's throat and felt her muscles swallow my seed. She gently removed her head, my wet, still throbbing cock from her mouth when the two maidens commenced to lick my sticky manhood dry. Several other maidens appeared and we were both washed, dried, and clothed in lose robes. Once seated back on the couch, the maidens departed only to reappear shortly thereafter with trays of fruit, water and wine.

For three sunsets I was kept entertained in the glorious splendor of fornication and sensuality. I was introduced to voyeurism, maidens pleasing other maidens in every way imaginable, sometimes using objects. They were allowed to touch me, massage me, but not fuck me. They were there for my arousal and only Agrippina enjoyed the penetrations without any inhibitions, screaming often with delight especially when my thick cock was ramming her tight anal abyss. The only private time was to relieve my bowels in a knee-high pot and even then, the maidens were close by to wash my anal cavity with a sea sponge. When I needed to urinate, I was followed and the same cleaning performance took place. Agrippina must have taken her private time during my period of sleeping as she was always there in my waking hours. Occasionally we conversed, but only in regard to pleasurable things, no third party or political subjects and certainly no mention of Caesar. We slept only in dozes, awoken each time to caresses and further indulgent pleasures.

After one such slumber and one of my vivid dreams, I awoke without the touch, alone and Agrippina was gone. I never saw her again. I was then clothed without bathing by dressed maidens and escorted to the front door. The six horsemen and chariot awaited me and climbed onto the platform. I knew I smelled strongly of bodily juices but my escorts showed no indication of recognition. The ride home was swift and in the usual silence. After bathing and still with an ache in my groin, I fell into a deep sleep even though it was only midday.

CHAPTER 13

The Pompei Distraction

Primus apologized for awakening me but I had an urgent message from Cassius. I enquired how long I had slept and was informed the better part of a full day and a whole night. He was only too aware of my escort's presence, departure, and return but knew better not to ask of the purpose, nevertheless he happened to mention his joy of my safe arrival back home.

After reading the dispatch from Cassius, the advance column had left and if all goes as planned, the main force would depart early at sunrise in two more days and would I inform him of my intentions. Handing the communication to Primus for immediate delivery to Cassius, my second directive was for him to pack traveling clothes with no less than six social garments for an extended stay in Pompei. After due consideration, I sat at my writing counter and conveyed to paper my full objectives and instructions to Primus seeking his future services. Being my most dependable and faithful of servants, Primus would remain in Rome, manage the household and local affairs using best judgement in my absence. After giving him my written instructions, I named two manservants to escort me for the four-day journey and although I saw a look of surprise, he did not question my command.

The next morning two legionnaires arrived at my home to accompany me and my manservants with very specific orders from Cassius that needed no discussion with me. Final preparations were made and we set off on the South Road before most of the city were awake. Both my servants were inquisitive as to why we started this journey so early and my only response was because I wanted to. After the third morning had passed, within ten miles of Pompei, we stopped under some shady olive trees to take some refreshment. I bid my servants to approach and as they stood awaiting my command the legionnaires quietly approached them from behind and they were put to the sword, accurately and swiftly.

They were chosen to travel and to die as they were spies for inquisitive others in the palace and it was a golden opportunity to be rid of them. Their possessions and clothing were removed then buried naked immediately behind the olive trees. Aside from that event, this was not an unusual journey as I had interests in the city including a partnership in a popular and upscale brothel called Lupanar, roughly translated from Lupa, "she-wolf," a slang terms for prostitute. At the entrance was a statue of Priapus, the divine God of Lust with an enormous male organ.

Julia Lucilla Quintianus, a once attractive but still a wealthy middle-aged woman and owner of several eating establishments was my business partner. She owned numerous properties and lived in a large home with as many as fifty servants close to the main entrance gate on the north road and I would be her guest whenever I was in the city. Our arrangement was purely a commercial one, especially since her sexual preference was very young juveniles, both male and female. She handpicked the prostitutes and catered for every taste and deviant pleasure with either sex. Some she purchased and others she trained using other slaves and never received any complaints other than the client's sometime incapability. I would often find a new addition in my bed, some I took advantage of, others I had no interest. Julia learned from my rejections the type that interested me and in time I rarely sent any away. There were few people who I trusted; Julia was one of them. We hastened into the city to the home of Julia where I was expected.

After my discussions with Cassius, I had sent a messenger ahead of my arrival and nature of my business. Julia listened with interest of my plan for a long expedition to the Orient and it was unlikely, we would see each other for many years I commanded her to collect my earnings that would be collected twice a year by Gaius Gavius Silvanus of Verona or his authorized accountant. I conveyed how much I trusted her, that she was a true friend, and if there was anything I should know in my absence to convey by messenger to Gaius Gavius Silvanus. My final subject of discussion was the possibility of either of us wanting to break the partnership, so that she would evaluate a fair price for consideration. Without questioning my reason, it was agreed such said sum would be paid in a combination of gold, silver, and coin. Although offered a concubine before leaving, I declined and after a long embrace, took my leave. With haste we rode north to catch up with Cassius's column.

CHAPTER 14

Escape to Verona.

It was a full five days before we caught up with the army marching north. We had to bypass the main part of the city and took every precaution not to attract attention. My companions returned to their ranks after I paid them well for their unconditional support and silence. After some eleven days the main force caught up with the advanced columns outside of the city limits of Verona. They had been busy replenishing supplies from the city garrison and ready for the continued march northwest the following morning. I bid farewell to my friend Cassius and quietly left the camp at dusk. Cassius, already passed his sixty-fifth year, would lead his last expedition and die of exposure in the harsh winter of Gaul.

I entered the city unnoticed and approached my neighbor's villa where the night watchmen were guarding the front gate. I dismounted and they raised their lanterns to ascertain my identity. I had visited my neighbor Marcus Gavius Apicius numerous times in the past and the night guards recognized me. One of them left to inform their master and I made it clear to him to convey my apologies for such a late hour (it was not that late but I had learned such polite apologies was always a good gesture).

Soon after I was led into the villa and immediately greeted by Marcus dressed in some form of cloak-stained garment. "Come, come in my friend," he said. Clapping his hands, a very young what seemed to be girl appeared and Marcus commanded wine, two goblets, bread, cheese and fresh fruit. Making haste the youth returned with another and upon studying further noticed they were twins. Studying further I realized they were boys but with feminine features, dressed as girls, facial coloring with shoulder length girlish curls. They quickly placed several trays on the table then one requested permission to pour whilst the other laid plates, cut the cheese and bread and waited for further instructions. With a wry smile he grasped his wine and apologized for his appearance but he was experimenting in the Culina and maybe I would care to have a brief excursion later of what was obviously his pride and joy. I said that I would be delighted.

"Meanwhile, I hope you enjoy what little I can provide for a late supper and relish one of my favorite breads made with rosemary, dried grapes and olive oil." The combination of the bread, goat cheese, sweet red grapes and wine, though simple was delicious. I listened with joy and amusement his cuisine experiences and in particular having entertained the Emperor Tiberius for three full days of gastronomic delights. At the end of one such story, his son Vitellius appeared and after the appropriate greeting he enquired what had his father had prepared as he was famished.

The culinary arts to Marcus were like my experiments with remedies and so it was of great interest to see him at work. Many of his recipes were well documented and copies would be found in all the wealthy family households. He had designed the extremely large Culina Complex to eliminate clutter and make it more efficient. A mill attached to the bakery, livestock pen adjacent to the slaughterhouse, meat and vegetables cooked in separate pits in well aired rooms to release the smoke. "I'm afraid I didn't roast anything only baking today as I didn't expect you home this evening," Marcus barked, "But please join us in what we have, plus there is some cured pig in the pantry. "Gaius smiled, removed his blade and disappeared for a short while with the intent obtain some nutrition with more sustenance. I liked Gaius and we would establish a strong and lasting bond together.

Once again, Marcus showed that cynical look then asked me, "Can you see any difference between these two boys he asked."

Wanting to say something appropriate the only answer I could muster was they are well trained and unusual to have waiting servants so young, I said. Marcus scoffed and carried on by saying they were his little bedtime pillows and it was time for him to retire for the night at which time Gaius returned with a large portion of meat on a plate. Marcus once more clapped his hands and the twins rushed to his side clasping his hands and walked out of the room.

For many hours until early morning I discussed business opportunities with Gaius including the management of my home overlooking Gardens and the River Adige before begging my leave. I eventually departed with my keys and guided by one of the night guards to my property. Absolutely fatigued, I went to my bed and slept for some hours but after a series of visions I awoke in a heavy sweat having seen Primus tortured by Canidia's witches. I spent the next many days documenting my instructions and met regularly with Gaius to ensure he understood them. Although he comprehended the directives, I could see from his expressions some concerns and confusion as to why I needed so much planning but he did not ask why. In the meanwhile, I sent a messenger to Vitellius Quintas Gallus requesting news of my dwelling and in particular of my servant, Primus.

My visions and nightmares were happening more often and I was not aging. I should be more than fifty years old but did not look or feel older than twenty-five. I had no explanation one of my greatest fears was the awareness of others. I wanted answers, I needed to get somewhere safe, away from everyone I knew, so I could think this out, document my revelations and understand their meaning.

It was ten days past when a rider arrived but it was not only my messenger returning but also Vitellius Quintas Gallus in person and six legionnaires from his father's personal guard.

I made all welcome especially Vitellius and offered them refreshments, rest, bathing facilities and change of garments. Vitellius handed me a fairly thick pack of documents bound in two leather tied boards with an inscription on the outside saying, for my reading only. "Whilst I clean and change we shall discuss the contents once I feel human again," and with a smile followed my servant to my personal bathing room.

Once refreshed and almost immediately Gaius Gavius Silvanus appeared as I had already sent for him shortly after my visitor's arrival.

I opened the portfolio and started to read them one by one, then passing them to Gaius. Each one conveyed information and news from my numerous observers and infiltrators in Rome, some dealing with political intelligence but for the most part specifically that which dealt with me. There was an obvious vendetta by Lucius Junius Silanus Torquatus and the more I read, seemingly his whole family was involved through gossip and spreading rumors of self-importance and keeping selfish knowledge of fountain of youth potions. I had not read all the documents when Vitellius returned and I introduced Gaius as one of my trusted friends and shared the same with Gaius to Vitellius. "Let's pour some wine, "Gaius said. "I believe we shall need more than one!" and we all chuckled.

It was many hours later before all the information was digested by all three of us and numerous suggestions were deliberated and examined. Finally, we reached a unanimous agreement for a plan forward with a most brazen solution. There had been one piece of news that upset me the most that filled my heart full of hate for Lucius Junius Silanus Torquatus and he would pay dearly.

CHAPTER 15

Primus

P rimus was very proud of his position as keeper of his m/aster's household, but more than that he was trusted and relied upon in many ways. He worked with Simon Gallus on his potions, tended to his gardens and relished the teachings he was offered. Simon was a passionate man and he had visions of following his example.

Several days after his master's departure to Pompei, he ventured into Rome and to his favorite brothel. When it came to sex, Primus was a shy and personal individual and as it transpired over the years his preferred activity was that of a spectator. He had no time for brutality otherwise he was open to most everything else and as per his long-standing instructions to the madam, his viewing pleasure was always a surprise.

The viewing room was divided into two sections—that of the observer and that of the participants on an elevated small stage separated by a flimsy curtain. The onlooker had a comfortable couch and a table with choices of refreshment and various warming oils. The onlooker was in the darker side whereas the stage was lit by candlelight and reflecting mirrors shining on the playful activity. Occasionally, Primus saved enough money to be the only voyeur but that would have reduced the number of opportunities to visit, so sharing became an, option although sometimes a nuisance.

On this particular evening, two couches were in the room some three to four meters apart and when Primus went through the ritual of payment and entered the room there was enough light to see he was the first to arrive. This meant he had the couch preference and chose to be on the right-hand side of his yet to be companion. Pouring himself a glass of wine, he made himself comfortable and loosened his clothing. Hearing the rustle of movement beyond the curtain it was obvious they were preparing the scene and at that moment a young, hesitant man entered the room, getting used to the shadows before he sat on the couch to my left making himself at ease.

The curtains opened, showing a living room scene with an attractive slim woman and a young eleven or twelve-year-old petite girl sitting having a light conversation. In stormed a man in an obvious temper wanting to know if they had seen their son who missed his schooling, grasping a note from his tutor. Heads were shaking from side to side when a boy of around fourteen entered the room. The father immediately became aggressive and abusive stating he had been too lenient and time to teach the boy a lesson. Tearing the boy's garments until he was naked, the father grabbed a birch and placed the boy over his knee taking two swift strokes on his buttocks and shouting more abuse. Both mother and daughter ran to the Boy's aid when the mother slipped and fell, falling with her head on the floor and between her husband's legs. On looking up, she saw her son had a sizable erection and stared in amazement. Without thinking, she reached up and started stroking his cock. Whilst this was happening, the daughter came face to face with her, father pleading him to stop. The father responded quickly that if she didn't start behaving, she would receive the same treatment. The daughter replied he would not dare! By now the boy's cock was in his mother's mouth as father quickly stood up and grabbed his daughter pushing her face down on the table thus releasing the boy to the floor.

Lifting her clothing, exposing her bare buttocks, he slapped her hard several times.

About this time, Primus observed movement from his left and his cohort was standing just a few paces away stroking his own cock rapidly. He too had released his clothing but was massaging himself slowly. He quickly took a mouthful of wine while keeping an eye both the event and that of his companion. The father in the performance was fully erect of average length but thin, and about to enter the daughter's anal passage at which time his neighbor turned to face him. Suddenly and with complete surprise, Primus felt the warm spray of semen hitting his face time and again and attempted to stand when he was overcome with giddiness, blurred vision, and unable to control any body movement. Collapsing to the floor, he lost consciousness. The wine did its work. Slowly raising his head and opening his eyes, Primus looked directly into a beautiful face, then immediately noticed he was restrained to a wooden chair.

"He's awake," the woman announced when a man approached but Primus. He was having an issue with his vision so could not clearly see the man. He shook his head, blinking hard before casting his eyes again on the man.

"You know me? the man asked. Primus looked into the face of Canidia Albinus, healer to the court but to most people in service, his reputation was far more demonic. Primus had seen Canidia many times in the company of his master so recognition was obvious. "You have met Martina and my other assistant Locusta will join us shortly," he said.

"What is it that you want of me?" asked Primus. "I have nothing of value," he continued. "That is for me to decide," was the response.

Canidia started to pace back and forth when he asked his first question. "Do you not help your master preparing potions and compositions? Do you not have his confidence?" was his second, without waiting for the answer for the first.

"Well, yes, I treat the garden under the instructions of my master and grind the necessary components by his strict measure, package and deliver to his customers."

"You know the names of the ingredients?" Canidia asked in raised tone.

"Of course, I do," responded Primus. "Cats Fir, Dog Paws, Pigs Ears, Rats Tail, Goats Beard."

"Stop, stop," screamed Canidia, swiping the face of Primus with the back of his hand splitting his lip, then again with the other hand puncturing the veins in his nose. "You dare jest with me?"

Wincing with pain and bleeding from his nose and mouth Primus pleaded to cease the beating and that he could explain. "This should be good," thought Canidia. Primus rambled and tried to explain in the fastest manner that he had difficulty saying or even remembering the real names, so his master gave them easy, fictitious names to make it easy for him to follow instructions. Canidia could not contain himself and burst out in a fit of laughter. "I always liked Simon," he blurted out and continued chuckling. "Well now, I do not have the patience to examine you further and what you might actually know but I leave you in the capable hands of my assistants, Martina and Locusta."

CHAPTER 16

The Purge

Lucius Junius Silanus Torquatus had a very corrupt and tainted history and originally came from a sizable family in the southern part of Italy. Over the years, he and other relatives fought and assassinated each other mainly over greed and possessions. The last known fatality was his Brother-in-Law which I heard from the drunken lips of Canidia Albinus. No doubt Canidia played his own part for the right sum of money.

Lucius, his sister Octavia, his wife Livia, three sons, Marcus, Octavian and Augustus, and two daughters Scribonia and Clodia, were the sole survivors of once a large family and for the most part all lived on the same estate. His eldest son Marcus serves in the Pretorian guard and presently enjoying the flesh of his Superior's wife, obviously without her husband's knowledge. His second son Octavian is a high-ranking leader of the TL Gang (T for Torquatus and L denoting fifty members), a group of thieves and murderers formed from ex-soldiers, gladiators and mercenaries founded and financed by the Torquatus family. The third son Augustus, in his mid-teens, was still being schooled but already has a reputation as a bully, mistreating the house servants and impregnated a maid by force. The two daughters, Scribonia aged seven and Clodia aged five, both from his present wife Livia, were relatively innocent but spoiled. However, they could not have been totally oblivious to every day home squabbles and devious planning. The same evil would have been implanted in time.

For the plan to work, I was to stay very visible in Verona even though I very much wanted to quench my vengeance and participate in the action. As it would turn out, none of us would need to. We planned to reverse the technique of rumor and gossip and play the role of informant. Stage one, informant and so the first son of Lucious was killed by his higher-ranking officer in the bed and home of the officer. The officer took his own life after beheading his wife and only son as she confessed in her anger that he was another's child.

Even though Lucius's second son was dealing with speculation and accusations of his family taking more than their share of their acquisitions, he had a gambling problem that made it easy for us to elaborate his losses beyond his means by using some of the gang's share. Through various members of the gang in social places we were able to make convincing tales of vast fortunes being held in a secret room of the Torquatus residence. Considerable share of this fortune was swindled from the TL gang.

After a raid on a small caravan inbound to Rome with treasures from the East, the TL gathered at their warehouse to divide their ill-gotten gains and Lucius's son was controlling to proceedings. From the rear of the building came raised voices and a group of men were manhandling two others. They were pushed to the ground within the main gathering and more shouting ensued until one of the gang leaders demanded silence and an explanation. We caught these two loading some of our plunder into a wagon and believe they are in the employ of the Torquatus house-hold, blurted out one of the gangs. All eyes were now focusing on one man— Octavian.

It was early morning; the sun was rising from the east and all was quiet at the Torquatus estate. Domitia, the governess for Scribonia and Clodia, had already departed for a field learning trip to the College of the Vestals. Which was just as well, whilst funeral arrangements were being prepared for their eldest brother Marcus, who was presently lying on a cold slab in the cellar. Livia was still in her bed whilst Lucius awoke before the dawn and made his way down the living area and pondered as to the whereabouts of Khammu and Hmong, his personal bodyguards. Since my personal incident with Lucius, I spent considerable time investigating and collecting knowledge on history of his very large and intimidating protectors. Purchased in their youth, they were already larger than other juveniles. They were brothers and slaves brought from the far north of the Kmer region south of China. Lucius acquired them under dubious circumstances and trained them in gladiator school to eventually become his exceptional and very recognized guardians making him known as someone not to be played with. His downfall was not treating them right or with respect. I befriended them through others before making myself known and played on their desires and aspirations. Appropriately, the brothers would not be on duty that morning.

Not knowing what to think, Lucius made his way to the cellar to where his son lay at rest. Suddenly a commotion could be heard above stairs and he made haste to understand the source of the raised voices. As he arrived at the top of the lower stairs he came face to face with several armed men and within moments knew their identity.

"What is the meaning of this intrusion?" he cried and then noticed two more men walking towards him escorting his son Octavian with a choke around his neck and chains secured to his wrists. Again, he raised his voice just as Octavia, Livia, and his son Augustus appeared on the upper stairs. More noise as other members of the TL gang escorted servants into the main auditorium and Ummidius, now appointed leader of the pack approached Lucius and demanded to know where the treasure room location was.

"What treasure room?" Lucius replied with an obvious tremble in his voice.

Ummidius had no patience as he removed his dagger and sliced the cheek of Lucius inciting the laughter and cheers of the crowd. Livia screamed, begging Ummidius to cease his attack and that she would show them where the fortune was kept.

Livia was led to the cellar stairs and Ummidius followed with eight gang members, Lucius and Augustus in tow whilst everyone else, including Octavia, remained in the main hall. Passing the body of Marcus to the cellar far wall, Livia pulled hard on the wall torch fixture revealing a hidden room beyond. The chamber was small—no more than four meters by three— with brick like shelving flush to the walls. Every layer was stacked with leather purses, jewels, and gold artifacts with hardly empty spaces bringing smiles and glaring eyes from the intruders. Augustus grew angry attacking the nearest assailant, withdrawing his blade and thrusting it into the man's gut. Lucius ensued, breaking loose from his captors and moments of mayhem followed, however it was short-lived. Additional men arrived in the cellar with swords drawn and within moments thrust and cut into the bodies of Lucius and Augustus. Livia collapsed to her knees falling onto her now deceased husband and son. Ummidius bellowed to remove her to her chambers for the pleasure of his men and to remove the plunder to the waiting cart outside.

The wounded man was also put to death as others scurried in haste grabbing purses, scooping gems, jewelry and ornaments into baskets as quickly as possible.

The riches were gathered by the main door and with a slight nod of the head from Ummidius his followers commenced slaughtering all the servants except Octavia. He personally delivered the fatal blows to the chest and neck. After the bloodshed and other than the sound of multiple footsteps, the only noise were Livia's screams echoing from the upper chambers. Everyone cheered. Under the instruction of Vitellius Quintas Gallus, centurion Stephanus and his troops walked quietly the last fifty meters to the gates of the Torquatus Estate as the TL gang were loading their cart. Their arrival took the rogues by surprise and combat quickly followed as the soldiers overwhelmed the less numbered forces outside then entering the villa in swift and well executed fashion. The skirmish was short and no prisoners taken with a loss of four foot-soldiers and two more wounded. By the time Vitellius arrived, forty-three members of the TL gang had been slaughtered and four of the Torquatus family executed. Lucius and Augustus in the cellar, Lucius's sister in the hall and the naked body of his wife Livia in an upper-level bedroom with her throat cut. The two youngest children were nowhere to be found and a search of the estate produced no evidence they were at home during the invasion.

Clodia, the youngest daughter was getting irritable and bored whilst Scribonia was mumbling about how dumb this all was, especially when informed that vestals were pledged from the age of six, certainly before puberty, and sworn to celibacy for a period of thirty years. Scribonia was seven and inquisitive, spending much time snooping around the house and watching her family and servants perform a wide range of physical pleasure. She was eager to reach an age when she would be able to achieve these sensual indulgences.

Domitia sensed their tediousness, and knelt in front of them grasping each one of their small hands. "I have a surprise for you but let us go to the gardens and eat our packed lunches first."

The girls squealed in delight and kept asking, "What is it, what is it?"

"We are going on a journey far away from Rome to visit your aunt," responded Domitia,

Clodia just smiled but Scribonia quickly responded, "Aunt, what Aunt?"

"I will explain when we reach the gardens and during our meal," said Domitia. And so, the tale was told of their father's sister and many reasons why the knowledge of her existence was kept secret from them but it was time to meet her.

After eating, a quick visit to the baths, and a short walk, they reached a carriage with a driver who was introduced as a servant at their aunt's estate. The girls climbed in with a little help and their excitement was very obvious. After getting settled, the horses and carriage moved off at a rapid pace towards the south road.

After what seemed many days to the little sister's they finally arrived at their destination well past sunset and both were starting to drift in and out of slumber. Domitia quickly and quietly left the carriage under the watchful eye of her husband Casperius and approached the gate of the villa. There she was met by a watchful guard and words were exchanged and he entered the premises leaving Domitia to wait. Shortly thereafter the guard reappeared and bid her to enter.

Some time had passed and Casperius started to be concerned when the main door opened and she advanced towards him and the carriage. At this time the children were starting to stir and Domitia smiled at them, telling them they had arrived and their aunt awaited them. As they entered the villa, Scribonia noticed the warm colors of the walls and the decorative frescos, lavish furnishings and huge ornate pillows. Unlike their own home where their father preferred plain fixtures. Sitting in the middle of the room sat a well-dressed lady that had a pleasing face and charming smile. Hello, she said with a welcoming voice, I am your Aunt Julia she continued. Come make yourselves comfortable and almost immediately Clodia flopped onto a huge inviting chair and rolled up into a ball. Scribonia was very much awake and curious placing herself next to her aunt on the lounger. You must be tired after such a long journey, are you hungry? Or would you like a bath? Noticing little Clodia was already fast asleep. I am tired replied Scribonia but I could eat some fruit and a small piece of cheese. Domitia picked up Clodia and Julia directed one of the servants to lead them to a sleeping chamber whilst issuing instructions to another to bring a selection of eats and milk. Having arrived and placed on a table, Scribonia busied herself with the selection that was much more than she could consume when Julia and Domitia took their leave to a distance where they could not be heard.

"What is your instructions? Julia asked Domitia.

"To deliver the children and return to Verona," she said.

"Stay the night, refresh yourselves and leave early in the morning," Julia replied, as she looked at Ciboria, who was obviously having a hard time staying awake.

Once everyone had been shown their rooms and all was tranquil, Julia immediately reopened the letter from Simon. As usual, he was to the point and precise as to the fate of the two little girls. Other than their names, no other relative information was given other than they were orphans from a prosperous family. They were to be raised as refined ladies and tutored in what was Julia's most formidable asset, the teachings in the art of sexual excitement, desire, persuasion, and temptation when ready, only available to the finest of men or women. She smiled and was filled with delight knowing she would make these girls the finest of whores at the Lupanar, Pompei.

With Canidia at the palace of Caesar, Martina and Locusta were bathing, rather inebriated and under the influence of hallucinating mushrooms when the soldiers entered the bathroom. Without hesitation, they slaughtered them both without mercy when the assailants noticed they were both eunuchs. As they looked on at the dismembered corpses, they all laughed in glee, sheathed their swords and left as quickly as they had arrived.

CHAPTER 17

Last Meeting

As prearranged, a year later, fifty-four years after the crucifixion of Jesus Christ, I gathered with Gaius Gavius Silvanus, and Vitellius Quintas Gallus at the home of Julia Lucilla Quintianus in Pompei. I had arrived in Pompei with my acquired protectors, Khammu and Hmong a few days earlier than Gaius and Vitellius in order to discuss my local business venture and curious to see if Julia had any new delights to offer. She did. I also needed some time to infect the skin under my eyes and on my brow to give the effect of aging and using a combination of ash and bleaching agent to color my head and facial hair. My application proved highly effective.

Within a few days, we were all together and met over a sumptuous dinner, making small talk and each of us getting more knowledgeable of the other. On the second day in the garden and away from possible listeners, we shared news and reports from our informers. The recent death of Claudius, aged sixty-four, reportedly poisoned by Agrippina, was not proven. Canidia had suspiciously vanished whilst we discussed the appointment of her son Nero as emperor. Nero was persuaded to marry Claudius's daughter Octavia by Agrippina to secure his status whilst his advisor and tutor Seneca became her lover. She had become the most powerful woman in the Roman empire, but created many enemies and some say not only was Nero jealous of his mother, but had a desire for her, and he was suspicious of everyone. It was dangerous times.

With financial help from me, Gaius purchased more land to develop future vineyards and new olive groves whilst Vitellius and I planned a trading venture to the east within the next few months and meanwhile sell my assets in Rome. As for Julia, she had purchased a neighboring tavern from a patron who lived well beyond his means and was infatuated with one of her more demanding ladies. His demise came shortly after in a disagreement over the same lady. He was found in an alley with his throat cut. Julia was to demolish the tavern and rebuild a series of themed cabanas, catering to all whose taste and imagination was beyond the norm and were able to afford to indulge themselves.

My request to Julia not to expose the little girls to us was upheld at all times and we spent a further day together reviewing our future business relationships and enjoying each other's company. I informed her I wanted to sell my interests in Pompei and would she start thinking about a suitable price and sole ownership rather than a new partner. Julia understood and would advise Gaius within a few months. Before parting, I spoke for some time of my own expectations as this was likely the last time we would spend together. My friends were shaking their heads in disbelief and saying, "Nonsense!" and other like comments. "Nevertheless," I continued, "My journey to the Orient will very much take me many years and I may even reside there for learning purposes and investment opportunities."

I produced four bronze seals hung from silk cords, giving three to my friends and keeping one for myself. This seal would be used on all correspondence and will expect dispatches from you all that transpires in the empire, news of Rome, our ventures together and Julia's intentions for the girls. After all the customary goodbyes, we left Pompei, parting with Vitellius on the road to Rome whilst Gaius, my bodyguards and I continued to Verona.

CHAPTER 18

Kahmuu and Hmong

Kahmuu and Hmong remained with me since being released from their bondage with Lucius Junius Silanus Torquatus even though I had granted their liberty. They were trustworthy, dependable, committed and I had made it clear to them they were free men, they felt an obligation to me no matter what I said. In the few years we were together, I came to enjoy the company of my guardians and I developed a special bond with them, learning some of their language and had meaningful conversations with them on a regular basis. With their help, I studied their way of life, their culture, their beliefs and discovered they were rare men amongst men. They came from the far north in a country called Laos, close to the Chinese border at a place called Kuang Si Falls south of Luang Prabang and for many years their whole village had been born into slavery to the local Chinese warlord and the warlords before him.

I had given it a great deal of thought on our journey from Pompei to Verona and due to my future plans, it was time to let them go back home. Not as slaves but with letters of authority granting them travel, documents showing they were free men and enough silver from one of my hidden wagon compartments to somehow trade or fight for the liberation of their people. As in my dreams, I knew I would meet them or their dependents in the distant future.

CHAPTER 19

The Gathering

I had some experience with India trading in the past with mixed results but Vitellius Quintas Gallus and I had gathered much information and contacts there of lucrative commerce with possible China introductions and this excited us both. Although I had gained both wealth and reputation in Verona, I could not overlook this potential long-term prospect not counting the enormous profit and so I responded to Vitellius's correspondence with a request to join the expedition. Some weeks later a lone horseman arrived with numerous dispatches including a very enthusiastic letter from Vitellius.

Once winter had passed, I would seek an appropriate site and coordinate the collective groups. The dispatches listed the lead individuals, numbers of wagons, herdsmen, troops, horses, cattle and trading goods. Camels and goats would be purchased along the way. It was a well-planned and organized venture and immediately took to the task confirming same to Vitellius with the lone horse rider. I had no knowledge of ships but Vitellius did and he confirmed in his notice to leave all the negotiation of vessels to him. All I needed to confirm was the additional personnel, slaves, animals, stores, provisions (live and dry), weapons and total amount of wealth to be carried to ascertain the number of crafts and sailing crews.

The river Adige meandered through Verona heading northwest and an appropriate undeveloped site was accessible and without cost on the east side banks. It was important to have major access to water and to dig enough latrines, cleansing areas for the whole caravan and the nearby forest would provide timber as firewood and minor construction. As other expeditions were planned if this venture was a success, this site would be developed as a permanent starting location. I drafted a dwelling layout which I modified several times before I was satisfied with its design and function. It was time for the next step, labor and construction. My main concern with the start of the camp foundation and sewer groundwork was the weather. The previous winter was not only very cold but the snows settled for many months. Fortunately, this winter was mild and when it did snow melted very quickly, so with an acquired slave force and local architect/builder we started work early. The first of the caravan groups arrived prior to completion of the works but for the most part it was a working facility.

Over the next weeks, many more of the expected parties arrived and only three more units were expected when the surprise arrival of Vitellius Quintas Gallus with a large contingent of cavalry appeared. Greeting him with delight I offered him my hospitality and my home. For the next few days, we toured the site and it was obvious from his gestures and cheerfulness how delighted he was with the result. In conclusion, he had made a decision that was deluding him until now making me the caravan Leader and sole controller of this venture. Before I could make my protest, he listed all the positive aspects of my actions and would not take no for an answer. I had no argument nor option but to accept. The Gallus family had strong associations with the Roman Navy that had its base in Ravenna since the development by great Augustus. Based on my facts and figures he and the naval commanders designed and fitted out the number of the fleet totaling seventy-two. I was staggered at the number but was quickly informed it still might require a few more. Vitellius also stated that there were more than five hundred available and different designs to suit our purpose. It would be better explained when arriving Ravenna and seeing for myself and the conversation was left at that.

The rest of our time we discussed the expected investment return, the risks and expected duration. He would not be taking the journey himself but would leave sixty of his soldiers under my command and only under my command. It was expected some policing would be necessary. I would choose twelve of these men to become Immunes and to train them as healers plus the necessary slaves to oversee the medical health of all travelers. All the groups had arrived and a full inventory of man, beast, and trade goods were taken and the journals kept in my pavilion.

The evening before our departure, Vitellius and I had a lavish feast at which time I handed him my will and commands for my Rome properties and interests elsewhere for his supervision in my absence. My written instructions also included the names and details of my other two trusted friends, Gaius and Julia with the firm directive they meet annually to review our fortunes and my estate. Whenever possible and or necessity they are to find a way to communicate with me with the provision I would do likewise. Even though I knew the caravan would have an early start, we talked very late into the night enjoying the pleasure of each other's company.

Just as the sun was rising, I forced myself to awake, washed myself with river water and sent for all the group leaders. I purposely had my gift given guard stand strategically around my new home and erect their colors high on my dwelling, making a statement of command to all and respect to my sentinels. Vitellius had already appointed the head of the guard, Anthony and two direct subordinates who attended all my arranged meetings. The relationship was kept strictly professional having learned it was the best path to mutual respect. Over the past months I had met with all the commanders on an individual basis and managed a written journal on each of them, their likes, dislikes, demeanor, character, attitude, and above all performance and management of their unit.

When all the group leaders were assembled, we shared official introductions and some wine. When the group was called to order by Anthony I stood on a specially prepared podium before speaking. I introduced Anthony as commander of the guard and that he reported only to me. Now that we had established chain of command, I addressed each leader by the order they arrived, requested they give a singular name for their group and select a color or colors as their banner. Seemingly simple it actually took quite a while before all was said and done.

Stones with numbers were put into a pot and each leader withdrew one that established their rotation in the caravan for the duration of the expedition. This was the first of many gatherings that proved valuable in sharing issues, suggestions, grievances and learning from experience that would benefit future ventures.

CHAPTER 20

Journey to The Red Sea

And so, at early light we started our journey and proceeded some one hundred leagues (222 km) east to the port of Ravenna adjacent to the town of Classe. It was slow and uneventful for the five-day journey, other than one guard put to death for sleeping on his watch. Otherwise, we arrived safely and camped just outside of the west part of Classe. Vitellius had informed me this harbor and fortress was originally developed by Emperor Augustus for military purposes and home of the Roman Navy with a reported fleet of around five to six hundred ships of assorted designs, troop barracks, armories, beast stables, consumable control and distribution, and dry goods storage to name a few. In support of the fleet, a work force of up to ten thousand was made up of tool makers, carpenters, repair craftsmen, oarsmen, weapon masters, sailors, and naval officers to name a few and their families lived in Classe. The Roman navy was initially designed to support Rome's armies, but it never achieved the might it could have been. To generate funding, they were used to protect merchant ships or carried freight and caravans throughout the Mediterranean. The offer from the Gallus family to venture through the Nile and on to India was indeed a challenge for the Navy committee, but the rewards were too tempting to refuse.

The morning after arrival our caravan, the leaders and I met with the naval commanders to settle on the final number and type of ships to engage. Sixty-seven in all were engaged. I was assigned the vessel Athena along with my scribe, personal guard, various servants, and most important of all my bullion of silver and metal Ingots. I had never given any real thought to sea travel before, but found out very quickly it did not suit me. The motion made my stomach nauseous and on numerous occasions my stomach contents ended up in a bowl or in the sea. It took quite a while to get my sea legs so to speak but not on this first outbound voyage. Not that we experienced rough seas, in fact from the Aegean through the Mediterranean and arrival at the harbor of Daneoi and entrance to the canal to the Red Sea it was pronounced by our Captain as unusually calm seas. Looking at the clear skies and bright stars my thoughts turned to my dreams and visions or lack thereof over the past half year. I felt a calmness that I hadn't felt in a long time but I had this sense that told me this would be short lived.

The next morning the flag masters were busy signaling each other with instructions how to proceed through the canal. It was wide enough for two vessels with oars fully extended, and would need four days to navigate, whilst anchored and well-lit at night. The lead vessels carried troops to ensure safe passage as we had been informed of piracy in the past. My ship and that of the senior naval officers followed. It was quite a sight to behold. Arriving at the entrance of the Red Sea late afternoon it was decided to stop for the rest of the day and night and meetings were set to discuss our next part of the voyage to Muza and into the Erythraean Sea. The oarsmen, who were free men and proud of their profession, built large fires on the shore, roasting pig and the occasional oxen but no alcoholic beverage knowing they needed to be fit and with clear head at sunrise. In order to maintain the sobriety, they policed themselves. Anyone caught was put to death as his performance or lack thereof would hinder the overall crew. Oddly enough, this rarely happened.

The winds were favorable and it wasn't until the ninth day we used the oars. We didn't see much in the way of other crafts and those we did were far away. Most of us were quite surprised at the mighty width of the Red Sea and we hugged the center in order to avoid any possible conflict from the shore. As much as we kept many watchful eyes, we saw no other peoples on the journey to Muza. On arrival to much excitement on the shore, small boats were sent to the port with several of the captains and a military escort of one centurion, a hundred men with several interpreters. They were to establish a base for three, maybe four days, gain introductions to local leaders and merchants.

After receiving very positive news from shore, I decided to venture into Muza myself along with my personal guard, other investors, scribes and accountants. It was fortunate that many traders were in the city as they lived in the capital Safar some two days camel ride away. They had sent word of our arrival to others in the capital but would not be here until the eve on the second day. Meanwhile we were invited to see their storage areas full of fruit, spices, oils, grain but most impressive of all was the mounds of ivory tusks. The naval commanders and senior officers were extremely joyous to learn the Ivory traders were more interested to negotiate their stock for weapons. They knew our iron arsenal were far superior to their own made mainly from brass and would make a handsome profit from the various warring tribes in the north.

After much discussions, we filled seven ships with the elephant tusk and two with spices and oils. With three escort ships and much to my disappointment we were left with fifty-four ships with which to venture. Not having any interest with the ivory, I had purchased a full vessel load of the spices and oils to return to the Roman Empire with instructions to Vitellius. By the fourth day we had fully re-stocked water and provisions for the rest of our journey to Barbarikon, bordering Persia and India. Adding local sailors who knew the coasts of India we sailed on the fifth day.

After several days and hugging the coast to our left, we entered open seas in what is known as the Erythraean Sea and maneuvered to sail east still keeping the coast on our left and within sight of the eye. In doing so we avoided what looked like storms further south and the wind, weather and the environment proved favorable. Many more days passed and I was informed by our new crew that the coast of India would be seen on the following light.

Indeed so, on entering the deck I sighted land to our right and noticed we had steered north west and the rising sun to my right. Recalling the previous night's vivid dreams and after eating a breakfast of fruit and flat bread I examined our course arriving at our destination by the next full moon some twenty sunlit days hence. The winds were not in our favor which resulted in using the oars and arriving at Barbaricon later than expected. Just before light the fleet dropped anchors well into the bay having been advised of very shallow waters at the river approach to the city.

Before long, a long narrow boat approached powered by at least two score rowers with twenty-five armed and standing soldiers. As they became closer and seated in the center were four well-dressed envoys. I instructed my signalman to notify the naval leader vessel to send out a small boat to greet our hosts and guide them to their ship. Additional signals were sent to the other merchants to meet on board the same vessel. The sun was high in the sky by the time I arrived and some introductions had already preceded. It was a pleasant surprise to learn all of the four ambassadors spoke Greek, even some Latin and after the pleasantries we were informed our convoy of ships was the largest by far to visit their shores. When they ascertained our purposes, they were overjoyed and much discussion of what we had to offer and the goods they were able to trade continued till the sun was setting. It was agreed to send a large group of our representatives to shore in the following morning for further negotiations followed by an evening banquet in our honor.

CHAPTER 21

Barbarikon

The actual city sat on a river of many estuaries and marshlands which provided natural defenses and difficult to approach by sea. Our large contingent arrived early the next morning and after further greetings, assembled in smaller units according to their representation. The landing point was busy with activity that extended into a large market square surrounded by many storage buildings and we spent much time observing and surveying the many goods displayed. This was a community of traders, bringing their wares from eastern sources as far as China and was a delight to the eyes. Our scribes were busy making summaries in preparations for interest discussion and possible negotiations. By the days end, we were extremely satisfied with our progress and prepared our camp on open grounds presented to us. Our delegation of eighteen participated in the evening's festivities that included an introduction to their Tribal King, Nambanus and his family. A man of little words and I observed his stares resembled that of suspicion. During conversation I gathered he had every reason to due to many warring Tribal factions constantly battling each other with regular changes in their leadership. This, however, did not alter the activities of the much lucrative merchandising historic town of Barbarikon renowned for its function and purposely kept intact by each controlling king. There were many regional kings and they all served under the ruling kushan emperor, Kujula Kadphises

Trading continued for many, many weeks thereafter until all but three ships were fully laden. I spent much time with their holy men who were also their healers, learning the ways of making their medicines mostly from plants, roots and berries some of which I found useful, some I knew and although my own knowledge was far greater, I only divulged to them what I thought was beneficial under their way of life. Furthermore, I had decided to stay in the kingdom of Indo-Scythia, venture further inland to the borders of China and possibly beyond. This decision was not taken very well amongst my personal guard, senior naval officers or the other merchants so I requested only volunteers needed to remain. Although my personal guard were hoping to return home, they were also loyal and declared they would travel wherever I decided to go. All in all, almost one hundred and twenty would remain most of which were military with approximately forty others made up of several of my healers, scribes, linguists, map makers, woodcutters, hunters and cooks.

Most of the fleet had sailed, leaving a quiet void and somewhat of a hollowness in our existence for a short while. Meanwhile, the local leaders were busy forecasting their projections for future trade expecting another fleet's arrival in approximately another year. I spent the next thirty days assessing our caravan to be, speaking with every man, reviewing his abilities, leadership and creating a competent, organized force. Finalizing my decision of governance choices, I smiled to myself with a great deal of satisfaction. The next day I would gather those chosen and the disciplines they would be responsible for before deciding the time to depart Barbarikon for the Kushan capitol. I had known for some time I would not be returning to Verona or Rome, at least not in the foreseeable future and needed to investigate means of concealment and how to become someone else. My visions became more frequent again, repetitive, and waking up shaking and with a sweat became common.

Our caravan was given a fond farewell and soon the town of Barbarikon was far behind us. The terrain was mountainous and barren and travel with wagons on the stony, dusty road was slow and tedious. After five days we arrived at the outskirts of Minnagara, the home of the Tribal King Nambanus and many of the wealthy Trading merchants of Barbarikon. We were expected and a lavish banquet was held in our honor and it granted me the opportunity to obtain information on the Emperor Kujula Kadphisis and the Kushans values, beliefs and way of life.

The emperor lived in the city of Taxila located in the north west bordering on three trade routes, to the East and Central Asia, the west towards Persia, Greece, and Mediterranean, and north to China and what was referred to as the "Frozen Countries."

CHAPTER 22

The Kushan Kingdom

We stayed in Minnagara no more than a few days, replenishing stores, obtaining as much information of the route, making maps and the expected dangers we might expect on our travels to Taxila. The one thing I wanted to avoid was desertion and by staying in a metropolis there was always that risk. In fact, when taking the head count prior to departure we were one less military man and fortunately, he did not make up any of the critical ranks. Of course, there was always the possibility of foul play but we had no time to investigate and every man knew the rules.

We were to follow the River Indus and keeping it to our left as long as possible before the road would split and we were to turn north east. I marched everyone hard for more than 10 days and barring the usual sores and bruises we encamped to what I believed to be several days from our destination. It turned out I was right because we had barely set fires and the cooks started preparing the evening meal when a group of ten riders led by a ranking Kushan Warrior arrived.

After greetings and hospitable welcome, the Kushans felt more at ease as we conversed in the Greek language. We had been watched ever since we left Minnagara and waited until we camped but a day's ride before this meeting to establish our intentions. Although they were sure our goal was purely trade and we were hardly a large force to intimidate them, they were a suspicious people having lived with hostility and warfare for hundreds of years. Besides, how could they be sure a much larger military force was not arriving on their shores. We broke bread, shared our meal with ample refreshments and reassured them we had no other purpose than trade and learning their culture.

We dismantled camp before light and on our way as the sun rose from the east to our right and arrived at Taxila as the sun was sinking to the west on our left. Although rapidly losing light, the walls of the city were most impressive with steep slopes from the base of the citadel to the land. Passing through the vast gates the architecture and building designs were colorful, sturdy and from the activity it was obvious they were garrison quarters that ended abruptly at a bridge over a fifty-meter-wide river. Arriving at the other side we were guided to a large building with stables and advised these were our lodgings for the duration of our stay. Adjacent to the structure was a large open area where we started to pitch our Eighty-man military camp. The rest of us examined the accommodation and allotted the various rooms according to rank of importance.

I was making myself acquainted with my three roomed lodgings when a sealed communication was delivered from the palace. It was an invitation to dine with the Emperor, his family and a small group of Officials. The invitation was for me alone and it also made clear visitors could not bring or display any weapons. A herald and aides would be sent just before dusk to escort me and I should be ready without delays as the emperor regarded promptness in high regard and despised unpunctuality. I dressed in my finest linen Toga with embroiled gold threads, rope designed sash and the finest leather ankle footwear. No armor or jewelry but enough refinement to show my prominence.

As instructed, I was seated on a lounger by the main door when my escorts arrived. With four guards preceding me and four behind, we marched in unison to a waiting carriage. Normally my guard would escort me to my destination but in order to obtain the emperor's trust, they were instructed to remain in the camp. The herald introduced himself as one of Emperor Kujula Kadphisis' advisors and to escort me to the evening's festivities. I thanked him and bid him to lead the way to the waiting carriage. We exchanged pleasantries on the way which took a lot more time than I anticipated, finally arriving as the sun was setting and palace staff were busy lighting the outside torches. I had already reached the conclusion this was a city of considerable size and population.

Through the palace gates into a long, pathed street edged with statues and militia standing with their feet slightly apart at every twenty paces or so that went on for some while before we reached another large, tall doorway. The carriage came to a halt and I was bid to exit at which instant the doors opened. Once inside the room it was impossible not to notice it was enormous, circular in shape, with many passageways attached, descending in all directions and servants coming and going.

As I approached the center of this huge auditorium there was a sunken pool surrounded on three sides with furnishings and pillows of all shapes and sizes. The fourth side had steps leading into the pool and sparsely dressed men and women were busy placing floating timbers on the water laden with all manner of foods and fruits. When all was said and done, a well clothed man with a form of headdress ushered all the servants from the room except three who remained in the pool. Without further ado and invisible door opened on the far side of the room and an entourage of men, women and children entered who seated themselves around the pool seemingly knowing where their place should be. I was requested to join them to the right of the emperor and within touching distance. I bowed before seating myself which brought giggles from the children and grins from everyone else. It is not our custom to bow in private gatherings, only in public, nevertheless I respect the gesture said the emperor.

The servants in the pool glided without making a splash ensuring each dish stopped within reach of all numerous times around. Other servants poured all manner of refreshment and conversation flowed on many a topic but mainly the purpose of my journey and expected rewards. I was also curious as to how the room was kept warm as no fireplace existed. I would learn later. From then on, I nurtured a kindred relationship to Kujula Kadphisis and his family for the next four year. It was during this time I wed his daughter, Ahsan upon her fourteenth birthday. In reality I would be eighty years old.

Buddhist monks were tutoring the Ruler's family and many of them converted to their beliefs and way of life. Two of the monks were Herbalists, creating tonic drinks and potions to boost energy, improve stamina and enhance digestion. It was a new form of medicine and I spent much time learning their skills.

Three years had passed and there was great contentment amongst our travelers. Many had settled with local women, started businesses and even some became Farmers which meant the original intent to develop trade was lost. I too had taken a wife and already fathered a daughter, Kashi, now one year old. The herbalist monks, An and Batuo had a planned trek to the Mountains in the far north and extended an invitation which excited me but not my young wife, especially as she was with child again. She also became very needy and constant arousal required daily activity, many times more than once a day. If it were not for my monk's potions, I may not have been able to keep up with her yearnings. This was some-what diminished when during her early pregnancy she developed chronic morning sickness and fatigue. Opportunity to join the monks on their venture proved timely as my wife's sickness also took a form of revulsion towards me as if I was to blame for her condition.

Upon the advice of the monks, I dressed in the manner of a Huntsman in order to avoid curiosity and I bid my family and King farewell with the intent to return before my child would be born. Without refinery except wearing a solid pair of well-made sandals and a good pair of boots packed on the one horse with all our food supply, water, spare clothes, weapons and utensils, we departed on foot. I would learn a great deal from my new friends, the path to enlightenment, their obedience to meditation, morality and attaining wisdom through being at peace. They had no guilt, desires or unnecessary possessions and shared everything they acquired.

After many days, collecting flora and fauna along the way, we came across a group of nomads who had just slaughtered a wolf to eat and kept her cubs in a cage made of wood. After exchanging greetings and accepting their hospitality I was curious as to why they kept the wolf cubs. Simply to feed them until they were the size of eating was their laughing response as if I asked a foolish question. Could I obtain one of the cubs I asked and offered one of my long steel knives. After examining the quality, they were enthusiastic to trade and I could choose from the litter of three. In my journeys, I had seen wolves trained from whelps and remaining faithful to their masters in numerous capacities and so was my intention to guide this animal to hunt, protect me and be my quiet companion. My traveling brothers thought it unwise to take a beast from its normal habitat but said no more on the subject. After inspecting each animal, I chose what seemed like the alpha pup and the female of the litter. I named her Luna.

We saw no other pilgrims along the way except from a far distance and our final destination of Kashmir was a lot further than first advised. It was also the original birthplace of my Buddhist companions. The predominantly barren land turned into forests and rivers with mountains on the horizon. We stopped by a small village and Batuo walked to the water's edge striking up a conversation with one man then another. Upon his return he advised us a large river boat would be traveling northbound to Jammu and needed one piece of silver for passage that included our horse. Other passengers, beasts, including oxen and pigs, produce and goods would be on board. I produced the one piece of silver that was woven in my tunic and gave it to Batuo who promptly left to engage our passage that was leaving the following day at sunlight.

As scheduled the large, narrow, flat bottom boat departed as the sun began to rise in the sky. Animals were placed in make-shift pens and owners were responsible for feed and keeping the deck clean. Passengers were busy claiming their space for the duration of the voyage which for the most part done in orderly fashion.

After four miserable nights we arrived at a rudimentary landing point in the early hours of the morning but still in darkness and most everyone disembarked and as rapidly as we arrived the boat departed into the obscurity of the river. As we climbed the steps the early morning light started to appear as we reached a road and we could see the river below winding through the metropolis known as Srinagar and in the distance a vast range of mountains. The Himalayas.

We were the last group of people walking towards the city and arrived at the outskirts in the full morning light. A tall foreboding wall appeared and we could see an entrance to the city with a large contingent of armed soldiers searching all carts and random people as they entered through the large, presently open gates.

We arrived at the entrance and without a murmur ushered to pass. Batou spoke quietly, we are recognized as holy men and regarded as innocuous and without threat. The road meandered and our leg muscles gave strong indication of gaining height as continued up the main thoroughfare. After a while we stopped to rest by a water well where others were drinking and waited our turn to drink. From this point we could see clearly below the river separating the city and many bridges spanning between the two sides. With my eyes following the river and I could see it ended at a huge lake as far as I could see towards the mountains. After satisfying our thirst we continued and after a while I could feel the rumbling of my stomach reminding me, we had not eaten in a while. Almost immediately, my companions stopped, climbed some adjacent steps to a door of a small building and entered without knocking and I followed. The door opened to a small open-air garden and looking beyond was a long room as wide as the house itself and smoke filled the chamber and I could smell this sweet and pleasant odor that I later learned was from the flower known as Jasmin.

I had learnt many words and a few sentences of Koshur, the language of Kashmir, and after giving the formal greeting of Anjali Mudra to our hosts I was received with a hearty welcome. When I first met my Buddhists companions, they taught me their respectful gesture of greeting by pressing the palms together in front of the chest which is referred to as Anjali Mudra. I also learned that Buddhists claim that four communication ideologies must be preserved in order to reach harmony amongst other human beings. They being, kindness, peace, truthfulness and usefulness. I had become very respectful of their way of life and embraced much of their conviction and faith.

After washing myself, fruit and flat bread were served for the main meal. Soon thereafter, I was shown to some humble quarters where I could rest. For many moons I spent time acquiring knowledge of both the language and local plants, vegetation and herbs. I ventured many walks throughout the town which was much larger than I first supposed. I crossed many a bridge over River Vyath as it meandered onward to Lake Wular. Lakes, swamps and lush forests surrounding the city and wildlife of every kind was in abundance. What I did not see was any real sign of poverty or hunger as they lived of the land and hunted only for food.

I had returned from one of my strolls with Luna to be informed that a rider had arrived from Taxila with urgent news for my ears only. Whilst being led to the messenger, I was advised that he appeared with a fever and confined until my arrival. Once in the room I approached with caution covering my face as I grew closer to him. I recognized the symptoms not unlike the affliction I had experience during the Eastern Campaign and ordered all who came in contact with him to gather until I could examine them further. The courier lifted his arm with difficulty and pointed to the leather satchel on the table but before I would carefully inspect the contents, I questioned him of the situation and how he became unwell. In a brief summary I was informed that the city was engrossed in this pestilence that emanated from the visiting force that I brought the city. It ravaged everyone from the general populace to the heads of the rich classes that included the Emperor, my wife, and daughter. Stunned with grief and anger, I could not compose myself but knew I had to return to Taxila to see for myself the devastation and what I could do to overcome the sickness.

The messenger died in the night before I left early the next morning, carrying the dispatches without opening them. The journey was tedious and delayed due to monsoon weather but I arrived during heavy rain and noticeable lack of people in the streets. Upon entering the palace, I was greeted with both delight and apprehension, but I made it clear I was aware of the disease and the necessary courses of action to take place. I made a list of demands and actions to start the control and separation of the stricken and a process in place of cleanliness rules. It took some time to pursued the governing power to accept my demands but soon realized I knew more about the issue than they.

It took several days but the strategy was taking place. Volunteers were drafted on the basis of rewards and training was administered under my administration. After many weeks the numbers of afflicted was becoming less and after three months we had the situation under control. By this time, I was exhausted and thoughts of my future started to worry me and I knew serious decisions and arrangements for my move forward had to be made. To protect my life, I decided that I would produce false dispatches to all my interested partners by introducing a son and my upcoming adventures in Asia. By doing so, I would protect my legacy and give me time to understand my existence and path forward.

BOOK 2

CHAPTER 01

Letter and Dispatches

My first dispatches to Gaius, Vitellius, and Julia were sent with the returning fleet, detailing the events to the time of our departure with particulars of my intended venture to the north. My instructions were to address all future correspondence to me care off the Port commander, City of Barbarikon. My second and third dispatches were conveyed by caravans overland and knew not if they arrived at their destinations as return letters made no mention of them. I sent another dispatch to all three recipients, detailing what was in my previous communications that included taking a wife and the birth of a daughter, both who perished in a plague. It was almost five years before news reached me from Rome, Verona, and Pompei and I was unsure of each one's arrival at Barbarikon.

Gaius

Initially the news was brief from Verona, mainly around the selling price agreed with Julia (although, as agreed no mention of the price in dispatches) and that the silver had arrived by caravan hidden in secret compartments in wagons. The olive yield was good and the new grapes vines did not produce a very palatable first year wine due to incomplete water irrigation. Nevertheless, the new crops were showing plump and juicier grapes and improved harvest each year. In later letters he asked me if I heard from Rome and the major changes without giving me any detail other than Nero had become Emperor and a centurion and his soldiers had arrived in Verona seeking my whereabouts and had ransacked my home. My fortune was safe as it was well hidden and he was instructing his son, Marcus of his affairs as he was suffering with an inhalation problem, shortness of breath, and difficulty keeping his food digested. He finished by saying they had no word from me and concerned.

Vitellius

I hastened to open his dispatch. Much had occurred since my departure the saddest news of which was the death of Agrippina at the hands of her son, Nero. Brutally clubbed and stabbed in her villa, she was cremated on her dining couch without any formal ceremony. Vitellius feared for his family and likely to leave Rome as Nero was assassinating all those close to Claudius. I should also know that my name was on Nero's list and to be wary of Rome's long reach. Silence followed and I worried for my adopted family in Rome.

Julia

She wrote that most of her news was through customers from Rome and that fear had gripped the empire once again with many associated with Agrippina executed or perished in the gladiator ring as entertainment. That included the family of Vitellius Quintas Gallus who all perished and that there was a list issued of wanted persons that included my name, Simon Gallus. soldiers had also visited her premises seeking my whereabouts. I quietly mourned them both, Agrippina, Vitellius, and his family.

Time moved on and I wrote nothing. I did however, receive numerous notifications from Julia;. A great fire had consumed much of Rome and soon thereafter Nero committed suicide with the help of his guardsmen, although indications where the Praetorian guardsman were at the point to murder him anyway. Servius Galba succeeded Nero, albeit for less than a year. The plague had gripped the nation when Marcus Salvius Otho became emperor of Rome on the death of Galba in 69. He was succeeded by Vitellius. It was Vitellius who proclaimed certain families to be vindicated who were assassinated by Nero. This included the exoneration of Vitellius Quintas Gallus, any member of his family, and me.

The eldest daughter of Lucius Junius Silanus Torquatus, Scribonia, now aged twenty-two, became the understudy to Julia, trained and highly efficient in the arts of love, becoming the most demanded by the wealthy senators of Rome. Julia discovered that Scribonia was asking questions of her family. She had remembered Rome was her birthplace and was determined to investigate the roots of her family. The opportunity presented itself when an introduction to a senior member of Senate during a visit to Julia's establishment. Scribonia spent the full summer in Rome at a discreet property owned by the senator, well away from his own home and family. Little by little she learned the identity of her parents and slaughtered brothers. The Gallus family were the main perpetrators, most of whom were eliminated under the instructions of Emperor Nero with the exception of one Simon Gallus whose whereabouts and family status were unknown. Scribonia quietly spread the word of a large reward for his location and I knew it was only a matter of time before she would be rewarded.

Titus Flavius Vespasianus was ruling Emperor at the time and had been for a number of years when Julia travelled to Verona with Clodia now twenty years of age where she started a loving friendship with the son of Gaius Gavius Silvanus, named Marcus, after his grandfather. It was during this time that Mount Vesuvius erupted destroying everything in Pompei including all of Julia's assets, ladies and all. It was 79AD. As fortune would have it, Julia traveled with a large amount of silver coin with for payment of my partnership plus he owns fortune with the intent to keep in my safe keeping in Verona.

It was time to reappear as my invented son Agrippa and sent a dispatch in that name to Marcos hoping it would reach him before I did in person. It was another year prior to my arrivals and I was greeted with the news of Julia's death.

CHAPTER 2

Verona, Clodia and Scribonia

M arcos made we very welcome as the son of his father's closest friend. Clodia was truly a delight and I must say under different circumstances I might have pursued her as I felt a chemistry there, but out of respect did not. Julia had left my father (me) sealed letters but as his heir Marcos thought it acceptable for me to open the documents. Most of the contents were making Clodia her heir and the rest of the papers were detailing Julia's life through diary's, the activity of Scribonia and her marriage to a member of the Senate. She also left me a list of names in Rome, who, for sums of money would spy for me. I decided to pursue this avenue, if nothing else for peace of mind.

I knew that I needed a long-term plan and decided to return to my beloved India via Rome and to see what Scribonia's intentions are and to what end she was scheming. Meanwhile, I would relax and enjoy the company of Marcos and Clodia whilst devoting the rest of the time reviewing my fortune, how to transport it and contemplating my future. I spent long periods in the company of Marcos and much discussion around our futures and that of the Roman Empire. He still owned the seal of friendship I had given his father and we agreed to use them not only for ourselves but generations to come.

Traveling to Rome, I bid farewell knowing I would not see them again. I had grown fond of Marcos and Clodia but knew through my dreams that they would have long, happy lives and produce six children—five sons and one daughter.

I met with several of Julia's contacts giving them instruction to provide whatever information of Scribonia's activities surrounding her investigation into my whereabouts and to send to Marcos. I paid in advance with promises of further payments from Marcos Silvanos of Verona. Scribonia was murdered by her husband who himself committed suicide and I never knew the reason why.

Passing Years

I once again ceased to exist with the exception of the occasional dispatch to Marcos, his children and his children's children. Another hundred years passed and once more I had indirect contact with the Roman court during the reign of Marcus Aurelius, a formidable Emperor, a passive philosopher and due to his health became addicted to opium which he took every night to get some sleep and I happened to be the supplier. Due to controlled supply and demand, and very expensive cost, opium was only available to the higher classes of Roman society.

The Roman empire died some thirty years later after the rule of Commodus, who was the worst Emperor of the Antonine dynasty. He was alike Nero, the idol of the masses spending most of Rome's fortune organizing gladiator exhibitions and unlimited death.

The visions, dreams and nightmare continued through the years and I did not return to Italy until some 160 years later as Marcus Quintas Gallus.

CHAPTER 4

300AD - My Wife Octavia

I cannot say that I have experienced real love, but I loved women, enjoyed the chase and the excitement of the relationship, companionship, and good conversation. Such a woman I met at one of the many celebrations of the emperor's return from Britannia. Although I had not known her long, I threw caution to the wind and made Octavia my wife. I learned over time I had married a deceitful, cunning, scheming, and unfaithful woman. She had been married before whose husband died of an unidentifiable disease but as I ascertained later, most people believed he was poisoned.

One night she arrived home very late from reveling with lady friends of disrepute and started to flaunt herself in order to tease and offend me with an outcome she did not anticipate. I had a goblet of red wine in my hand and with unexpected rage threw it against the wall then rapidly approached a traumatized Octavia. Slapping her in the face sent her reeling to the floor when I quickly followed landing on her reluctant body letting out a deep sigh from the impact. My face touched hers and I could taste the blood from her lips. The combination of her scent and the taste of her blood ignited my loins and I could tell she had little or no undergarments. She sensed the situation and started to struggle which increased my lust, and I tore her clothing until her pelvic hair was visible. I too was only wearing a loose silk vestment that I easily discarded showing my very erect and throbbing penis. She started to thrash and shaking her head from side to side but I proved to be too strong for her when the head of my cock discovered the soft flesh of her cunei lips then thrusting hard into her love canal that was surprisingly wet.

After a while as I thrust into her with mighty vigor, she started to relax but I continued to hold her arms firmly to the floor changing my tempo from time to time and moving my pulsating cock from side to side. She started to moan, getting louder and louder and even though I could feel the ache in my testis, I withheld the release of my load until I heard the scream of her orgasm and warm juices engulfing my hard phallus. Moments later I released wave after wave of bursting semen as deep as I could until the last throb. I did not withdraw and continued to lay on top of Octavia until I allowed her to push me off at which time, she rushed to the washroom crying on the way. For several days I took her when I wanted, how I wanted, and she never fought back. Then as suddenly as it started, my anger and passion ceased, I avoided her, and we lived in separate parts of the villa.

When Octavia discovered she was with child she despised me even more and avoided me until the arrival of our son whom she named Aquila. I briefly tried reconciliation but quickly discovered it was a waste of time. As time passed, I traveled often and according to my spies she took every opportunity to turn my son against me, spoiling him rotten to the core and displaying incestuous tendencies. I did not contest the issues and when I was at home, they shunned me.

CHAPTER 05

323 A.D. SILK ROADS

The journey from China was always a challenge, from bandits, traveler theft, injuries, sickness but most of all the extremely difficult mountainous paths, deserts, weather conditions and its consequences. Fortunately, on this my seventh expedition, spanning twenty years it was less arduous than all my previous ventures. Nevertheless, between raids, accidents, disease, disputes and executions fifty-nine men were lost. Under my rule, Women and Children were not permitted. Some 120 years before, the first rulers of China during the Han Dynasty opened trade outside of Asia. To develop such trade a road needed construction on which traders could safely travel the thousands of miles to reach other countries. Commencing in Luoyang, central China, then following part of the Great Wall, through numerous mountain ranges, passing through deserts all the way to Antioch and the Mediterranean Sea. From there, boats carried the goods across the sea to Europa. Since the first enslaved labor force started the first road over 5000 miles of varied routes were developed to many countries where trade proved profitable albeit named singularly as the Silk Road.

Obviously, from its name, silk was one of the primary goods traded from the East but it was far from the only item. Tea, rice, spices, paper, dyes and even medicines (many I kept for myself). We traded with silver but also many large herds of animals, camels, horses and dogs (some of which were bred on the route). Furs, Skins and Seed were also in demand.

Our caravan consisting of three hundred plus wagons, one hundred and twenty Camels and almost a thousand men, some quarter of the size of the outbound journey. It was but a day's travel to our final destination of Nicaea in Byzantium and already merchants were greeting us to purchase goods before we reached our destination. I had already received Constantine's list of demands from his herald some days before and subsequently separated those items and others that I thought would please him. After all it was, he who financed the caravans and supplied the personal guard. I also received a personal letter from Constantine but I did not need to read the letter immediately as I knew very well the knowledge of its content. My son, Aquila. I first met Constantine during a hunt many years past in Britannia where he was serving under his father in the rank of Augustus. He had fallen from his horse and I tendered his scrapes and bruises. We became friends and shared nightly adventures, wine, women (sometimes the same woman), interesting, and sometimes gripping conversation, much around what he believed to be the future and the role in which Religion would play. I listened intently but often did not share his beliefs.

His father, Constantitius was the senior Western Emperor of three such Emperors, governing by region but immersed in turmoil and civil war. After his death in AD 306, Constantine the Great as he became known was declared senior Western Emperor by the army.

I had lived a life of fear, fear of the unknown, living for over 300 years and not aging, not having answers to my questions. I maintained the habit of eating breakfast with my daylight guard and dinner with my dark hours guard sharing conversation whilst listening and observing the characters of each man, the good and bad traits. We had camped for our final night before entering the city and the excitement, bartering and celebrations began. As usual my tent was placed in the center one hundred paces from all others except my six personal trusted bodyguards and their fifty-man guards strategically placed in ten smaller tents. They were some of Constantine's elite guard, highly paid, treated and fed well, many of which I knew by name and gave respect to as they did for me.

CHAPTER 06

Aquila

I had retired to my tent to read the last of many dispatches sent by Constantine's herald and poured myself a glass of wine when I heard a voice requesting entrance. I immediately recognized the voice of Cornelius, one of my elite guards and bid him to enter. Behind him by a few paces was my son and another young, if not younger boy. Aquila nervously embraced me then taking a step backwards, he introduced his companion, Marcellus. We acknowledged each other by a slight nod of the head. Turning back to stare at my son's face, I looked deeply into his slightly bloodshot eyes and asked in annoyance, "Why are you here?"

He took a moment to speak and blurted out "I took it for granted father that you would be busy on your arrival in the city, meeting with the emperor and members of the Council so I thought it would be opportune to greet you beforehand."

Not taking my eyes away from Aquila, I commanded Cornelius to bring some more wine and goblets. He quickly returned with another guard, Livius, bringing two flagons of wine, two goblets, a bowl of fruit and assorted olives. Cornelius was always thoughtful. No words had been exchanged between the time of order and arrival but I gestured the two young men to sit.

"What of the journey?" young Marcellus enquired. I gave an in-depth overview of the main events and perils we encountered, whilst consuming our wine and assorted fruits. It didn't take long however for Aquila to request their leave to venture around the camp. I pondered for a moment then offered an escort of one of my guards. This was quickly declined as unnecessary and so I gave them permission to leave.

As they left, Cornelius re-entered. "Have one of your best men discreetly follow my son and companion and report back to me," I instructed. He rapidly took his leave to follow my orders. I took another gulp of wine, recalling the events of the past in Byzantine with Constantine. I laid down, closed my eyes for what I intended only a brief moment. Almost immediately I drifted into one of my semi-conscience visions looking down on a heavily smoked campfire. Hemp sacks were burning and the small group were inhaling the essence. Wine was being consumed and breathing in another substance from a palm leaf. It became apparent that three men were highly intoxicated, naked, with their members erect. Suddenly, one man tripped and fell on his back whilst another threw himself on top, pinning him to the ground. Forcibly spreading his legs open, the aggressor penetrated the body of the fallen victim. It became clear that both men were in rapture, one fondling himself while the other thrusted his penis aggressively into the willing body. The third man moved closer stroking his cock with vigor. The assailant reached up his hands closing around the victim's neck and as he tightened the recipient spurted his juices all over himself. Almost immediately the standing man started groaning loudly as his semen exploded onto the two bodies below. The hands gripped the neck tighter as his body kept thrusting as he was reaching new heights of passion. The victim was flailing his legs in resistance and with bulging eyes passed out. This did not stop the strangulation and within minutes a wail of delight filled the air as his orgasm filled the lifeless body.

As with many of my visions, I jerked my body up with sweat rolling down my face. This nightmare was unusual inasmuch I dreamt it for the one time only and I immediately knew I was having the revelation as it happened. Whilst I proceeded to pull myself together, Cornelius entered my tent with a grave look on his face. As instructed, he had one of his scouts follow Aquila that led him to a campfire. He watched them for some considerable time as they consumed wine and what seemed like some substance from a palm leaf at which point, he needed to take a piss. Thinking this spying could take some time he quietly retreated to some bushes where he began to relieve himself but taking his time and looking up at the stars. Upon returning to his vantage point, he witnessed the events that took place which was interesting to watch, but not sexually arousing having a preference for the feminine flesh. Besides, he was not close enough to see all the activity in detail with the most aggressive man showing his back. It was not very long before all three naked men were laying down seemingly in deep sleep when the scout decided to move closer. As he approached the now dimming fire, the early dawn was approaching. Stepping cautiously, he came upon what looked like a very young male lying seemingly lifeless. Once past the smoke, the body became clearer, with vast amount of blood around the genitals area. He then noticed his penis was missing. Casting his eyes up the young man's body, he saw severe bruising around the throat but what attracted his sight was the bulging eyes. Looking over at the other two men he saw the severed penis in the nearest, now snoring man's gripping fist and a bloody knife in the other. The third man lay further away and had vomited that still laid in his mouth. He quickly left the scene to report back to Cornelius.

I shivered as Cornelius told me of his scout's report, not of the event, but the fact I dreamt of it. I immediately rose to my feet and instructed Cornelius to make haste back to the campfire and establish who the killer was, move all three bodies to one of the guard tents, restrain the two live ones, cover the third and remove all evidence. I washed my face and my thoughts reflected back to my vision. It wasn't long before I heard the voice of a guard bidding to enter. "Pass," I cried. The guard entered and introduced himself as the scout, Marcus. He requested I follow him to where Cornelius was waiting outside the guard's tent and relate to me the evidence of his discovery. My son was the perpetrator, over and over I said in my head. What should I do? The fact Aquila was my son should not cloud my judgement but the irritation in the pit of my stomach was telling me to be lenient. Suddenly I returned to reality.

"I await your instruction my liege" said Cornelius, realizing the predicament I had been placed in.

"I need to gather my thoughts and strength," I said. "Meanwhile, this tent is off limits to all except the three of us. Is that clear?" Saying nothing both of them gave me the Roman soldier's salute signifying complete obedience. "Do we know who the third man is?" I asked.

"A Camel merchant who also had considerable amounts of herbs, spices, and other unknown powder substances, but we suspect it is opium."

After brief consideration it was clear this man had no knowledge of the murder but he must surely know what manner and danger of the powder they were all digesting. "Try not to waken him fully and bring him to the surgical tent", leaving Marcus to guard Aquila. I made my way quietly to the surgery tent knowing it would be empty and away from the main encampment. It seemed like a lot more time had passed than necessary and I was starting to get impatient when the third man arrived looking soaking wet followed my Cornelius with this sword drawn. "What took so long?" I said angrily.

"It took me a while to awaken him and needed to make a brief stop by the stream and push him in. He became aggressive, hence drawing my sword and ordering him to walk ahead, giving him no reason why."

The interrogation commenced and without pressure proved to be extremely talkative and a willing informant. Learning he was originally from Egypt and although he bought and sold camels, his real profession was dealing in recreation drugs for wealthy clients in Byzantium and Rome. We gathered from him that Aquila was seeking a supplier in Byzantium but was informed there was no supply and waiting for a large shipment on the next caravan due to arrive any day. Aquila forcibly obtained the Egyptian's name and presented himself with a friend the previous evening. Normally he would not deal with an individual but as the son of noble Simon leading this caravan it was sensible to oblige. The Egyptian then proceeded to instruct Aquila and his friend Marcellus the process of diluting the drug and warned of the serious aggressive side effects of mixing wine at the same time. The Egyptian was invited to participate, initially declining, but Aquila was quite persuasive declaring it would be at his expense. After a while, additional doses were taken, adding the wine when issues arose. He did not recall most of the evening to the point when he could not stand anymore and passed out. "Why were you naked?" I asked. He did not remember. "Quite convenient," I stated. "Bind and gag him, Cornelius, then go get Aquila."

"Shall I clean him up?" he asked.

"No, bring him as he is and tell Marcus to bring the body of Marcellus but not visible to the camp."

Cornelius returned with Aquila wearing a very disheveled robe and bloody hands looking confused and disoriented. He became even more so when he saw the Egyptian bound and gagged.

"What is happening, why am I being held?" Aquila asked

"All in good time" I responded

"Now be silent" I continued

" Even though I had little or no contact, I had tried over the last eighteen troubled years to educate him with the best advisors and tutors, Aquila turned out to be a narcissistic bully using my position and friendship with Constantine to manipulate and hurt others. His mother spoiled him, possessed and influenced him to the point of incest, whilst protecting him from all his wrong doings. Truth be known I disliked the boy, and often wondered if he was from my seed.

Marcus arrived carrying a rug over his shoulder which he placed immediately on the ground. "Marcus," I instructed. "Please tell us the story

106

of last night's events." I was quite surprised as to the detail Marcus maintained during the narration and gruesome detail, almost like he enjoyed telling. "Marcus, "I directed, "Unravel the rug," which he did. The Egyptian's eyes narrowed as he reclined his body away from the naked lifeless body of Marcellus. Aquila stared in disbelief, shaking his head and denying any responsibility then repeating, "No, no, no it wasn't me."

"Cornelius," I said loudly, "Kill the Egyptian through heart." With swift movement he withdrew his sword and thrust it in his chest. Sliding sideways, the Egyptian fell, taking his last breath.

"Father," Aquila squealed. "It was the camel dung of a so-called Egyptian who killed my friend as our identities were confused in the dark." He was sniveling as I produced the knife used to castrated young Marcellus and he recognized it as his own. Marcus stood motionless with Cornelius close by his side still holding the bloody sword. Both were staring at me with anticipation but knew not of what would happen next but expected a cover up. After all, he was my son. I moved in front of my son and put my left arm around him drawing his body to mine placing his head to my shoulder. Whimpering for his own sake and simultaneously, without saying a word, I thrust the knife into his side parallel to his heart that ended his life. Momentarily shocked, Cornelius and Marcus stared at my action before reaching out and catching the dead weight of Aquila.

As they let him slowly drop to the floor, I spoke clearly and decisively. "You caught the Egyptian in the act of killing Aquila and Marcellus while under the influence from the poppy flower. This shall be documented so and only the three of us will know what really happened.

If it had been anyone else other than my son, justice would have been taken by another hand. His mother will be informed by me on arrival and not before. My gratitude will be generous and will grant any reasonable request." I looked them both in the eyes and commanded a response; are we agreed? With their clenched fists on their hearts, they agreed. "Bury the Egyptian, clean the bodies of my son and his companion, cover them with oil of eucalyptus, and wrap them in cloth ready to transport to Byzantium. We will inquire on arrival who to notify of the death of Marcellus."

Drinking my final glass of wine before sleep when I cast my mind back to the last three hundred eventful and sometimes terrifying years. Having been wounded, beaten, captive and tortured I managed not only to endure but healed with wonderous haste. I had learned to survive, learned to kill that included family, friends and those who started to know too much. My conscience was unbelievably clear, my secret needed to be protected until I understood my purpose.

Constantine and The Council of Nicaea

We set camp by the river in an area kept for traveling caravans and traders. Tents were assembled and goods were distributed and stored according to type and value whilst camels, horses and other stocks were taken to the holding pens. For obvious reasons I selected Marcus and Cornelius to accompany me to my home in Nicaea and bare witness when I informed Aquila's mother of her son's death. Their concurrence of our contrived account to Octavia would bind them further to me.

Octavia stared at the lifeless body of her son in disbelief, glared at me, then collapsed to the floor, her body moving convulsively and screaming from the top of her lungs. Her maid servants rushing to her side to console her but had difficulty getting to her as she squirmed vigorously, screaming even louder. Octavia stiffened when she was raised up by her servants. "Take her to her bed," I said. "I will bring her a tonic to help her rest." They carried her away sobbing.

I prepared the potion and took it myself where Octavia was lying face down weeping between deep sighs. I sat beside her when she turned abruptly staring at me with a resentful look. "This was you're doing!" she screamed. "You never cared for my son," she continued. "Aquila was my joy, my only child, my friend, my lover!" She gasped when she realized what she had said and her face turned red and expressionless awaiting my reaction.

I handed her the potion saying, "Drink, it will make you feel better." She took the goblet in anger and before leaving I asked for information regarding the family of Marcellus so I might inform them of the tragedy, but received no reply. Without another word, I took my leave. I sent word to Constantine of my arrival and awaited further news. The next morning, I received a reply to see him on the morrow at the high rise of the sun in the city of Nicaea. I instructed my supply administrator to deliver in advance a complete list of the Emperor's trade and an optional list that may be of interest.

During this time, I had no contact with Octavia other than keeping her appraised of Aquila's funeral arrangements through my affairs supervisor, Arius. I would have to be rid of Octavia and I thought I know how. She would not survive the night; it would be staged to look like she took her own life due to grief. I would not mourn; in fact, it would be a great release for me.

Arius also maintained a meticulous record of information that took place in my absence, the civil wars with Maxentius and Licinius finally coming to an end after four bloody years and under singular rule of Constantine for some months now. The city had many new guests, religious leaders summoned by Constantine and at his expense in particular Bishop Hosui of Cordova. Although I knew the civil war was religious in nature and dissention amongst its leaders, I couldn't help wonder what Constantine was up to? The meeting with Constantine was not as I expected. He was dressed elaborately in purple clothing adorned by many jewels and acting excitedly. We quickly reviewed his caravan contents and extra objects he had chosen for a price beyond reasonable that I did not contest. He was so caught up in a frenzy to greet his daily guests and without debate bid me to join him.

The last thing I wanted was to listen to all these so-called spiritual scholars but I would not dare deny my Constantine. He went into a great deal of detail as to who was attending, some 200 Christian Bishops from across the Roman Empire, and their ensembles of Deacons, Priests, Scribes and followers debating the doctrines of Jesus Christ and many issue surrounding contested and acceptable scriptures. He had actually invited many more, some 1000 or so, which would have been madness if such a gathering took place.

The Council of Nicaea was held in the palace Grand room and before we had arrived voices could be heard quite loudly from several chambers away. On entering the vast main hall, the noise diminished when the congregation noticed Constantine had arrived. He stood momentarily but what seemed much longer before slowly walking forward and the individuals bowing and nodding in his presence. He quickened the pace stopping from time to time to formerly greet some of his guests and introducing me to them.

Constantine the Great was no idiot; in fact, he was a master negotiator and mediator. He did not merely petition the bishops of the churches in the empire appear before him for he called a council in a city easily accessible to all the bishops of the empire. He also paid their travel expenses, lodging and welcomed them with formidable grandeur and enthusiasm. He simply appealed to their vanity and greed. It became very clear that Constantine played a meaningful function even though he was not a man of God. The privilege was granted by the Bishops and he played a significant role in their discussions through tact and diplomacy. Multiple subjects were presented by each delegation, which stirred up controversies from the very start. The emperor listened to all with patient attention, deliberately and impartially considering whatever was advanced. He partially supported the statements which were made on either side, and gradually softened the severity of those who opposed each other. Little did he or I know how the Nicaea council meetings would have a profound and significant influence on the future of the world.

As I listened a shiver went down my spine with the thought that these individuals would represent our future, most of whom were bigots, extremists, zealots and fanatics. I needed to be far removed from this scene, and soon.

It was the year 325

CHAPTER 08

Aragon

After my discrete departure from Nicaea in 325 AD I was in a turmoil as to my next steps in life. I finally decided to return to Verona where I would clear my mind and spend time planning the future. It was 326. Playing the role of an ancestor, I enjoyed the peace and solace for the next eighty years.

It was the turn of the fifth century and news from Rome was unpleasant and disturbing.

For some time, I had developed my own ring of paid informants, some I paid in cash, others in kind. Over time I had learned the art of observing other people's traits, needs, anxieties, desires and I succeeded to manipulate and influence them to the point where I became a necessity.

It was a time of great turmoil in the realm where, due to internal strife Emperors lasted but a mere few years. It was time for a life change. Many years ago, I had met a visiting Germanic merchant residing in a region of the western Pyrenees of Spain called Aragon. His name was Petrus Sabbatius, an influential local governor. This area was rich in the mining of metals and we entered into a partnership for the purpose of the making of coins. I had only visited the area once for half a year and loved the remoteness and beauty of this mountain region. Whilst there I purchased property in a small village called Astun just ten miles from the capital, Jaca.

The empire's northern legions had their encampment just outside Verona and made it my business to infiltrate their senior ranks and gain their trust and in some cases friendship.

As Aragon formed part of the Roman Empire, the northern armies had an allegiance to its citizens, or at least those who had influence and fortunes. I had indicated to my new companions that on behalf of the Emperor I had invested in in mining and a newly developed coin making facility. I backed this untruth with forged documents and a large purse to those that would accompany me on the journey from Verona.

It was a matter of a few days before I was approached by a military tribune and two centurions that they would undertake the mission for a substantial sum of silver. The amount was somewhat more than I anticipated to pay and as much as I expressed so, showed reluctance, but agreed. Half to be paid on departure and balance upon arrival Aragon. With smiling faces, we had an agreement and would leave in the spring, some three months ahead. In the meantime, we would send ahead a troop of fifty men carrying dispatches and substantial funds to my business partner Petrus Sabbatius instructing him to set up an encampment for the troops and plans to start building a large fortified dwelling on my property in Astun. It was the year 410.

The spring flowers were in bloom as the caravan of over forty wagons and oxen carrying everything from tools to silk, gold, silver and jewels hidden within. Supported by 225 cavalries, 300-foot soldiers, 175 carpenters, and stonemasons the expedition took fifty days to travel 900 miles. It took three years to build my home with secret passages and rooms with a subterranean floor and a cellar below it. I had seven different crews working so that nobody knew except me the full design and layout of the Chateau Cassius. In parallel, closer to the river we built quarters and barracks to house fifty officers of various ranks and 1,000 soldiers. It was a number of years before Rome became aware of this outpost but quickly acknowledged its strategic location and fortifying the garrison with another five legions. We called the town Saragoza after the great city of Caesar Augusta. Petrus and I developed a large trading warehouse, a blacksmith and an infirmary with healing training under my direction.

As our partnership blossomed so did our friendship. Petrus was blessed with six children when his wife died in childbirth with their seventh child, who also perished. He took his grief very hard and drank himself to sleep most nights. His drinking began to impair his decision and after a blunt discussion with his children I locked him up in a bare room to free him from his curse. He hated me at the time but it did sober him up enough that I was able to speak with him clearly and honestly, what he was doing to himself and to his family. Leaving him with his own deliberations and the welcome sight of his offspring turned him into a deep sobbing outbreak. It took time and the wonders of happy, determined adolescent were the key. Viola, his eldest child at seventeen was betrothed to a Roman officer and Ophelia at fifteen was blossoming into a fine young lady that it caught my sincere attention. To my surprise when I approached Petrus with the possibility of taking Ophelia as my bride, he was filled with joy and sanctioned such a partnership. However, I insisted that I court Ophelia in my own way, to capture her love if I could. My second surprise was that she was receptive, even overjoyed to such an advancement, claiming she had desires in my direction. She gave me such a bracing hug I could feel my penis growing with eagerness. Upon release she had obviously felt my passion and gently covered my enlargement with her cupped hand and probing fingers.

We were married on her sixteenth birthday and gave birth to our son before she was seventeen. Arousal and sexuality came natural to Ophelia, which fulfilled my desires greatly. To my amazement she instigated fresh concepts to our love making, positions, independence, and toys. It seemed after each child was born, her obsession with sexual practice intensified and never ceased to astound me. Within hours after our fifth girl being born, she wanted to have stimulation and after self-indulging masturbation and subsequent orgasm, she had an itch at her anal spot and whilst soothing with her fingers noticed I had an erection. She continued to rotate one finger and inserted into her rectum followed by a second finger. I could not wait any longer as I reached out for the jar of palm oil and poured it generously over my genitals. I moved swiftly, first entering her vagina as she increased the thrusting of her fingers into her rectum muscle. She was extremely wet and discharging her juices with vigor when I withdrew momentarily then moving my phallus resting on her fingers. Removing her fingers, I pressed my shaft into her awaiting anal muscle which made her jerk with some pain. The pain turned to joy as she started to gyrate wildly. Screaming loudly, Ophelia had orgasm after orgasm while I filled her bowels with my deluge of semen.

Ophelia started to grow with our third child when I noticed she was paying a little more than normal attention to a young horse trainer we recently engaged. When I approached her on the subject, she grinned saying that naughty thoughts had entered her mind to entertain him in our sexual adventures. She surprised me but considering her sexual prowess, the thought could have happened sooner. After some considerable deliberation, I decided, why not! After all, due to her condition, she could not conceive.

Ophelia approached him with the invitation and casually over dinner she informed me of Dimitri's positive response and the encounter would be our dessert. For a three-way, it was a scorching experience. This relationship continued on a regular basis until Ophelia decided it would stop due to her increased size and discomfort. It was but a week or so later Dimitri and I were bathing when I saw his erection and he grasped mine. After extensive foreplay, I butt fucked him until he came and I was exhausted.

It was the year 420 and another daughter was born.

Although diminished in strength over a number of years, my visions during sleep returned with a vengeance, flashes of pain and demise overcame me. For the next five years and no additional children, we lived a peaceful existence although our evening entertainment did not diminish. Winter had come and gone.

CHAPTER 9

Bereavement & Diversity

I t was spring and Dimitri informed me of the arrival of a Nomadic caravan that encamped by the river. He added that he came upon them when he was taking two of the stable horses for exercise. He approached with caution but received by its people with courteous gestures and gladness. Their language was seemingly a dialect of Greek and it was his understanding they had been traveling west for some ten years fleeing pestilence and aggressions How many are there I inquired to which he responded four to five hundred, were poorly dressed, malnourished, transport driven by oxen and basic tent like accommodation. They had a leader spokesperson called Theodore who requested compassion and aid for he had sickness and hunger. I immediately ordered the slaughter of ten cows and ten goats, skinned and cut to be delivered to the roaming settlers tomorrow. I would personally pay them a visit the next morning to ascertain the severity of their infections.

Leading the small convoy of wagons loaded with beef and goat carcasses, blankets and footwear I entered the community and greeted by who I assumed was Theodore. His broad smile showed me his joy at the arrival of so much food, as he screamed out loud to his partisans. A mass of people suddenly appeared, advancing towards the carts of meat and screaming with delight. Leaving them to their preparations and cutting further of the carcasses into smaller pieces I dismounted from my horse and started to roam the campsite. On reaching the far end I noticed one large marquee distanced and close to the banks of the river. It was strangely placed with the entrance facing the waterway. Lifting the flap type doorway, the pungent smell of pestilence hit my nostrils like a hammer. As my eyes adjusted to the hazy light, I covered my face with my bandana and saw what looked like at least twenty women and children in attendance. Reaching back to the entrance I lifted the flap to allow more light into the den and what I saw took my breath away. Memories of my eastern Roman campaign flooded back to me of the same pox like disease as I moved between the infected group noticing several of the bodies were indeed corpses. Retreating instantly and taking a deep breath, I vomited into the river. I immediately came to my senses, jumped upon my horse and rode to the fortress.

Making my way to the Commandant's quarters where I was greeted warmly but after explaining the reason for my visit, his face turned visibly pale. We both agreed the caravan had to isolated and each and every individual examined. Every member of the guard had to wear hand coverage and facial covering their nose and mouths. A centurion instructed the guard accordingly and quickly moved his soldiers to the camp.in a rapid march His instructions were that everyone that had no reason to be in the encampment were evacuated but needed to register formally with our infirmary and observed in case evidence of the disease appeared.

After discussion with Theodore, it transpired they had lost half of their community over the past year or more but not having any knowledge of opposing the sickness, they chose isolation for the victims. I requested of him to provide me with volunteers who would work under my instruction, teach them sanitization and cleansing. He looked at me with a strange face until I explained that I had first-hand experience with plague type infections and how to treat them. He immediately took his leave to gather helpers. The Centurion who was standing by and listening approached me and nervously asked how serious was the epidemic. After a brief moment

I responded that it would depend on several issues: one, containment of the tent inhabitants and isolating the obvious sick, second, strip every one of their clothes and boil them in hot water and rosemary whilst I instruct my servants to mix large quantities of a solution combining aloe vera and chamomile. Thirdly, observe everyone who has had contact with these civilians in the hope that it does not spread.

In spite of all the precautions, within several weeks, new cases were quickly adding up to where it consumed almost half of the settlement, nine soldiers were diagnosed.in the barracks and four in the Chateaux, including Dimitri. Separate quarters were set up in both areas and within the month the death rate was alarming.

I was not getting a great deal of sleep especially when my family were overcome by the virus The sores first appeared on the baby, then two of the children before my wife, Ophelia contracted the blisters, followed by my three children. As much as I bathed them all in my emulsion, I watched them die, one by one, Ophelia being the last, closing her eyes, lying in my arms. They all perished within eight days of each other and I laid them all in a shallow pit, side by side, their mother first, then the children from the youngest to the eldest boy.

It took the best part of a year before the day, then a week, that we had no new cases, however, the damage was done. Many of the survivors decided to leave our once proud town, to where they did not say. Meanwhile we received word from Rome that the Germanicus had overrun the city and lands in Italy. All indications pointed towards the fall of the Roman Empire.

It was with a sad heart that I dissolved my connections with Spain and ordered the destruction of the above ground buildings of Chateau Cassius leaving the ruins scattered, leaving the majority of my fortune buried in the lower terrains of the estate. Only I would know where to find the riches, provided they remained undisturbed.

Once again tragedy followed me.

Once again, I would venture east as a traveling monk.

CHAPTER 10

Kmer Empire
and Twins

Many years had befallen as I journeyed tediously from country to country, seeing nothing that enticed my empathy for the future. There must be decency and goodness somewhere in this world of men. According to my calculations the year was approximately 490 AD. I reached Funan, close to the Chinese border at a place called Kuang Si Falls south of Luang Prabang, a warrior kingdom ruled by a vicious, brutal and sadistic man, Khoun Boulam. They treated foreign travelers with suspicion and usually killed them in a cruel fashion, normally by mutilation and dismemberment. Fortunately, they recognized my robes as a holy man and in order to let me live, they set a test for me. Torture was their only way of levying a result of one's resistance, hence a test in pain. A discussion ensued to what my test was to be, which seemed a deep and heavy debate until, a decision. I watched as they built a heavy fire and started to place stones into the flames. Even though I had a fair knowledge of their language from centuries past, I did not indicate so. A warrior took me by the arm and simulated what I was supposed to do. He pointed to his feet as he walked heel to toe, heel to toe. It was then I understood that I was to walk on hot fire stones, as he flashed his hands showing ten fingers, clenching his fists and once again showing ten fingers. This indicated to me I was to tread twenty times over an unknown distance. Through more body repetition from my foe, if I failed, I would be put to death but if I could endure and still walk, I would be spared.

My brain was working rapidly and the only remedy I could think of was for some form of protection for my feet. Suddenly I noticed Calendula flowered plants growing everywhere, sometimes known as marigolds. Their leaves carried a healing agent, especially for burns. I turned to my jailer, grabbing his sleeve to get his attention whilst pointing to the blooms. He frowned as I grasped a handful of the flora and started to rub on my toes, under the arches to my heels. He started to laugh and allowed me to continue as I crowded the petals between my toes and smothered my feet with the residue of the flowers. From the corner of my eye, I could see they had finish laying the hot boulders that measured approximately one meter by two meters in length, which I calculated about six to seven paces per crossing, one hundred and twenty to forty in all.

I was beckoned to stand and guided to the short end of the coals feeling the heat at my toes. If I moved at a quick stride and maintained a six-step progress each-way, I might endure less pain. At least that was my mental thinking! I know not how I prevailed, almost like a dream, I walked backwards and forwards smelling the occasional burning of flesh but I felt little pain. Suddenly I felt hands grabbing me that stopped the torment. More hands were patting my arms and back as I was seated and there was a sense of excitement. As I looked up, I saw the twisted face of displeasure as Khoun Boulam grabbed my chin and screamed as saliva hit my eyes and forehead at what I thought could only be profanity. He turned in disgust as others were tending my feet and I never saw him again. Suddenly hands were offering me water with more smiles and greetings from others. As promised, if I was still walking after my ordeal, I was to live.

I later learned I had saved others due to be executed or tortured that day. It had been declared by the Council of Chiefs that if I succeeded, the sons of a village chieftain would be spared. His crime was to provoke rebellion amongst his people against oppression, ill-treatment and exploitation. As my senses restored, they dragged the tribal chief not five paces in front of me and cut of his head from the throat backwards that took skill and effort with an extremely large knife. His skull rolled to my feet as I closed my eyes.

I awoke naked and to the smell of honey, As I raised by body staring at my heavily bound feet drenching in deep brown essence, 1 noticed two young men squatting close to me. They both wore brightly colored loin cloths and their upper bodies shone in the sunlight. They raised themselves and I could see their bulging muscles but what was extraordinary was their height, however, their faces were covered but there was something about their eyes that looked familiar. They kept bowing until I gestured them to stop and after looking at each other, they did so.

Many more days passed and my two masked devotees tendered to my lesions, bathed me daily, brought me meals and beverage whenever I wanted. They never left my bedside as I encouraged them to converse in their language having sustained a good knowledge it from the past. They did it gladly, even supporting it.

After a few months and after a walk through the forest, my two companions sat me down and told me a story handed down to them of how their ancestors were slaves to the Roman Empire. They were befriended by a healer named Simon, who made them free men and their names were Kahmuu and Hmong and then they revealed their faces. Memories flooded back to me. They told me that the names of Kahmuu and Hmong had been passed from father to sons. It seemed their ancestors named their firstborn twin sons by these forenames and that someday they believed Simon would emerge as per the prophecy of their predecessors. I stared at my attendants who looked identical to my original guardians who served me. Why do you believe I am this benefactor, I asked. Hmong raised himself and shortly returned with cloth bundle. Unwrapping the fabric revealed a wooden carving of a very distinctive face, my face. I took a deep breath and was lost for words. Through many absorbed conversations and by some mystique I learned that twins occurred in their family approximately every other generation.

CHAPTER 11

Misfortune,
Mining and Jade

A number of events took place over a short period of a year. One, the war lord Khoun Boulam was killed and his family slaughtered by another faction from inland China. Most captives were taken as slaves and the remaining survivors had severe wounds or mutilated bodies, which few endured. Fortunately, our settlement was across the river and some distance away from Boulam's encampment that we escaped unnoticed. Two, destructive and unrelenting storms that persisted for many, many weeks, causing flooding, casualties and countless wounded victims, losing life and limbs. Thirdly, infections and sickness descended upon us like an epidemic in the form of a mosquito invasion and water contamination. I tried many compounds that included garlic, cinnamon and turmeric and in many cases, it stopped the infection growing but it was not a remedy.

Kahmuu and Hmong were by my side practically all the time as we applied bodily mastic balms and fed potions to the stricken populace. Then, they too fell to the infection and at one point I thought I was losing them. One night after a long day and a previous night lack of sleep, I found myself next to my two companions in an experimental sweat tent and laid down between them. I passed into sleep when I experienced a powerful and vivid vision. It was seemingly some-time in the future, somewhere in the orient and outside a large building with giant size lettering K & H and Sons, Import and Export. I could see my friends dressed in a style unknown to me in a busy market environment next to a tall uncharacteristic sailing ship and looking very prominent. I woke up in a sweat as I usually did after one of these visions and found my two comrades, awake, grinning and free of their condition .A strange sensation came over me that made me shiver but in a blissful way as I sensed a long and everlasting friendship between us.

Everything progressed and improved from that moment forward and somehow, we started to deliberate and examine our path forward in life. It was if they knew that they were destined for something extraordinary.

As time passed, we developed our mining skills, both copper and jade. Previously sold in bulk to merchants, we reviewed our options and decided to develop finished products. We expanded the jade market to include fine polished jewelry but we needed to venture into known large bazaars to sell our products. Kahmuu and Hmong proved not only to be knowledgeable of their products but developed skills in the art of negotiation and diplomacy .Without interference I allowed them to take the reins and was truly content to do so. It was truly remarkable that within six months of each other, their respective wives gave birth to twins, all male. After much discussion and mediation, they agreed to teach one child from each twin to serve me, for life once they turned sixteen. They would also take the names of their fathers, Kahmuu and Hmong. The other two boys were named Somnang and Kong-kea and follow in their father's business. All four children would be taught many skills from languages to the art of war. Once in my service my two young men would learn new skills, obedience without question, fearfulness, assertiveness, and resolve, executing my needs for twenty-four years until they turned forty years of age. All the Chai family would learn to know of my miraculous magic of life. As inexplicable and puzzling as it was, it was acknowledged without question.

Whilst Kahmuu and Hmong remained in my service, they took no wife, however, Somnang and Kong-kea each had twin boys and one of each was promised to me as successor. By some phenomenon, this cycle of life continued through the ages even though we were not always together—which was my choosing—often for protection of my identity and for the well-being of each other. K & H and Sons grew and the Chai's expanded to many townships as did their development in trade, silks, spices and agriculture, especially the poppy, or opium, as it became known. To manage the distribution, it was necessary to be close to their market, therefore, it was decided to move the base of operation to Guangzhou. Fortunately, this was not too great a distance from Laos and it was chosen as an established port with plenty of storage and excellent road access to inland China. They would become a powerful and influential family and I would be their guidance, moreover the major financier. With my counselling and leadership, K & H would expand throughout Asia into many fields of enterprise.

BOOK 3

CHAPTER 1

Sant Gall

O ver 300 years had passed since Laos and for the most part I trav-elled the Orient in obscurity, often with my companions, to new countries, much through wars, hostilities, feuds, met many rogues, thieves, experienced pestilence, plagues and diseases that I had never seen before, yet we suffered not. Thirteen descendants had passed since the original Kahmuu and Hmong and although every twin-set were slightly different, their resolution and tenacity remained the same.

My dreams and nightmares tormented me the most. Many were persistent, some repeatedly, many of Yeshua, or better known as Jesus and memories filled my head whilst religion festered over the land like an epidemic.

It was time for me to travel west once more, but alone. I spent many hours, days and months deliberating and reviewing our options with what has become my family. Their persistence and stubbornness proved to be quite challenging but we finally agreed my legacy would continue in my absence no matter the time we would be apart. For the most part, they had the wisdom and expertise to regenerate my heritage.

Although missing my companions, I ventured to Rome returning from my eastern travels as a wealthy Greek merchant only to learn of large-scale treachery where life expectancy was brief for many. It was a forbidding time when happiness was found rarely and the disparity between the wealthy and poor was immense. It was the dynasty of Charlemagne and according to the Papal church it was the year 822 AD as I left Rome traveling west, alone, in the guise of a priest. Many months had passed and on a cool day, the autumn wind blowing from the Alp mountains as I approached the city of Gallen in Upper Bergundy, a Roman territory. I was on foot having lost my donkey to thieves some days ago in the night. I didn't hear them due to the wine I drank and was relieved they didn't kill me in my sleep. They had searched my belongings but found nothing of value as I had learned on my travels to find a hiding place for my coin nearby so I appeared to be traveling in poverty. Fortunately, sleeping outside did not happen very often as I could find refuge in a Monastery, sacred ground or even a stable.

At the edge of the city, I arrived at a large building and from its design it was an Abbey, Monastery or Friary. With a clenched fist I banged on the door four or five times and waited and waited. On grasping the handle, the door opened and I entered to a large open area with a footpath leading to an inner building and another door. I approached and above the door written in Latin was the name Sant Gall and to my right a rope was hanging which I pulled to the sound of a loud ringing bell within. Within a short while and after ringing the bell for the second time the door opened and a bonnet covered head peered around the entrance. After a moment the access widened and the woman smiled seeing I was a priest. It was a very pleasant smile and I could see beyond the full working apron she wore a fine linen blouse which told me she was no impoverished maiden. She bid me to enter speaking in a Germanic tongue. To put her at ease I informed her I was an Italian cleric who fell on hard times quickly explaining my robbery encounter.

She expressed my fortune in arriving at their Abbey of Sant Gall, and explained that her name was Wiborada and that her brother, Hatto, was the resident Benedictine monk. She apologized for her clothing as she was milking goats upon my arrival. At this point, her brother arrived and after introducing myself his enthusiasm was overwhelming as he quickly explained that it was after a pilgrimage to Rome, he had decided to become a monk. I was quickly led to a kitchen where bread, cheese and fruit was offered. I indulged myself as my hunger was very real. After much conversation I was invited to stay and maybe assist them in some of their upkeeping undertakings at the abbey for bed and board which I gladly accepted. One could tell Hatto and Wiborada were brother and sister for both had the same short stocky nose between their striking stone color eyes. It was prominent, even attractive, and under different circumstances I might have succumbed to my desires, but quickly removed it from my thoughts.

At the evening meal it was just Hatto and I. He explained that Wiborada ate with an eight-year-old orphan girl and besides women talk bored him. I accepted his explanation but I somehow thought there was another reason.

A day turned into weeks; weeks turned into months until a year had passed and it was 823 AD. I had roamed the abbey and best of my knowledge there was not a room I had not been in but in all that time I had never seen the girl in the whole year and knew her only by the name of Rachildist. In all that while I dined alone with exception of ten days when Hatto was ill but even then, no child. It was shortly after Hatto's illness and over dinner that he asked me of my familiarity of confession? Although I did not tell him, I had a great deal of experience in this field. Confession was a fine tool used by the church to own secrets, secrets used to influence, even control their flock. I used my own opportunities well! Hatto had learned whilst in Rome that servants of the Lord must confess their sins at least once in their lives and to another man of God. I held my arms open with the palms of hands facing up to show I would gladly be his confessor. He grasped both my hands and with a smile thanked me although he told me this was his first step. He would be in serious prayer for thirty days to glorify his confession with complete honesty and sincerity. "So be it," I replied.

It was also about this time that I saw more of Wiborada due to my excavating rocky ground to make way for vegetable and herb growing. It was here in the garden that she spent a great deal of her time. The more we spoke, Wiborada revealed her expertise in languages, and that she was well versed in history and spent many an hour repairing and binding old books. She had much knowledge of herbs and spices which helped in the art of healing and on one day of the week local villages came to the abbey with their ailments.

The thirty days passed and Hatto approached me once again, revealing it was time to repent his sins and that he charged me with the responsibility of showing God's forgiveness. I suggested that should take place in the prayer chapel after our evening meal. To this he agreed enthusiastically.

CHAPTER 2

The Confession

Redemption, salvation, release, liberation, freedom were the tools of the confession. Give the confessor the feeling of release and salvation at the same time with feeling of complete emancipation. In his eyes I would be the hand of God and my blessings and sacred words would release Hatto from any immorality or guilt. He thanked me stating that in this life and in heaven I would be forever his intimate confidant. At the time I did not fully understand his meaning.

Hatto took confession to a whole new level. He had been led to believe disclosure was physical, emotional, as well as spiritual, and had given his revelation a great deal of thought.

On the anointed day I was waiting for him in the Chapel when he arrived wearing a white very finely made smock which I could see his naked body very clearly beneath. He held several written scrolls which he described as the main events of his life and intended as part of the ritual to burn them. He handed me small container which I should open on the morrow only. I nodded.

I told him to tell his confession in his own words, without interruption and so he did.

Hallo was born as the second child, having a sister four years his elder. His childhood was not memorable but neither was it unhappy even though his father did not pay him any attention. He was about ten years old when he noticed how much his father was getting really familiar with his sister Gilda, then fourteen years old. He also saw his mother had noticed too. It was six months later that Gilda was getting sick all the time and unknown to Hallo, his sister was pregnant. At this time Hallo was separated from Gilda and then one night his mother came to his bed and explained in great detail what his father had done to his sister and the tragedy didn't finish there because Gilda died giving birth to a baby girl. Hallo cried in disbelief, that his father would do such a thing and the loss of a sister that he was very fond of.

Several years had passed without Hallo seeing his father. His mother raised his sister's daughter who they named Wiborada. He learned from the kitchen staff that his father lived in the town, whoring and drinking most nights at the local tavern.

Hallo had reached fourteen years of age, but not without issues. His father had collected his tenants' rents but provided nothing to support his family. The servants were first to go, then there was less and less meat, and relying on the vegetable grown on the property. Hallo eventually achieved enough courage to go to the village in order to confront his father. It was early evening but by the time he located him he was already consumed by alcohol and was in no mood to be confronted by his offspring and assaulted him using his fists at first then raised him from the floor, walked him to the door, kicking him from behind as he threw him into the street before slamming the door closed. Hallo raised himself to a sitting position as the rain poured down and he shivered with pain and disgust. He walked the several miles home arriving soaking wet and bewildered. The following day he told his mother he had fallen from a tree he was climbing. She didn't believe him.

It was several months before he returned to the village, only this time it was to observe. After numerous visits he could see a pattern in his father's movements and decided his fate. It was easy, he didn't even hear me and without pause he used all his power to put the sickle in his back time and time again. Panting heavily, he looked around but could not see anyone just the dull noise from the tavern. Turning the body over he searched for his money pouch and found it quickly and bulging with coin. Looking at his father he could feel the hatred burning inside and plunged the sickle another dozen times in his chest, repeating over and over again, "This is for Gilda." Running from the scene, he felt a sense of relief then realized he was covered in blood. There was a small pond on the way home where he stripped himself naked and spent quite a time cleaning himself in the warm summer evening. He would have to burn his clothes and hide the coin. Many days passed and Hatto wondered why no word came from the village then one morning a group of men came by to see his mother, giving her the news of her husband being robbed and murdered.

We paused for a few moments and my head was in a spin when reaching this part of the confession. This man had committed murder at aged fourteen. and his father no less. He then continued.

The group represented leaders from the village including the Prefect of Police who described the scene of the assault and determined it was likely committed by two ruffians from the local tavern. They thought it was two persons because of the wounds both front and back. They had rounded up all the known regulars and were interrogating them all. They brought with them a large chest with the deceased's belongings and a set of books that was the accountability of his collections from his estate. There was no coin and assumed it was stolen but there were sums due from some of the leasing farmers. After they left, his mother started to weep, not for his father's death, but tears of joy that they were no longer impoverished.

Another year passed, the good life and happiness had returned. Hatto had noticed his mother taking more care of herself and looked attractive. The other thing that changed his life was getting an erection and masturbation. At fifteen years of age, he was stroking his penis every day, sometimes twice! He had a very vivid imagination and getting audacious as to where he would play with his relatively new found plaything. Then the inevitable happened, he got caught, by his mother. Hatto was in his mother's room thinking she had left for the market but she had returned having forgotten her shawl. He was smelling her clothes with the sweet smell of honeysuckle whilst his right hand was firmly around his hard penis, jerking in slow motion. He wasn't sure how long she had been standing in the doorway but as soon as he saw her, he attempted to cover up himself with his mother's clothing. "How long has this been going on?" she asked. Hatto was lost for words but then told her it was half a year. "Let me see," she said decisively. He mumbled when she spoke again rather firmly, "Drop my clothes and let me see," which he did sheepishly. By this time his erection had gone, displaying a limp sex organ. His mother started to walk towards him, stating that she knew this day would come and that she needed to guide Hatto in the matter of sexual practices. Sitting him down and removing his clothing so he was exposed, she grabbed his phallus. "Before I discuss this issue further," she said, "We needs to remove this arousal with the use of my hand through stimulation." In a matter of moments, he felt the growth as his mother stroked him up and down. It wasn't long before his sperm was spitting out over the floor, which brought a smile to his mother's face. The only thing she said afterwards was that Hatto had to clean up after himself.

This happened every day well past his sixteenth year, until one day in the garden he noticed Wiborada was watching from behind a bush just at the point of ejaculation. He pretended not to see her and wondered at her early age of seven what she made of this performance. Apparently, he was not the only one to see her. His mother raced after Wiborada and Hatto could see a lot of hand gesturing from his mother then giggling between the two of them. Well at least there was no floor to clean. Later, his mother told him she explained to Wiborada that he had a pain (hence the shouting and groaning) and that she was applying an ointment for relief. A few days later and anticipating my usual attention my mother took the by the hand to the bedroom and there on the bed was a naked blonde voluptuous maiden. "Her name is Greta and she will teach you in the arts of the flesh as I will no longer be relieving you. Be patient, listen to her advice, treat her with dignity and absolutely no violence." With that said his mother left the room and he walked sheepishly towards Greta and the start of a wonderful adventure in lust and love which lasted for the next three years.

Hatto had reached twenty years of age when smallpox ravaged the village and his first love Greta died. A short time thereafter the same disease took his mother and he lived in sadness for quite a while until a severe winter set in.

Wiborada had turned eleven and she followed Hatto everywhere. He was the only family she had and was afraid of losing him. She would not sleep alone at night and found great comfort in being close to Hatto, sharing his bed, feeling his warmth, hearing him breath. Hatto also relished his little half-sister's affection. It brought contentment and solace at a time of despair and desolation. It would soon be his twenty-first birthday and he would be officially owner of his mother's estate and the revenue it would bring.

One morning upon awakening he happened to look over at Wiborada and noticed that there was growth in her little breasts but even more astonishing was the size of her nipples. He immediately experienced an erection and started to stroke his cock until he exploded all over the eiderdown. Wiborada looked innocent as she slept when Hatto felt a sense of guilt, then quietly left the bedroom to clean himself up and get dressed. By the time he returned she was awake but still in her nightdress. He found himself staring at those cute buttons, rigid and enticing. Wiborada noticed his look, laughed and said, "You observed too," as she grasped her tiny mounds with both hands!

"Yes," replied Hatto. "It's the start of maturity and adulthood." This followed by question after question not giving him the time to answer when he finally said an explanation would be forthcoming and maybe their housekeeper would be better, woman to woman so to speak. With that said he abruptly left. He approached the housekeeper, a stout, homely woman who had seven children of her own. She blushed slightly but understood the issue, especially as Wiborada was at an age when she is likely to get her first period at any time. Hatto had not even given it any thought, after all, what man would be concerned with feminine matters. The housekeeper agreed she would take control to ensure transition into womanhood.

Wiborada continued to sleep in Hatto's bed until a few months passed and one morning he awoke to find her gone and a smear of blood on the bed linen. He learned from the housekeeper that Wiborada had experienced her period cycle and she was guiding her through it. The housekeeper had recommended that under the circumstance Wiborada would be better off in her own bed so as to not disturb Hatto.

At this point in the Confession, Hatto paused. "Do you need some rest," I enquired.

"Yes," he replied. "Just a few moments to consume some water, set my mind straight and burn some scrolls." I waited patiently and pretended to be in prayer.

It was but a short period when he interrupted my prayers and he continued with his confession. A number of months passed when having stomach cramps and during one of her periods that Wiborada came to Hatto's bed looking for comfort and he welcomed her with open arms. It was a wonderful feeling having her close to him, her warm embrace that took them both to a magnificent slumber.

Subsequently, they reverted back to their old habit of sleeping together but it would not be the same. Hatto could not ignore her body and suggested to Wiborada to modify her night clothes to a heavier garment. She did not like the suggestion but followed the request, at least for now. This went on for months until one morning Wiborada awoke early and hugging Hatto face to chest and feeling something hard against her pelvis. Reaching down with her left hand and lifting his tunic she touched, then grasped his manhood at which time Hatto awoke. He moved his right hand over the left hand of Wiborada and started to glide it over his penis, up and down, stroke by stroke and she silently followed in awe what was happening. She was not unfamiliar as a great deal had been explained by

138

the housekeeper. Nevertheless, this was all new but exciting at the same time. Hatto was guiding her hand with more rapid motion as she looked at his wonderous and swelling gland. She could not help but stare, then all of a sudden, a white liquid spurted out time and again and she realized some had landed on her face and body as well as covering her hand. Hatto was breathing heavily, removing his hand as she let go then feeling the sperm on her face as is dripped into her mouth. She tasted a slightly salty but not unpleasant savor, then licked her hand to relish it some more. Hatto was watching and it excited him to see Wiborada's delight at his aftertaste. He felt a growth in his groin and he whispered to ask if she wanted to do it again. She smiled and just nodded as Hatto removed her nightrobe displaying her nubile young body in all of its magnificence, those little mounds of breasts, erect nipples and little virgin cunny.

Every day for twenty days a month they would play, a little more daring as time went on until full fellatio and cunnilingus were performed. Hatto had a difficult time trying to explain why his penis would not perform all of the time and he often sexually stimulated Wiborada with his tongue without reciprocation and she enjoyed it so, having a rather sizable and sensitive clitoris in addition to a high carnal appetite. He was thankful of the rest during her time of period and often she spent some of that time alone. With all the massage and caressing her body was changing from a girl to a woman even though she was barely twelve.

One afternoon, they were drinking wine and Wiborada was naked, dancing very seductively as he sat, legs wide open with a full erection. She danced closer until she was hovering over his phallus and her clitoris was touching the tip, then suddenly he was entering her and hearing her gasp. Momentarily, they both froze and he could feel her wetness as her hymen broke. She shuddered as she started to move up and down very slowly at first, wrapping her arms around his neck. Hatto could not stand it any longer and needed to take control, turning her on her back, thrusting into her tight succulent embrace. He had no restraint, the glorious surge through his loins until he exploded into her with unimaginable extasy. It was the only time he copulated with her but the damage was done and she became pregnant. She became extremely moody and was afraid. On top of that she was always throwing up, going to the toilet to pee all the time, and lost total interest in sex. Hatto knew they needed to leave their home and was able to find a buyer, albeit at a lower price than he had anticipated.

When they left their home Wiborada was already changing her shape but it was winter and baggy clothes covered her swelling belly. They had purchased a small wagon with two good horses making their way northwest going from inn to inn until they arrived at the city of Gallen where they found accommodation at the Rooks Inn. It was here they learned of the local Abbey, in need of money and repair. On enquiring further, there were only three persons living there—the elderly Abbot and two lady followers of the church. Hatto decided to investigate further and paid a visit. They took with them wine, venison, cheese, and bread as a gift and were well received. With the offer of monies to reestablish the buildings and obtain sufficient labor, the Abbot agreed to the residency of Hatto and Wiborada. The church lady clerics were informed that Wiborada had been violated by a nobleman and that they were seeking refuge. The women sympathized and offered every assistance and as such, a huge burden was lifted from Hatto.

Hallo spent his time overseeing the restructure of the Abby and hiring local tradesmen, which made him very popular as he paid them in silver. He set up an agricultural program, had woodcutters, and a foundry make tools and furnishings. Wiborada gave birth to a daughter who she named Rachildis. Hatto kept his distance.

And so, he came to the end of his confession.

I gave a huge sigh of relief as he waited for my absolution. I passed my right hand in the sign of the cross whilst saying, "God, the Father of mercies, through the death and resurrection of His son has reconciled the world to Himself and sent the Holy Spirit among us for the forgiveness of sins; through the ministry of the Church may God give you pardon and peace, and I absolve you from your sins in the name of the Father, and of the Son, and of the Holy Spirit. Amen.

He smiled and stood up, his frock stained with semen, walked towards the door without saying a word, then closed the door behind him.

After regaining my thoughts of the event that just happened and shortly thereafter, I left the chapel going out the same door leading to the garden and there hanging from the oak tree was Hatto's lifeless body.

CHAPTER 03

Farewell and Return to Sant Gall

Staring at the body swaying in the breeze I saw Wiborada on her knees some twenty feet away. I walked ever so slowly towards her until I reached several feet from her as she looked up, turning her head in my direction. "Did he tell you everything," she asked.

"I believe he was honest, but as to the confession, I am unable to convey his words as they are sacred."

"I understand," she responded and stood up. After a brief moment she calmly spoke again, "I think you should leave this place and not because of Hatto."

She had learned from a Hungarian refugee of a predicted attack and told the other priests and staff to escape to the monastery at Reichenau Island taking with them books, manuscripts, and wine. I offered to remove Hatto's body, but Wiborada declined my assistance for reasons she did not explain. I took my leave and hastily packed travel clothes, as much silver I dared to carry, and the box Hatto had given me. The rest I would keep hidden in one of the secret rooms for I would return one day and the more concealed reserves I have, the better. I crammed all my goods on a mule and took one of the better horses without speaking a word to anyone and headed for Waldburg several days ride to the south east. On arrival, I opened the box Hatto had given me. It contained a letter addressed in my name, a deed to the monastery, and a detailed plan of the estate with all the secret passages and rooms. Reading the letter, it detailed where his gold, silver, and jewels were hidden so long as I would take care of Wiborada and his daughter.

My first thought was to return, but then I received word of the Magyar marauders reaching Sant Gall. For whatever reason Wiborada did not leave and the raiders embedded an axe in her skull as she was kneeling in prayer. Her daughter Rachildis was in safe keeping and in the care of the priests at Reichenau Island. They took what little in value and burned many buildings, however St. Gall was a solid structure so all they left was a destructive mess. Afraid of retaliation, the raiders departed as quickly as they had arrived. Meanwhile I headed for Reichenau Island, some twenty hours ride to ensure the safety and future of Rachildis.

On arrival, I met with the Abbot, giving him letters of instruction to make her a ward of the monastery and giving him enough silver to cover her living expenses for ten years, even though I intended to return beforehand. I did not see the need to meet with her and left the Island the morning after my arrival.

It was nine years later in 842 when I returned with my obedient servants Khammu and Hmong and was happy to see the Abbot had survived, recognized me, and was genuinely pleased to see me well. He praised Rachildis learning, a gifted attractive eighteen-year-old student with great promise in finding a fitting suitor amongst the local nobility. I was gratified, even delighted at the Abbot's praise and before I could give him thanks for his tutorial a loud knock was heard and entering the chamber was a young, alluring woman that I knew was Rachildis.

I immediately raised myself from chair and introduced yours truly as an Italian cleric named Simon which produced an elated reaction from her.

She curtsied with elegance, bowing her head and in a low voice thanked me for being her benefactor. I moved forward, placing my hand on her arm, lifting her up until her face was close to mine. What a magnificent creature she was and it was several moments before I spoke. "You are very welcome," I said and apologized for not returning sooner, and explained that my business took me far and wide and please excuse my heathen servants outside. She responded with many questions for which I replied, many of which were a fabrication.

For many days we spoke, took walks, and dined together. She was a fascinating loveliness; a knowledgeable well-educated conversationalist and I enjoyed her company immensely. Our discussions eventually turned to the future, suitors and marriage but her primary concern was how long I intended to stay. After a brief pause, I replied that my intention was to delay my departure until she had chosen a husband and married in the church. She was elated wrapping her arms around me feeling her warm excited body against my chest, feeling a twitch in my penis.

After a few days, at breakfast, the Abbot asked me what I intended to do with St. Gall which took me by surprise. Of course, I intended to return in the hope my secret rooms had not been discovered and retrieve the monies hidden there. "What do you mean," I replied.

"I thought you knew," he said. "The Abbey was left to you in letters written by Wiborada and left in my care."

"No," I lied. "I did not know," said I, also knowing the property had already been left me by Hatto. "I will leave in within a few days to inspect the premises before deciding what to do with its future."

Although Rachildis wanted to join me on my journey to Sant Gall, I explained that it would be challenging and dirty inspecting burned out buildings and destruction not yet known to me. Reluctantly, she agreed to remain in Reichenau Island.

It was indeed a mess so I set up a meeting with the town's development representative to agree upon a labor pool and payment terms. I could only get access to two secret rooms and thankfully the jewels and Silver we untouched. With the exception of obvious suspicion towards my companions, the meeting was very successful inasmuch revenue for the locals was in demand and I also agreed they could use the stones and brick to subsidize their own building needs. At first, I agreed to twenty men but after a week the advancement was slow so raised it to fifty men. I also employed carpenters to make tools and handcarts as well as women cooks to make them one good meal every day.

I wrote several letters to Rachildis detailing our progress and she wrote one back wondering when I would return. After forty-five days I was able to get access to the remaining three secret rooms and decided for the time being to leave the monies where they were. After all, it could not be in a better place. After many months I was able to install doors, windows, iron bars, fitted furniture, drapes, and linens, keeping many towns folk employed and contented. I even had a team of gardeners restore the grounds to some of its previous standards. Reaching 150 days into the project, I was satisfied with the result. I organized a grand gathering in the grounds, suppling all the food and beverages for all the workers, their families and local dignitaries to show my appreciation. It was well received.

I spent the next five days assessing my fortune which, even after the restoration costs was still considerable. I decided to obtain two pack mules to transfer the jewels and some silver to Reichenau Island, leaving the bulk of coin and bars in their secret places. Without telling a soul and with the assistance of Khammu and Hmong we packed the mules late at night, put cloth coverings on their hooves and our horses, walking them all through the outskirts of town before mounting our steeds and riding until through the night and the rising of the sun. We took some rest, ate some fruit and quenched our thirst with water before mounting our stallions again for the arduous twelve plus hour ride to Reichenau. It was my plan to arrive late evening to transfer the heavily laden mules to my chambers without being seen.

My protectors were tired and sweating from their labors carrying hessian sacks to the large strongbox in my lodging I bid them a good night, showing them their quarters and rested on my cot whilst quenching my thirst, allowing the water to dribble down my chin. I had the coffer purpose built in readiness for this purpose. Made from iron and the ebony tree, too heavy to move and with secure Chinese designed locks, I intended to disguise the box under a wooden cradle and sheepskins that indicated it was a lounge chair.

Once satisfied with my scheme I stripped naked, took a cloth, dipping it into a bowl of water and proceeded to wash my body. It was a warm night so I took a small stool, sat on the veranda to dry off and for some unknown reason developed an erection. Taking it in hand my thoughts drifted to Rachildis and I quickly reached a climax. Cleaning myself off, I took to my bed and drifted into a deep sleep. I awoke and the sun was already high in the sky. After making myself presentable I left my room and made way to the Abbot's cloisters, who showed great joy on seeing me alive and well. We sat and I explained in great detail what I had done to St. Gall which pleased him greatly at which point he advised me that Rachildis had decided on a suitor and eager to discuss her choice with me.

I took my leave and ventured in the garden where I knew Rachildis spent most of her time and it didn't take long to find her tendering the herb rockery that we had nurtured together; however, she had designed the plants in such a display that was extraordinarily delightful to the eye. She was so immersed in her nursery and humming to herself that she did not notice my approach until I was just a couple of feet away. In fact, I made her jump as I spoke. She quickly ascended throwing her arms around me in delight and holding me tight. We sat and talked, well, she did most of the talking asking many questions and only stopped to take a deep breath. I answered as best I could until we reached the subject of a suitor. She seemed nervous at first and stating the one person she could not lie to was me. She confessed that in looking for the right man she wanted someone like me, with my qualities, understanding and warmth. I was momentarily speechless when I said, "There are no two people alike and each shall be judged by their own merit." She smiled and said she had met a wealthy merchant some seven years older and had been married before whose wife died in childbirth. Her description intrigued me and expressed my desire to meet him. Rachildis informed me she would arrange such a meeting and then the subject was dropped carrying on our conversation of local matters and news as my guardians walked on by.

A dinner was arranged at the home of Hans Keller, the possible future husband chosen by Rachildis and there would be numerous guests. I dressed in my expensive silk robes as I wanted to give the best impression and was greeted in the hallway by a very beautiful Rachildis in a wardrobe of fine deep blue and yellow linen. Simple yet refined. She was also wearing a necklace that I had given her on her fifteenth birthday. Offering my arm, we made our way outside to the waiting coach. My bodyguards remained behind. On the way she told me she had met Hans at the County Fair, had a number of outings with him but always with others and only introduced to his parents recently that included a formal dinner. So far as she could tell his family liked her and up to this point had not been entirely alone with him although she wanted to. After all, she was a woman with natural desires She was anxious for me to meet him; to give my blessing so she could pursue her yearning but something else bothered me for which I could not quite fathom. Why was it necessary for me to sanction what was her decision in the first place? To give my consent did not seem essential so it must be something else?

The dinner was very agreeable and well presented with herb and garlic infused pheasant served with various vegetables, fruit, and cheese supported by a good choice of dry, slightly fruity red wine. The conversation was rather dull due to the lives they led and limited to local activity until I introduced one of my travel exploits that had them all listening intently that continued to another, then another, absorbing them in a totally new world. When I stopped there remained utter silence and then our host offered more wine. I politely declined saying it was time to return to the monastery, however we must have Hans and his family visit us at the Abby within the week. Pleasantries were exchanged and took our leave to the awaiting coach.

Instead of sitting opposite each other as we did upon arrival, Rachildis squeezed next to me gripping my right arm, laying her head on my shoulder and I smiled.

CHAPTER 4

The Wedding

The next few months were spent with preparations and discussions mainly around the location, style of wedding, decor and number of guests. Planning was progressing satisfactorily, when I found myself in the garden contemplating activities surrounding Sant Gall. Suddenly a voice was addressing me and as I turned, I came face to face with Hans's father. "Excuse me, I did not hear you clearly," I said. "Could you repeat it?"

"I thought I would take this opportunity to address the subject of the dowry that would be forthcoming on behalf of Rachildis," he stated.

The question came as a surprise as I didn't know that a dowry was required in this country. It is true that certain cultures and even Rome considered dowries to strengthen the wealth of newly married couples but mostly given to support the bride in case the husband abandoned his spouse. He continued to say it was expected that Hans would continue living in the home of his parents whilst deciding on their future dwelling and a dowry would help to make this happen. I paused before speaking, thinking that I needed to choose the right words. "Firstly, as my wedding gift, I intended to give a portion of land in Sant Gall to the young couple. I have for some time been modernizing the estate, running water, new secure doors, windows, furnishings, other comforts including workforce to run the home. Secondly, I have set aside a sum of monies to keep Rachildis in the lifestyle she is accustomed to and for her future children. Under these circumstances what objective would a dowry accomplish?" I asked.

He was speechless to the point his jaw dropped slightly and at this point I walked away.

I caught up with Rachildis and Hans having a discussion with the Abbot when I interrupted them with the news of my intended wedding gift. They were elated and gladly accepted. It was agreed we would make the trip to St. Gall to review possible changes and improvements, the feminine touch, I was sure. I needed the trip to review my other plans for my structures, modifications and reformations. For this, I had prearranged to meet an architect from Gaul specializing in deceptive design, secret rooms and passageways.

Time passed quickly and suddenly it was the wedding day in June of 844 AD. Everybody's efforts paid off, the ceremony in the garden with perfect weather, followed by a glorious feast and flowing wine, however I could see some disappointment on the face of Rachildis gazing upon her new husband getting rather intoxicated along with his young friends. I was not going to get involved. It was at this time that I took my leave of the festivity, making my way to my chambers. Removing my celebratory gowns, I noticed it was sprinkling with rain and walked into the garden to wash myself in the natural essence of rainfall. With my eyes closed running my fingers through my hair, I heard a familiar voice and turning my head caught a glimpse of Rachildis at the same moment reaching for my thin bedroom robe. Before I knew it, she was by my side dressed in her bedchamber attire and sobbing profusely. Grabbing my hands, she collapsed to grass beneath us dragging me along with her. In between weeps she spoke to me of her efforts to separate Hans from his comrades and when she finally succeeded in getting him to the bedchamber, getting undressed, and attempting intercourse, he passed out. She tried to revive him with cold water but to no avail.

Suddenly she raised her head putting her lips to mine and although I knew it to be wrong, I could not resist even more so when I felt her hand grasp my throbbing penis. "Please don't be angry," she said. "I have always felt this way about you," as she guided me between her legs. She didn't want the foreplay, she just wanted me inside her. Feeling the warmth and wetness, I hesitated entering her then slowly glided my thick girth into the abyss of pleasure that sent a shiver down my spine and a loud gasp from Rachildis. I opened her nightgown revealing her sumptuous body, pear shaped breasts, upturned large deep brown nipples, and her dark mound consuming my phallus. Starting slowly, I burrowed into her vagina gradually quickening and deepening my strokes while she was moaning and sighing louder every time, I penetrated her. I continued my rhythm for some considerable time, playing on her reactions, then feeling her arch her back upwards and screaming out loud as I felt the hot juices of her orgasm. Regaining her breath, she pushed me off, stood up holding her hand over her pelvic mound and rushed into the direction of her chambers. Confused and still with an erect penis I stood and watched her disappear into the night. Had I offended her or was she ashamed and a number of other reasons were going through my head then suddenly I could hear running steps as I picked up my robe to cover myself only to see I still had a noticeable growth. Rachildis reappeared with a sly grin on her face then kissed me full on the lips. "Are you ok?" I asked. "Did I offend you?" She looked down and couldn't help notice a bulge through the thin wrap, then reached out with a firm grasp. I felt another quiver and a wanton ache as she stroked my swollen shaft. "Where did you go in such a hurry?" I whispered.

"I was bleeding when you broke my hymen so I decided to cover my husband's penis and leave blood stains in the bed so that he thinks we had intercourse. Now fill me with your semen." Releasing her gown, she lay on the grass leading me to follow and like a sheep being led to slaughter I followed. We were in bliss for what seemed a long time unloading my seed twice into her womb and at one point she was on top ravaging me, screaming in delight. Totally exhausted, we lay in each other's arms, consumed with sweat and the smell of our essences in our nostrils.

The sign of dawn was approaching and Rachildis disengaged from my body and said she needed to return to her marriage bed before Hans awoke. Pressing her firm lips to mine and pushing her tongue into my mouth she then ascended, putting on her robe, then departed.

I was in rapture, not remembering when I last felt such enchanted wicked and criminal pleasure. Nevertheless, I needed to return to my chamber and get some deserved sleep. Later that mid-afternoon everyone was milling around in a sluggish fashion, some nursing appalling alcohol after effects, except Rachildis, who was full of the joys of spring.

A few days passed when walking in the garden, Rachildis approached me and guiding me to a place well out of earshot informed me that Hans woke her up not remembering anything of the previous evening but evidence on his limp manhood and blooded sheets suggested he accomplished what was expected of him. However, due to the severity of his hangover he was not in the mood to repeat his performance. In fact it took several days before he took her body, only once and hurriedly. It was obvious he was still ailing from the excessive wine and other liquors on the wedding night. Hans had in fact arranged a trip the following day to a mountain hunting lodge so they could spend time alone together. Smiling, she left me to my thoughts.

CHAPTER 5

Years 845 to 1300

Although I never returned to St Gall during the life of Rachildis, I kept in touch by letter although it often took a year before news caught up with me. I had invented a new life, that of my invented son, Maurizio. Rachildis gave birth to seven children, the first a boy barely nine months after the wedding followed by four daughters, another boy, then finally a girl. During her life, two daughters and her youngest son died of diseases and after thirty-two years together her husband Hans met with a hunting accident. Her eldest son, named Simon was apparently a fine figure of a man and it was he that wrote to me of the death of his mother, Rachildis by an unknown pestilence. Enclosed in the dispatch was a sealed letter addressed to me from her confessing Simon was my son. The year was 885.

I wrote a letter to Simon Keller expressing my sincerest condolences and that I was unable to travel due to back and hip issues but I would send my own son, Maurizio within the year. Khammu and Hmong had returned to continue the dynasty and would be some years before I met their descendants but would exchange correspondence as to their accomplishments.

It was almost a year later departing from Verona in 886 that I left with a small caravan of stonemasons, iron foundry blacksmiths, locksmiths, design furniture carpenters, a host of servants, male and female, in addition to a large amount of gold and silver hidden in the wagons. Such was my influence in Verona that we were escorted by a centurion and one hundred skilled infantrymen. The journey was estimated to take fifteen days, maybe longer, traveling almost 500 kilometers of steep roads often disturbed by avalanches of fallen rock and heavy rains.

The journey proved to be arduous and early in the morning twenty-two days later we reached the outskirts of Gallen and started to erect tents by the river. It was already getting cool to cold being end of October especially at night but we were fully prepared and equipped for almost any eventuality. A small but well-armed military group greeted us as soon as we were making camp then they sent a messenger to inform the Abbot that Maurizio, son of Simon, had arrived with a Roman legion. Later that afternoon another group arrived from the city and escorted to my majestically imposing tent surrounded by legionnaires. Spying on them from my private chambers the church and wealthy citizens were well represented and so I entered my auditorium making my way towards the new Abbot. Polite greetings and introductions were exchanged when I bid them all to make themselves comfortable. Almost immediately a host of female servants appeared with wine, breads, cheeses, fruits and offering each guest a polished wooded bowl with silver inlays.

It was obvious the Abbot was their spokesperson, still standing whereas everyone else had made themselves comfortable on cushions or covered benches. He was asking the reason for my visit when a large, well-dressed gentleman with a large beard and receding hairline entered the tent requesting that he enter and apologizing for his late arrival. Looking at this man's features, his mothers' eyes and his mouth and jaw line it was obviously Rachildis's son, Simon. I bid him welcome.

"To answer your question Abbot, I have come to transform the part of Sant Gall that I own into a multi-city lending institution for the merchants, farmers, to handle foreign trade and to securely store their money's . Such institutions, mainly temples exist in the Roman Empire and the system works well. The Legion that accompanies me is to safeguard the large some of bullion that we have transported here from Verona."

As more questions were asked of me, I noticed Simon was staring at me. After much discussion they started to converse amongst themselves and many of them were realizing the benefits of my scheme except the Abbot, who was already providing such services but at a huge profit to the church. I then I found myself in front of Simon.

"Do you look like your father?" he asked.

"Well, yes, I suppose I do resemble him. I was born to his second wife as his first died in childbirth and he remained unmarried for some time."

"We have the same father," he said.

"How do you know this?" I enquired.

"Just before my mother died, she told me so and briefly the circumstances of her wedding night."

A shiver went down my spine. "We must talk some more but not at this gathering," I said, seeing the Abbot becoming fearlessly confrontational with the other townspeople. The debate continued and I learned that many of the merchants and farmers owed the church major sums with large interests, some as much as one hundred percent which did not allow their businesses to grow and in some cases had their lands forfeited due to changing lending terms. I pledged to them all I would review their loans and based on the amount they had outstanding would offer to pay off their debts and introduce a much lower interest repayment rate. With this statement the Abbot and his clergy were disgusted and upset and quickly departed but not before he made it clear I would feel the wrath of the church and the legal system. Raising my arms, I requested silence then made it abundantly clear I would not jeopardize anyone's legal position and would examine their indebtedness on a case-by-case basis.

They disbursed rather speedily and found myself alone with Simon. "I think you have presented a wonderful business proposition," he said. The tradesmen and growers have suffered so long at the hands of the Abbot.

"Don't be hasty. We must be diligent and accurate in evaluating the documents," I said.

After a moment of silence, I said in a low tone, "Do you want to talk about your mother?"

For many hours we, he talked about Rachildis, how a wonderful human being she was, how she helped the local community and spoke highly of his true father in the last months of her life. I listened, choking on my memories even after fifty years. Simon wanted to hear more about his father but I suggested the hour was late and we would talk further over the coming days. Which we did, and as brothers we bonded, except we were really father and son.

For the next months, work on the depository building progressed, although local craftsmen were upset the workforce was imported from the city of Verona. I was able to subcontract some work from the district, but none on the inside of the structure. In parallel, I reviewed loan documents from borrowers, many of which were fraudulently staged by the Ecclesiastic brethren and elected my associates to present new contract terms fitting to their needs and economical status. I was about to receive the wrath of his grace the Abbot and knew I was in danger. Since the treaty of Verdun in 843 the Monasteries were important bases for maintaining law, rule, and instruction including lending monies but all too often they took advantage of their status.

The Abbot's next move was to get support from Fraumunster Abbey who maintained the rule in Upper Burgundy, however, I knew they were engaged with Magyar marauders. I thought such a journey by the Abbot a dangerous one but he thought fifty well-armed Horsemen would be sufficient strength to ward off a few bandits. Nevertheless, I sent my own instruction to Verona to dispatch a substantial force in lieu of a possible attack. As it involved the church, I sent a fully documented report to newly elected Pope John V111 who I knew well in his previous capacity as the Bishop of Rome.

Within a month, a centurion and his force arrived from Verona with instructions to report to me and me only. A couple of days passed when a much larger armed Company arrived from Rome with similar instructions, which made me the most powerful man in the territory. My first course of action was to send a small brigade of a commander and twenty infantrymen as a scouting expedition in search for the Abbot. In just under ten days, an emissary arrived from the scouting expedition carrying a detailed report from the commander. They found the Abbot's burnt-out coach and every member of his unit's decapitated heads piled on an elevated rock but no sign of their bodies. They searched within a large area but no to no avail, no sign whatsoever of their corpses. As the search party had no knowledge of the Abbot's features the centurion instructed his men to construct a sled and place all the skulls upon it, hitching it to his horse. Their estimated arrival would be up to a day behind his messenger.

Upon return of the expedition, it didn't take long to identify the Abbot and his clergy amongst all the mutilated heads. From the commander's verbal report the site was only twenty leagues away which meant the Magyar's were not far and we had no idea of their numbers. I summoned all the ranking officers and we reviewed our defensive strategy. We sent out scouts for many months but there was no sign of the enemy nor did we ever see them. When word reached Rome of the massacre, additional Legions were dispatched to Sant Gall giving the township a formidable sized army.

As the years passed, moving into the tenth century, battles in the north took place between various settlements and the Magyar's but never near to our location. As the population grew so did the problems with sanitation, then the plague hit us in a very big way, killing whole families including that of Simon's. Although it was sad, I had learned to keep my emotions in check as cold as it may sound. Even though I had made numerous trips to Verona over the years, it was time to move on and create a new identity but I needed to put controls in place and had been planning for some time.

My dreams, visions or rather nightmares persisted, for the most part uncomprehensible.

I had been grooming a number of men with different mathematical abilities to work as a team and under them trained deputies and under them juniors. In this manner the Bank Controlling Organization would remain secure. Each senior board member would have an individual seal of authority that would be handed down to their deputy as they leave the organization for any number of circumstances. I myself had a special seal to which I, or my descendants could make any changes deemed fit and made this very clear to the board before saying my farewells.

The night before my departure I had the most vivid of dreams and felt I was actually there. It was a raging battle and I saw Jeshua, as a brutish warrior, slaying many in his path and I heard him screaming at the top of his lungs "I will destroy the city of Ur, death to all" I awoke shivering with sweat dripping from face and body. It would be many, many years before I understood the history behind this dream.

158

CHAPTER 6

The Crusades, Templars, and the Plague

O ver 200 years and seven identities had passed, spending most of my time in Southern Gaul and Hispania. Gaul was divided by kingdoms and continually ravaged in the north by the Vikings and in the east by the Magyars whilst the south prospered with shipping trades to the east. It was the reign of Louis, the Sixth such self-imposed Monarch of the Franks. Having already a vast knowledge of languages I took to Hispania Latin dialect very easily. Although I possessed numerous properties, Montserrat in Catalonia was my main residence, a mountain top city with a strong Christian faith and enough distance from the Muslim states to feel safe. I regularly traveled to La Sarsa and Carthage to minimize my exposure. Traveling between the two countries was close enough so as to remain inconspicuous. It was also a time of many conflicts and diseases that I found myself losing acquaintances without any effort on my part. I was still and continued to question my life, doubting my purpose but clinging to the possibility of all being revealed in the future.

I decided to make the trip to Verona via St. Gall renewing my association with my businesses and wealth. I was a merchant once more discarding what had been many lifetimes wearing the cloth of the church. It was 1120 AD I and getting established once more as a respectable trader when I was introduced to a Monastic military Order called the Knights Templar. The large army were passing through Verona on their way to Jerusalem and I was fortunate enough to entertain Crowned Heads, Lords, Nobles and Bishops. It was at such an evening that I presented my proposal to serve them as a Bank and displayed my secret developments at St. Gall as a fortress to store monies, jewels and other valuable items.

To my surprise, adulation and excitement my proposition was welcomed with open arms, seemingly an ideal solution to their challenge.

150 years later, in the year 1270, I was preparing another caravan to the east when I was approached by Jacques de Molay, the Knights Templar Grand Master, asking to accompany me. For twenty years we remained friends before he returned to Paris, spending the rest of his life until his unfortunate end. By this time, the Knights Templar had become one of the wealthiest and most powerful assembles throughout the lands establishing a system of banks, churches and castles throughout Western Europe and Arabian Countries. It also made me a very wealthy and concerned man.

The tide had turned in the Muslim world, at the very end of the 14th Century as the last Crusade was a failure. Through my circle of contacts and informants, intelligence reached me that the French King Philip IV was becoming very irritable with the Templars, their reluctance to loan the ruler additional funds and their plans to establish their own kingdom within the realms of south eastern France. I was forewarned of a purge on the templars led by Pope Clement in collusion with King Philip and I tried to get a warning to Jacques de Molay who was now the Grand master of the order but failed to reach him in time. On what was to become the infamous date of Friday, October 13, 1307 the assault on Templar estates began that continued for three years. They were charged with fictitious and fabricated offenses, tortured and burned at the stake in 1310, dispelling the Templars as an organization by the Pope in 1312, with Molay suffering the same fate in 1314. I, however, played an important art in assisting many to escape, along with their treasures. Right up to the late 1300's the Popes resided in Avignon albeit still part of the Roman Empire.

It was at this time that the Black Death plague developed in East Asia brought to Europe by rats crossing from port to port. For many, many years I studied the disease, how it manifested and its progress from rats to fleas and lice. It was ferociously spreading as I passed from city to city, towns to towns. The worst I saw was in Constantinople where it was reputed to have lost as much as ninety percent of its population and we could find no cure other than confinement, Tragically, many of the volunteers succumbed to the same fate. Symptoms of the Bubonic plague causes fever, fatigue, shivering, headaches, and giddiness. As the condition worsens, sufferers also endure hemorrhaging, bloody sputum, vomiting, and delirium.

All the major ports of the Mediterranean suffered similar catastrophe decimating the population by huge numbers. Paris alone lost over 80,000, around forty percent of its inhabitants. By the late 14th century, the spread had substantially dropped mainly due to the shriveled population. It was several centuries later that I learned that it was estimated up to fifty million lost their lives in Europe alone, which was close to fifty percent of its citizens. Totally despondent and miserable, I became a recluse but not after ensuring my fortune was safe, organized, meticulously and carefully structured. As such, it was thorough and impossible to intrude without my networks and complex passwords. A system of authorized and trusted individuals acting in the capacity of power of attorney As time passed, I would make changes accordingly to the adjustment of personal or business status.

As it transpired the shift in power from the royalty to the Church worked very much in my favor. It was a time of suspicion, of the dominance of faith. Muslim set the standard for structures but Christian formations were developed with religious architecture and story-telling glass windows. The vast majority of the lower classes could not read and write, consequently, churches and cathedrals conveyed through strong images the accounts and chronicles of the life of Jesus and the Holy Mary.

As a Holy Man, a monk, a friar, a priest, and even a bishop, I captured faithful followers and political powers over the centuries lasting through the Gothic period of the seventeen hundreds. It was about this time that religion was becoming more prominent than ever and time to blend in as a merchant once more.

CHAPTER 7

Darkness and Accomplishments

I had spent many a night pondering my fate and asking myself the same question—why? Why me! My dreams and nightmares continued to plague my darkest hours, some very vivid and repetitive. I could sometimes tell by the surroundings and people whether it was likely to be the past or the future. Some were obviously confusing and others very clear, especially the past and over time I would understand the purpose. I had learned from my early Roman days it was not wise to be so visibly prominent and over a long period managed to remain invisible, so to speak.

Nevertheless, along the way I became prolific as a healer, studied pathology (diseases), became an expert surgeon and bone doctor (orthopedics)—although this was an ongoing learning curve. I also trained as a therapist /masseuse and became skilled in psychiatry and a proficient psychoanalyst.

From my time serving in the Legion, I was capable and adept in the art of war, a trained horse rider/soldier, archer, swordsman, and knife fighter/thrower. As a priest and a monk was taught and practiced wrestling, boxing, hand to hand combat, Chinese Kung fu (Shaolin and Wudang), karate/kumite and taekwondo. Throughout all my travels, amongst other things, I studied botany, entomology, zoology, mathematics, strategy, architecture, banking and accounting. All that being said, I exceeded as a linguist of both ancient and modern written languages. It became an art, a passion, learned without any effort. I also achieved the capacity of memory, I mean everything.

This also had a down side, for I have executed and murdered, under numerous circumstances and undertakings. I believed in what I did, some for survival, some out of necessity and some because they deserved it.

As for relationships I had many and loved them in my way, but less over time as I played the game of life. I had my favorites who stood out not just because of their beauty, but compassion, thoughtfulness, generosity, in particular love and care for all things. Very few of my children survived and those who did, their children did not. I remembered them all due to this burden of recollection, their faces so vivid and graphic. It seemingly was my destiny and misfortune not to be otherwise.

CHAPTER 08

Knights and Treasure

W hat started as an investment became unbelievable wealth within a concealed network of financial institutions. It was truly amazing how the original Knights Templar treasures were kept as a closely guarded secret, even from themselves. All but a few knew of the actual whereabouts of the bullion that ultimately left just one Grand master and myself controlling the resource. The Grand master, Jacques de Molay was tortured and executed by King Philip, taking his knowledge to the grave.

Shortly after Pope Clement disbanded the Knights Templar and forbid any resurrection of the order. Nevertheless, the Catholic church continued to search for the wealth for centuries and even had suspicion the Swiss Bankers were possible suspects, they were unable to find any real proof of their association I had set in motion individual and corporate accounts with easily falsified certification and credentials, which was relatively easy to do with my international endorsements. Maintaining family and corporate journals enabled the continuing dynasty of the Swiss accounts without having to touch the financial records. Over time, they became richer and richer.

CHAPTER 09

Peter the Great
1672 - 1725

I just adored the fresh smell of cut timbers as I wandered through the shipyards of this naval city. Some 400 years earlier the Arsenal, full of private shipyards was born in Venice. Between the fifteenth and seventeenth centuries, Venice progressed and established fleets of war ships that matured into one of the most significant and dominant marine authorities in history. The proficiency of its labor, the skills, techniques of all the crafts made them superior to any other.

In the course of these centuries, starting from the twelfth century in particular, the Senate of the Republic of Venice decided to build a state squadron to carry out the work of the private ones. the beating heart of the Venetian navy in which all types of workers and activities related to the fleet were carried out in total dedication. The Arsenal was organized as a modern factory, with an assembly line layout in which each department worked independently and with a rigid organization to ensure the efficiency of the shipyard: in the periods of greatest splendor an exorbitant number of workers worked there, between 2000 and 3000. I had seen Peter from a distance which no one could miss because of his height being over 2 meters (6 feet 8 inches), however never acquainted or met him even though I was familiar with a number of his friends and comrades. His educational and training principles in the Russian Navy were well documented as well as the expansion of their fleet. I followed his life with a great passion and envy as he designated his life to mother Russia both socially and military

Count Ivan Golitsyn was a pompous, egotistical man, full of his self-importance, however, he was a brilliant tactician in seafaring affairs. A Russian admiral of Greek descent who had the full assurance and support of the Tsar. He resented my age and being assigned to him by the Venetian Board as construction and repair advisor. Over a period eighteen years, I carried out my occupation and performed my duties that in the end gained the respect of Golitsyn. Notably, during the Finnish and Swedish campaigns I was known as Alexander Dimitrios Gallus, of Greek descent and Roman aristocracy.

We spent many years living in St. Petersburg which as a bachelor, I enjoyed many a philandering female, including the daughter of the Count. It kept me occupied and demanding socially whilst being conscientious in the art of war. When Golitsyn was near dying and I did not sit well with Bruce Roman Vilimovich, the chief commander of St. Petersburg so I contrived my fatal accident in the repair yard, at night, feigning the collapse of a scaffold that hurled me into the cold waters of the marina. As a doctor, merchant and advisor I wandered through the vast Russian and Chinese and Indian countryside for almost one hundred years. In all that time I did not take a wife, although several lovers along the way. Made numerous friends but one in particular, Lovji Nusserwanjee Wadia, a Parsi Indian with whom we shared the love of ships, designing and building. Wanting to stay longer with him I was faced with the same old problem of not ageing so at the turn of the eighteenth century took my leave and returned to Russia.

Generally, I was not enamored by the things that I experienced over this period of time, poverty and sickness was everywhere I traveled.

The French Revolution had come and gone and Napoleon having failed in Russia was now a prisoner on the island of Elba where he was likely to remain for the rest of his days. Meanwhile, Grande Britania was fast becoming a force to be reckoned with.

But I kept asking the same, tedious question—what was I doing here?

CHAPTER 10

Princess Natalia Petrova Alekseyava

The year was 1804, ninety years after the death of Peter the Great. Having become an excellent forger and resourceful individual having imagination and inventiveness, there wasn't anyone I could not pretend to be. Being an exceptional linguist and a historian made me unique and I was proud of my creativity. Once again, I became a privileged doctor, favored by the tsarist regime when I was introduced to Count Christoph von Keller a Russian aristocrat of German descent who was seeking a physician and I came highly recommended by the Russian Court. It was shortly thereafter between spring and summer that I was formerly invited to their stately home to meet his noble family. They were made up of barons, princes, princesses, countesses, field marshals, diplomats and other Tsar relatives. Most notably, there was a strong contingent of females compared to men.

As I mingled, I gained a strong sense of coldness and indifference to the point of condescension, arrogance and to put in one word, snobs. I had never met a group so pretentious and I kept away from frivolous conversation until I observed a lady sitting alone and starring out of a large bay window. She had her back to me but somehow, I was drawn to her. As I approached and was within a couple of paces, she turned around. I was stunned by her beauty, her long raven black hair, partly tied in a delicate bun with the rest flowing down over one ear. But it was her eyes, piercing green eyes on a dimpled cheek face and gloriously parted red lips showing a glint of sharp white teeth.

For a moment I was lost for words. She smiled as I introduced myself. She stood up and held out her gloved hand which I immediately took in mine firmly. "Grand Duchess Natalie Petrova Alekseyeva," she replied, looking straight into my eyes. "I have been informed you are a highly reputable doctor," she continued. I don't get embarrassed easily but I could feel my face turning a bright red and hoped she didn't notice. She turned back to looking out of the window and she asked if I didn't mind answering a few questions.

"If I am able," I replied.

"Walk with me into the gardens," she continued and abruptly walked towards the open doors to the veranda without waiting a response from me. Like an obedient dog, I followed.

After a short walk I could see she was heading towards an open pavilion with a single table and two bench seats surrounded by ornate rose bushes. I assisted her in getting seated then I sat in the other bench on the other side of the highly polished wrought iron table. Almost immediately a servant appeared and requested what refreshments we required. "Red wine," Natalie replied.

"And I will take a cold straight vodka with a glass of water," I added.

"Do you believe in fate, Doctor?"

"Please call me Simon and no, I do not believe in fate," I replied.

"How about destiny, a calling, or a purpose?" she asked. I responded, "If I may humbly state in my opinion that is the same question as before."

"Rightly so Doctor, I mean Simon," she exclaimed. "As soon as I saw you walk into the room, I watched your every movement until you presented yourself and what if I revealed to you in that moment, I knew we were destined to be deeply romantic and passionate souls."

In astonishment, I stared into those alluring eyes and felt a strange dryness in my mouth. Our refreshments arrived. Silenced overshadowed the slight noise of placing the glassware on the table and I reached out to pick up my tipple and quickly placed to my lips, eagerly swallowing a mouthful of vodka. I realized I had failed in my etiquette and was about to apologize for my ill-mannered behavior when Natalie stood up and walked away. Had I offended her, I pondered. Still seated I gazed at her sleek figure as she gracefully walked towards the veranda. Dinner was about to be served and twenty-eight hosts and guests were seated. I was sat between the Count von Keller and Baron Sergey Ivan von Engelhardt and opposite the Countess Marie Wilhelmin1e, the Count's wife. Natalie was at the opposite end of the table and as much as I tried to get her attention, she did not look in my direction. Baron Sergey noticed my gaze and said, "Beautiful, isn't she?" looking in her direction. "She is to become my wife, an arrangement made when we were still children even though we are cousins."

"Oh, "I responded. "And when do you intend to make her your bride?"

"Sometime this spring, a date yet to be decided by my mother." Just like that the subject changed to that of politics and warfare. Although I knew much of the conflicts and struggles of various nations and I could hold a rather solid conversation on the matter, my thoughts were elsewhere. Dinner was at last over, the men all headed for the library for cigars, brandy and coffee whereas the ladies headed to the Sun room .

It didn't take long before gaming tables were set up by the servants and some serious gambling was taking place. As I wandered from table to table, I noticed the different sets of cards used. The Russian and Germans preferred the thirty-two card pack consisting of the six cards through to the ace but one table was using the conventional fifty-two card pack. Nevertheless, I was not an enthusiast and would rather play chess. Coincidently, and in passing a Field Marshall invited me to play, warning me that he was a true master of the game. Of course, there was a wager and I let him win the first game being the best of three. I won the next two games which infuriated him.

It was the early morning hours as I made my way to my allotted chambers. Peeling of my clothes I sat in a chair, naked and thinking of nothing else other than Leonilla. Eventually, I climbed into bed and fell into alcohol bliss. Startled, I was awakened with the soft touch of a hand on my cheek. I could feel the warmth of her body as she sat next to me on the bed and the aromatic scent that teased my nostrils. "You are to be the love of my life," she whispered, "And I want you to consume by body as I know not how."

I sat myself up grasping her around her waist and pulling her close. She wore a very fine and delicate wrap and I sensed very little else. After taking a deep breath, I expressed myself very slowly that I felt the same way and I would be very tender, adoring in my manner, compassionate and caring. First, we must learn by touch and with our lips, kissing her gently on her eyes, cheeks and finally her mouth. After multiple long kisses I parted her mouth so she could feel my tongue on hers and she eagerly responded. After a short while, I stood up and guided her to do the same. Removing her flimsy garment, I guided her to explore my body with her hands as I did the same, feeling her soft pear-shaped breasts and raised nipples. I briefly took my leave going to the table to a box containing a covered pottery decanter which I removed. I drizzled in my had the mixture of Ylang and Jasmine and proceeded to cover the body of Natalie, expressing her to do the same for me.

She was quick and eager to learn as her hand fondled and stroke my phallus and I played with her vulva and pressing her vagina lips with my forefinger. She gasped and it was obvious, becoming excited as I plied soft strokes. I was delighted to feel the same euphoric bliss as she applied gentle but firm caresses. Slowly, we released each other and returned to just kissing each other into a frenzy. I kissed and caressed every part of her senses, from her toes to her ears, finally blowing softly on her genitalia before placing my tongue and lips over her clitoris and gently sucking on its tip. I could feel her body tense up as tugged on her flesh until in a frenzy I could tell she was about to climax. In a matter of moments her juices were flowing into my mouth as I flavored her nectar. She finally relaxed and understood it was my turn. She very gently followed my pattern until I guided her mouth and tongue over the head of my phallus. I instructed her to caress my ball sack and apply as much of her saliva over my shaft. She was indeed quick at perfecting her skill. As I was reaching my own peak, I warned her that my semen may not be pleasant either in her mouth or to swallow but she was in a state of ecstasy, enjoying sensations of her own. Suddenly, I exploded but she did not stop her performance until I spent all my seed. "That was astonishingly pleasing," she said.

We relaxed for a while then captured our enactment all over again before drifting into blissful sleep. When I awoke, it was the slight noise of the waiting staff delivering fresh tea and water, but Natalie was gone. This day, gentlemen were to shoot wild boar after an early lunch but the ladies were off on a picnic and as planned neither party were to dine together that evening.

It was a long afternoon and I had to put my medical skills to work as several of our beaters were gored by an aggressive bull. One of them badly and died before the hunt finished. The other was trampled and gouged in the leg but it was a clean wound. Nevertheless, there were two kills that were large and heavy and needed to be dragged by horses back to the chateau.

Obviously, there was a considerable amount of vodka and apple brandy consumed especially after each slaughter of the hogs. The bloodshed and butchering were mostly unnecessary but most of the huntsmen felt they needed to strike the animals, with swords, spears arrows and even knives were used. Any means to get blood on their hands and tunics. It was expected of them.

The evening was of tales of the day and more drinking, many until they could not stand or crawl. I discreetly took my leave and ordered a manservant to prepare me a bath. I waited patiently as it took three servants to organize and transfer the hot water from the main kitchen. They waited for me to test the heat and left a number of essences for me to choose from. Removing my clothes I immersed into the bathtub. Suddenly, there she was, standing over me wearing the flimsiest of see through nightgowns. Staring at her beauty, I was dumbstruck. Then I uttered, "How did you get in here undressed like this?"

"Known to only few, there are secret passages," she responded with a smile. After stroking my hair, she moved to the bed and making herself comfortable she said, "Will I have to wait long?" Rushing to remove myself and hastily dry some of my body, I dashed to the bed and awaited bliss.

We repeated our ecstasy and harmonious pleasure of the night previous and although I was in seventh heaven, I still did not penetrate her. It was almost sunrise when the picturesque Natalie departed, the same way she had entered.

I awoke as the sun was reaching high above the sky, washed my body, dressed, and was suddenly ravenously hungry. As I entered the dining hall, I was surprised at the number of guests seated and busily consuming a feast. I was unaware that a number of guests were leaving today and wondered if Natalie was one of them. Just then she entered room with her handmaiden and after courteous acknowledgements from the other guests, one of them who's back was turned to me, asked if she was departing that day. She answered promptly that she was not but leaving the following morning, I sat at an open spot, sighing with relief. She stayed for a short time, drinking tea and a scone but remained silent barring a few whispers to her maiden. She exited without saying anything but glanced briefly in my direction.

I took a long walk in and around the gardens desperately trying not to think of Natalie but the scent of the flowers filled my head with thoughts of her that sent a shiver down my spine. Clouds quickly covered the sky and I suspected a rain shower was imminent. I picked up my pace, heading for the estate and arrived just in time before the heavens opened up. Heading for the Library, I hastened to pour myself an apple brandy then seated myself by a window whilst watching the storm.

There didn't seem to be anybody about as I climbed the stairs heading towards my quarters. I pushed the heavy door, peering inside but no Natalie. I quickly stripped myself and proceeded to hand wash my whole body, spreading fragrance as I went. Wrapping a toweled garment around my waist I sat on the bed. It was getting dark when I heard the screen door open and this sensation stood before me. Standing up I let the towel drop to the floor with an already building erection. We wrapped in an embrace with our lips and tongues searching each other's inner cheeks. I laid her on the bed and my tongue suckled her left breast whilst my fingers caressed her clitoris. She was already getting wet as I lowered my body and my mouth covered her vaginal cavity. It was not long before I could tell she was reaching a climax and her deep breathing led to a loud scream of ecstasy. During the height of her passion, I arched my body until my firm growth was at her entrance of her orifice and I entered her slowly. She stiffened, letting out a huge sigh as I started to move slowly, withdrawing and inserting. She was indeed tight and I could feel her virgin lips bracing around my girth. Her juices were flowing and to find out later blood also. Her breathing was intensifying as she was close to another impending and stronger climax. As I felt her amazing highpoint of elation, I felt my shaft swell and expel my seed with such fervor and intensity. Feeling spent, I lay on top of her with my penis still inside, I could hear her crying, but gently and upon looking at her exquisite face, she was smiling. "It could not have been more wonderful and superbly pleasing," she said. I smiled back and could immediately feel me getting harder once again. She could feel it too and so we took our bodies into an adventure of erotic heights till the sweat from our bodies intertwined and our energies spent.

I slept heavily and didn't feel her leave, again. As I raised my body and rubbing my eyes, I looked around the room. On the bureau was an envelope. I dressed in a suitable fashion in case anyone came a knocking then slowly meandered towards the very visible package with my name on it. Opening the folds, I read only the first line, "To My One and Only Love," then reading on, "I travel to meet my destiny, an arranged marriage by my mother to my cousin, Baron Sergey Ivan von Engelhardt. We are to be wed within days of my arrival which is practical as I may be with child, your child. I shall give pleasure to my husband, but it is you that I will be dreaming of, always and forever. I pray that we will meet again, ending with her signature, Natalie

I could not help my painful emotions as I wept.

CHAPTER 11,

François Victor Mérat
de Vaumartoise

I t was nine years later in 1813 as I was traveling through France doing my best to assist various townships with numerous epidemics. After treating the people of Lyon, I moved on to the capitol, Paris. As always, impoverished sanitation had proved to be a major issue in large cities and Paris was no exception. Cholera, smallpox, typhus and yellow fever had taken its toll since the end of the eighteenth century in all classes of life. There was indeed a race by physicians to find a prevention or even a cure. One such man, Louis Pasteur, had reasonable success, however, it took considerable time to reach the general public.

I called upon an old friend together with whom I studied in Rome, François Victor Mérat de Vaumartoise. He was not only a renowned physician but a highly celebrated botanist and held many titles as a senior member of the Académie National de Medicine. We discussed many things but in particular the problem that was scavenging the French aristocracy and he could do with my help and knowledge to treat what was an epidemic of gonorrhea and syphilis, commonly called clapier, which funny enough also means brothel. Francois discussed with me a particularly tragic case, that of the Engelhardt family and my ears immediately pricked up! This unscrupulous Baron, who frequented the lowest of the city's bordello's acquired syphilis and even though he was aware of having contracted some form of disease, continued to have sexual relations with the Baroness Natalia. Nevertheless, it was some time before she was introduced to him as a patient and he could tell from the tests that she had been infected for a while. It was already clear she was infertile with considerable damage to the uterus. Not before telling me Baroness Natalie had been abused by her husband having a preference to deep throat fellatio and sodomy that I told him I knew of the lady from nine years before. Later in their confidential interviews, her ladyship divulged her husband waged her body for the night to two degenerates in a game of cards. She was bedridden for many days after the ordeal.

It was difficult to control my anger but I was determined to get retribution for Natalie. Would she see me? Let me treat her? I would rely on Francois to reveal to her that my knowledge on the subject disorder would be beneficial to her life expectancy despite our past. Meanwhile, he was aware of the gaming club that the Baron frequented and he would gain me membership. I waited patiently for several weeks to attain news from Francois and it was bittersweet. Firstly, the Baroness was distraught and saddened that I was informed but knew in her heart that if anyone could develop a treatment or ultimately a cure, it would be me. Therefore, she agreed to an appointment within the week.

On the day in question, I was nervous to say the least and could only imagine how Natalie felt. Francois agreed to receive her but left her unaccompanied in order to meet me alone. I entered the doctor's study and as soon as she saw me burst into tears reaching out for me with her arms. Aside from additional lines in her face she looked as beautiful as ever, taking her in an embrace. It was a while before releasing her as I covered her face in kisses until or lips met sending a shiver down my spine. She continued to weep as we staired at each other, then she said I didn't look any older and I replied that the years had been good to me. She smiled. I informed her that this meeting was to re familiarize with each other, establish my purpose and commence treatment at our next appointment which I will set for tomorrow. We continued with small talk. Her eldest son, my son, had died aged six of typhoid, then her daughter did not survive childbirth, leaving a final daughter now aged five. By the end of our reunion, we both felt a sigh of positive relief. We parted with more kisses and a final embrace before I went looking for Francoise.

CHAPTER 12

Baron Sergey and the Merchants

I had been a nightly visitor to Cerce Gaillon, gambled little but made sure my present at the bar was visible and leaving large gratuities to be remembered. If you want to get word of mouth, depend on the bar staff. I had let them know I was prominent surgeon from Rome visiting on a sabbatical. On several occasions I noticed the Baron at one of the gaming tables, very loud and having considerable consumption of red wine I had observed. I walked past their table numerous times and although the Baron looked in my direction there was no recognition in his face. It was only a matter of time before I became friendly with couple of the senior members, especially as I was footing the bill. They in turn introduced me to the Baron and two of his companions, Adrien Beaufoy and Benjamin Garnier, both merchants. All three were very shallow and quite voluble by the fact they had no secrets, voicing their exploits in great detail, even that of the Baroness Natalia which made me fume and thought to plan their demise.

One late evening we ventured into the depths of depravity, the slums of debauchery and immorality of Paris. To my amazement, after excessive consumption of wine and cheap gin, Adrien and Benjamin swapped blows over a woman and had to be separated before they did serious damage. Their bloody faces needed some attention from me and I knew immediately how I was to implement their fate.

Whilst I further aided our two antagonists, the establishment did not need much persuasion to eject them from the premises escorted by a very intoxicated Baron. I finished my wine and made a quiet exit shortly thereafter. I found them a short block away, barely standing, quarreling and pushing each other with the Baron passed out on the ground. I saw my opportunity as I intervened coming between them both, drawing their blades from their waistbands, plunging the steel into the chests of the very startled and shocked collaborators. As they both fell to the surface with a look of astonishment, I quickly surveyed my surroundings to ensure we were alone. I quickly withdrew the dagger from the Baron's sheath, plunging his blade time and again into the chests and back of his comrades. Once again, looking into the street, we were alone. I started to cut the arms and faces of all three to give the impression of an intense dispute before thrusting the Baron's weapon firmly in the back of Benjamin. I made haste from the scene and needed to clean the blood from my hands and clothes, fortunately not seeing a soul on my way home. Stripping, washing with rubbing alcohol, I found myself shivering from the whole experience, but with no regrets. I took some large secateurs and cut up my soiled clothing into small pieces, burning them in the fireplace.

The next evening, I returned to Cerce Gaillon as though nothing happened. There was no Baron, so after polite conversation and a couple of glasses of wine I returned home. It was the third day of returning to Cerce Gaillon that I was immediately approached by a very nervous Baron . In an excited tone, asked if I had heard of the slaying of his two companions. "Not at all", I told him and continued to relay the events until they were all evicted.

"Incomprehensible," he mumbled. "I don't recall anything and awoke to find them both dead and I bloodied, so I made haste and left the scene. But fortuitus, as I owed them both considerable sums of money."

With that said, he requested a favor of me. "Could I treat him for the dreaded clap, discretely of course, especially as I had considerable medical experience in this field."

"Of course," I replied and with the utmost diplomacy. "Would an appointment suit for the next morning at the premises of Monsieur Mérat de Vaumartoise with whom I could rely his trust and confidence in such matters?"

The very next day morning, early, I called upon Francois, who received me immediately and I relayed the events of the past week to him, minus my involvement. Furthermore, I requested the use of his consulting room. He waived his arm in the air, as if to say, "Of course my dear friend." Francoise continued our conversation, divulging that he knew a, high ranking official and friend in the Prefecture of Police and would reveal our conversation and path forward, if I approved. "Absolutely," I responded, "And I would be willing to make a statement," I continued.

It was several days before Francois contacted me and he requested we meet at his place of business the following day at 10 am. I arrived somewhat early but he didn't keep me waiting and tea was served as I made myself comfortable on the couch. Apparently, the Baron has some good relationships with senior members of the Prefecture so there is some reluctance to proceed further, Francois stated. His contact belonged to the same catholic church as the Baron, even though he did not attend very often unlike his spouse the Baroness.

"Do you believe your contact has high morals, being Catholic and all?" I asked.

"Why, yes, I believe he has. Conversation around the dinner table would indicate so. Why?" he questioned.

"If you introduced me as a medical colleague with unsavory information regarding the Baron's disposition, it may change their perspective."

"Brilliant," he applauded.

Meanwhile, I had treated the Baron three times using a mild salt of silver and a special additive of mine, a mild dose of strychnine, enough to make him nauseous. I had informed him that the stomach-churning was a normal reaction to the medication and would in time cease. He only experienced a slight metallic taste as the strychnine was odorless and tasteless. Within a few days and whilst I was at Francois premises prior to treating the Baron to another session, I was introduced to Alan DuBois of the Prefecture de Paris. After a few formalities, he respectfully welcomed my account of events at Cerce Gaillon and concurred that I was assisting the Baron in dispensing treatment for the disease known as syphilis. I certified and validated what I told him was the honest truth and in fact was awaiting the arrival of the Baron momentarily. He looked deep in thought then announced he would also wait for the Baron's arrival.

We did not have to wait long; in fact, the Baron was early. He looked ashen and taken aback when the three of us greeted him. Carrying a large handkerchief that he was coughing into, I could see some blood spotting on it. Mister DuBois took the Baron aside but kept his distance, mostly through fear of the Baron's illness. A short conversation followed and we could see the Baron's head nodding before Alan DuBois took his leave with the Baron in tow.

Francoise and I were dining when a messenger arrived with written notice that our presence was required at the Prefecture on the next morning, at our convenience. At the meeting, Alan DuBois gave us a summary of the Baron's statement indicating he has no memory of the incidents at Cerce-Gaillon or thereafter. During the interrogation, the Baron was seemingly in some discomfort with spasms of chronic coughing, hence his vital need to comprehend how devastating was the Baron's health. In not so many words, the both of us revealed the intensity of the infection ravaging his body that in our minds would result in his demise.

What of the Baroness, did she carry the same catastrophe? Franscoise explained she had been getting treatment from him and with some success.

She had not had sexual intercourse or any other stimulating acts with her husband in more than a year since discovering she was afflicted.

Alan DuBois was pacing and obviously in thought. "I am thinking," he paused. "I am thinking." He repeated that it would be better for all parties that the Baron should cease to exist rather the troublesome trials and tribulations of a murder prosecution. Further striding by Alan as we waited patiently for his next statement, he asked if we could we alleviate the pain and suffering by inducement.

Francoise and I looked at each other but it was I who responded. "Yes, I believe we may have the solution, but it would mandate the authority of the Prefecture or at least their acknowledgement of the Baron's death by natural causes."

After a little hesitation, Alan affirmed that this would be so, finally announcing, "Let it be done." 0

Francoise felt unsettled to administer such a potion, however, I relieved him of any accountability and assign myself the task. Taking the silver nitrate and a major dose of strychnine from my medical bag, I followed Alan to a holding cell where the Baron was lying down on a bench. Leaving us alone I explained to the Baron that I was to administer an increased measure of formula, easing his pain and reducing his symptoms. After dispensing the mixture, lifting the Baron's head, and pouring it down his throat, I stood there, watched, and waited. It did not take long as I had ingested him with an extremely large dose of poison. He started to have muscle spasms which increased in intensity, respiratory complications, and I knew then it would be soon. I leaned into his face as his body started to suffer with paralysis and he started to foam at the mouth. Speaking clearly so that he would hear the last words. "Strychnine poisoning and syphilis has a defining conclusion to your embittered life Baron." He died of asphyxiation as I cleared the frothing from his mouth with his handkerchief.

CHAPTER 13

Lausanne, Switzerland

After the Baron's funeral I continued to treat the Baroness with new root compounds as well as the basic silver nitrate and she responded very well. A few years passed us by when a very healthy Natalia announced her conversion from Orthodoxy to Catholicism and moving to Lausanne, Switzerland. I knew she had devoted herself to goodwill and compassion in recent times and above all faith. I was pleased for her, that she found a purpose, unlike myself having endured many lifetimes and had no time for faithfulness. In truth I was very cynical. Whilst Natalia prepared her departure, we promenaded many walks, held hands, and possessed each other with many kisses. Finally, on the last evening we had a reminiscing dinner, sharing memorable, unforgettable moments and we cried. I wished her a long life knowing I would never see her again.

Natalia Petrova Alekseyava lived her long life with her convictions and to show her dedication, built a chapel on her property which became the parish church of the Sacred Heart of Ouchy. She died, aged 101, on February 01, 1889 in Lausanne, Switzerland

CHAPTER 14

India and the
House of Wadia

The history of the poppy is vague although popular belief that exporting began as early as the armies of Alexander the Great who first took vast quantities of opium south to Iran.

It was 1817 that I ventured once more to Bombay, India with the intent to meet up with a Parsi Indian Shipwright and exporter Nowrosjee Wadia. Besides being one of the largest Shipbuilders in south east Asia to the British, they had just started to cultivate the Poppy in large quantities. The Wadia family's Grandfather, Lovji Nusserwanjee founded the company back in 1736 and was a particularly good friend sharing our mutual love of ships and shipbuilding. Over the years we had maintained enthusiastic communication exchanges that sometimes read like manuscripts than letters. This continued through two generations of Wadia's with the exception of myself who portrayed my own induction son to son, so to speak as Simon reborn.

Meeting Nowrosjee for the first time was like greeting an old lost friend who had read with fervor all the letters we had exchanged throughout the years. What was unusual, he had a tall, beautiful Chinese wife Xlu Wen with whom they had nine children. Their eldest daughter Lilavati Wen, Hindi/Mandarin name meaning charming, graceful and elegance was also striking but had inherited her father's adventurous spirit. At fifteen years old, speaking abundant languages, including both her mother and father's native tongues and English, she had a thorough knowledge of her family business, their clients who were mainly British and American. The rest of the children varying in age between thirteen and three were still growing up under the strong teachings of Xlu Wen and showed little or no interest in the family's pursuits. Lilavati Wen was content.

Insisting I being a house guest, I saw little or no evidence of the children as they were lodged in a separated annex with their own entrance and isolated garden. I was also detached in the visitor's quarters on the other side from the main living areas. The design and planning of this large mansion was cleverly done. Nowrosjee and I started our business discussions alone but I was quickly informed Lilavati Wen would join us as and when we concluded the finer particulars of our agreement. He went on to explain she was the only individual outside of himself that he implicitly trusted and was non-negotiable. Although unusual, I accepted his request and as customary, we shook hands.

It was July, monsoon period, late evening, when the rains were particularly heavy, I was rocking myself in the porch chair when I heard a faint screaming from the other side of the compound. Standing, I tilted my head as to ascertain the source of the squeal, then heard it again and rushed out into the torrent of water falling on my head and headed in the direction of the whimpering sound. My vision was impaired by the ferocity of the water falling and had to wipe my eyes frequently with my hands when I perceived sobbing nearby. Pushing a bush aside I saw a semi-naked young man aggressively grinding on what I observed to be a young lady. Not hearing me as I approached closer, I recognized it was the body of Lilavati Wen and sensing she was being violated, I raised my boot and sent it crashing down on the head of the assailant again and again. Falling to his side and obviously unconscious, I hastily removed my jacket and placed it over the naked torso as she assumed the fetal position and still sobbing.

After a short while and gaining her composure, she moaned that it was all her fault, teasing the young man but got out of hand along the way. Salvaging her torn sarong and pushing her arms into the jacket, I kneeled to check the condition of the youth, bleeding above his left eye and even with the downpour of rain, it looked considerably like a broken jaw. Looking closer, he was dead. Sitting next to Lilavati, I hugged her as I whispered in her ear the condition of her aggressor and almost immediately, she burst into a flood of tears.

"Who was he," I asked.

"Just a houseboy," she responded meekly. "Just a simple houseboy," she repeated.

"Listen to me," I said boldly. "Do you know if he inseminated you?" Repeating the question as I took her by the arms and shook her gently.

"No, no I don't think so but I couldn't be one hundred percent sure," looking directly into my eyes as tears rolled down her wet cheeks.

"Can you get back to you room unseen as I have to dispose of the body," I said, looking at her sternly and waiting for her reaction. She nodded firmly. "What was on your agenda early this evening before this unfortunate incident?" I asked.

"I was in the library reviewing the monthly financial accounts and the records are still there," she replied.

"Not to worry, I will make sure they are all in an orderly organized assemble and look like you completed the task. Now go and entreat we do not get discovered."

Lilavati quickly took her leave whilst I pondered as to where to place the young man's corpse. It could not be too far; this is India and even during a monsoon there was always a mass of swarming bodies rushing here and there. That was it, rushing here and there! I made my way to the kitchen where one of the staff was sleeping by the door and sneaked into the laundry room and found some kurta's folded in a pile. I removed one that looked my size then searched for some sandals that would fit my big feet. Finding a pair but looking slightly small and collecting a sheet, I slipped by the same servant blissfully sleeping, stepping quietly to the veranda. Changing into the local costume, putting on the uncomfortable small fitting thongs I ventured back into the raving storm.

Picking up the lifeless body, wrapping him in the sheet, I lifted him up and threw the corpse over my shoulder, surprised at the lack of weight which would make my movements a lot easier. Exiting the garden, through the gates it wasn't long before I was mingling with other soles fighting the downpour that didn't notice what I was carrying. I came to an alley and I instantly dropped to my knees, releasing the young carcass from the sheet, departing as quickly as I arrived. Although I kept looking over my shoulder, I was sure nobody saw or noticed my movements. I hurried through the shower that was diminishing so I quickened my pace and arrived back at the manor just as it was ceasing. Looking around all the time I disrobed the Indian clothes and the sandals that had bitten into my toes showing bare flesh. Naked and shivering, I carried the wet garments, collected my robes that I left under the chair and tiptoed to my room. Sitting on the bed I drew a long breath followed by deep sigh and pondered on the incidents of the night. Then my thoughts turned to Lilavati, her naked and blood-ied body, wondering how she was coping with this intense situation then my immediate attention turned to the pile of water-soaked threads on the floor and pondering what to do with them. Shoving them under the bed I decided their disposal would wait until the daylight hours.

Surprisingly, I slept soundly, awakening to the sound of servant activity. Swinging my legs off the soft divan, my immediate attention focused on the bundle under the bed. Retrieving the sheet that wrapped the clothing and thongs, I placed it in a lower drawer inside the closet until such time I could safely dispose of it. There was a knocking on my door followed by a woman's voice requesting admittance which I acknowledged and two women servants entered, the elder carrying a bowl of water and the much younger soap and towels. Apologizing for the lack of running water due to the rainstorms, they had brought fresh water and linens for me to cleanse myself and continued to express regret as they left.

Smiling to myself I washed my body as well as I could, drying with one of the towels and lightly dressing myself as the humidity was overpowering, already feeling my sweat oozing from my armpits. Making my way to the dining hall I was delighted and thankful for the large rotating fans operated by four elderly men, two on each side of the room. The whole family were seated, including Lilavati and were well into devouring the first meal of the day which is considered to be the most important one and always amazed me the huge array and choice of foods. A chair was vacant between Nowrosjee and Lilavati and I was bid welcome as a servant indicated where I was to be seated. Surveying all the food I suddenly became conscious of my own hunger. Aside from all the variety of breads and pancakes made from rice and flour, steamed loaves made of yeast, stuffed with chilies, onion, poppy seeds, and coriander, not forgetting the Kanda Poha, a flattened beaten potato, onion, peanuts with spices. Curry was also well represented, some with potatoes, white peas with roasted whole spices, notwithstanding the big green chili peppers stuffed with spicy aloo masala, fried, served with green and sweet tamarind chutney and my favorite, a dish of potatoes softened with jamboo, a strong, spicy Tibetan herb. I tucked in heartily and the only noise around the table was the munching of food as speaking was forbidden unless Nowrosjee allowed it so or he was asking a question. Glancing to my right I saw nothing in Lilavati's face that would indicate the ordeal she had from the night previous, in fact, I would say she appeared her usual confident self.

With breakfast over and Nowrosjee dismissing the household, I watched Lilavati amble her way swiftly to the office closing the door behind her. It was my notion to follow but Nowrosjee spoke stopping me in my tracks. I have arranged for us to visit the poppy fields, he said, hopefully the monsoons will not occur until later and so I was unable to speak to his daughter, then and not at all.

A few days later the servants were having a large wood fire on the front meadow and to my relief, I took the opportunity to burn my bundle when they were not looking. Up to this point, there was no news as to the discovery of the deceased and could have easily been dragged of by wild hounds.

Within ten days, we had concluded our transactions and I waited for the arrival of Somnang and Kong kea from Guangzhou, China. Two weeks after the unpleasant incident and returning from a processing plant, I discovered a bloodied handkerchief lying on my bed with the embroidered initials of LWW. This was an obvious message and after considerable thought understood it to be the notification that Lilavati was not pregnant and evidently shamed and embarrassed to discuss this entire experience. I would respect her wishes, keeping the matter private and confidential

Some days later my friends arrived then spent time educating them in the opium trade and the Wadia estate. After much dialogue, it was agreed that Somnang and Kong-kea would manage the distribution in Guanzhou whilst Kahmuu and Hmong would remain close to me or obey my controlled demands, whatever they may be. Bidding our farewells, sailing from Bombay to the treaty port of Guanzhou it was a pleasant and uneventful voyage arriving before the dawn hours.

Returning to India five years later, with Kahmuu and Hmong, very little had changed, except I hardly recognized the Wadia children and Lilavati had grown into a fine-looking woman but received me distantly and reserved that was noticed by Nowrosjee. "You look well my friend, but I am troubled, Simon," he said and continued on. "Lilavati is a troubled daughter and as much as I have tried to understand, I am hopelessly confused. She has totally rejected a proposed husband who my wife carefully chose spending all of her time with women, some of whom I would put in the category of less than decent and respectable," then muttered something to himself and excused himself.

I sympathized with him but was quick to state the purpose of my visit, to understand the reason why the opium crop had been dramatically reduced over the past two years. Sabotage and fire had been the main cause but also ravaged by root weevil that compelled them to import fresh seed from Turkey. We concluded our subjective dilemma with a response to our problem. An introduction to the Turkish merchants was essential to maintain our ever-demanding consumers as long as we would return to Wadia supply once they reached capacity, probably within three years. In agreement, Nowrosjee decided to write a coded introduction letter that would satisfy the supplying merchant as to our legitimacy and service our needs.

Having informed our ship's Captain of our new destination of Izmir, Turkey, it took several days to provision the vessel. Leaving Nowrosjee again, I couldn't help wonder as to the predicament he was in regarding Lilavati but it was not my problem to understand her actions.

It was but a year later that I learned Lilavati had committed suicide with another woman, found in each other's arms. I wondered how much the violation of that night in the garden had an effect of her mental state diverting her away from men and into arms of another woman that eventually took her precious life because of a forbidden taboo.

CHAPTER 15

Russell

I t was 1823 at a particular trade meeting with the Turks in Izmir, on the
Mediterranean Sea that I, Kahmuu, and Hmong came across a young
Irish American in a smokey coffee house, Sitting at an adjacent table, he
looked despondent, distant and ill-looking. Whilst my comrades were
drinking gazoz and I a lhamur tea made from the linden flower, our neighbor was drinking Raki, a very potent aniseed liquor. We could tell by its
milky white color, a flask of clear Raki and a small jug of water accompanied his drinking cup that he held firmly in two hands. Looking away, I
suddenly heard a loud shatter of dishes hitting the floor and turning back
saw the collapse of our occupant on the next table. This was followed by a
bellowing shout from the proprietor who was more concerned how he was
to be paid.

Searching his pockets, we retrieved some letters and other documents, but no address and gravely, no money. Not knowing his misfortune
or wanting him to face the wrath of the licensee, I settled his account, which
was more than I believed owed. Kahmuu and Hmong lifted him from his
chair and thought it prudent to leave the establishment for our quarters. We
were housed in a large residence provided by our Turkish hosts that could

dwell twice our numbers so dropping our new acquaintance on the bed in an unoccupied room was not a problem. Whilst Kahmuu and Hmong were playing chess and I reading a medical magazine, our fresh found friend appeared. Rather sheepishly he asked where he was and who the hell were we? We explained. He then divulged what had happened a block from the coffee house when three ruffians robbed him and after a chase they disappeared into the same establishment. He thought if he waited long enough, they would show. Something was put in his drink as he had only consumed half a glass and the next thing, he remembered was seeing us.

"My name is Sean Samuel Russel, originally from Cork, Ireland but many years now in New York, USA. I am a self-made man from the trading of furs and skins in major cities. I came to Turkey on my own with a paid ship's crew to invest in the purchase of opium as I perceive an active market in China. However, it would seem my contacts here are far from reputable," he sighed. We understood his predicament and after a brief discussion decided to help our young friend. He was overjoyed.

Contacting our own source of supply and revealing Sean's account, they advised us that the proprietor of the coffee house was a despicable thief, villain and accused murderer not be toyed with. "Sounds like our type of justice is needed," Hmong stated. We all grinned at each, even Sean, who appreciated our aid. After several days of reconnaissance from outside and within, the establishment had a rear door access, but within the building, Kahmuu noticed various sly individuals were gaining entry to a cellar doorway with downward stairs located adjacent to the tavern serving bar. We decided a night watch would be practical and sure enough on the third night around 2 am a group of four characters emerged from the street opposite. Sean said they didn't look unlike those who assaulted him. This was our chance.

We followed closely behind them to the front door and was surprised to find it unlocked. We all had our shoes heavily bandaged with cloth so our steps were relatively silent and when we reached the cellar, we heard loud laughter and what we concluded was the sound of gushing liquid from a cask. Although the wooden stairs creaked, they did not hear us rapidly approaching. Sean was brandishing his colt pistol in his right hand that he retrieved from his ship and a vicious looking bowie knife in his left whilst I had a short-handled axe and a butcher's blade. Our Laos brothers carried their native long bladed knives and knew how to use them.

Immediately they came to view there were at least two to every one of us, Sean got off a shot, then two before I put my axe in the neck of one our foe. The were stricken by our surprise and remained in standing shock before realizing what was happening. Slashing with our blades we took down six dead or severely wounded leaving the last three raising their hands in the air that included their ring leader. Our opponents were nothing but thieves, not brave, not warriors and definitely no match for us.

Blood on our clothes and on our flesh, we cast our eyes around the room until they came upon a large table with jewels and coin. Sean recognized his leather satchel hanging from a chair nearby and reached out for it, raised the flap but it was empty. Hmong was standing behind the two remain robbers, looking at me and waiting for my signal which was a slight nod from my head, severing their heads with one blow from each of his knives. Before their boss could say a word, Sean raised his revolver and shot him between the eyes. This should send a strong message to the community, he told us. "Of that, I have no doubt," I responded.

Surveying ourselves, we seemingly came out of this ruckus unscathed until I noticed a large pottery splinter embedded in Sean's right eyelid and bleeding profusely. Sitting him in a chair I examined the wound closely before I decided to remove the shard. This caused Sean a great deal of pain as the blood poured from the injury. Covering his eye with a kerchief I took Sean's left hand and pressed it firmly over it. Raising him to his feet the rest of us gathered all the trinkets and monies in Sean's and two other sacks. Slipping back into the night, checking our surroundings as we crept back to our lodgings. Removing the temporary dressing from Sean's face, I inspected the laceration and concluded it was a deep incision which at this point could not tell if it permanently damaged his vision. Inserting a linctus to the eye, applying a heavy alkaloid compound within a covered patch and binding it to his head for support, the composite would ease his pain and aid in his slumber. Sean would lose his sight in his right eye but believed I saved his life even though I told him his wound was not fatal.

For many years Sean and the Chai became working partners and long-lasting friends using the same distributing warehouses as I and developing a more personal relationship. Attended his wedding in 1832 and became godfather to his first son, Ethan Samuel Russell in 1835 with whom I remained very close, especially when his father passed. Ethan was seventeen years old when his dad died in a duel, the reason being an insult to his wife. His assailant did not live long, I made sure of that. I became the guidance counselor to Ethan, his two younger brothers Clark and Jackson. Their mother, Margaret chose to remain close to her daughter Elizabeth and remained so until war came upon them. Some eight years later Lincoln was elected President during turmoil over slavery and subsequently their civil war started a year later in 1861. I had mixed emotions in regard to the servitude of the black race as did the sons of Sean Russell. By this time disguising my age was proving difficult and receiving comments helped me decided to take my leave and return to Europe, probably England.

The Russell family went through their traumas of war losing Ethan at Gettysburg and Clark at Sabine pass as part of the naval Union forces. Margaret passed of heart complications after Clark's death was reported. Elizabeth died during birth complications as did the child. Her husband was also a casualty in Virginia by ambush. That left Jackson as head of the family with a considerable fortune at fifteen years of age and me as custodian. Without force and by mutual consent with Clark it was agreed for him to take passage to England and study at Harrow school with further training in the arts of defense, language instruction and business management. He was a fine student. After ten years he returned to the United States along with three of my own investment bankers to guide him in the right direction. My instructions to him were to recruit his own trusted personnel and when he felt comfortable, my staff would return.

Clark turned out to be a formidable and respected entrepreneur in the financial market, making impressive purchasing decisions that frightened the competition. He was fierce and relentless, gaining a reputation of overwhelming intimidation over his adversaries. He had many investments from newspapers to railroads and developed a syndicate of journalists across the United States of America. He learned very quickly the importance of information and this was a focal point in a great deal of our communications. We corresponded practically on a weekly basis and I marveled at his progress. I continued to monitor his career, although communication became difficult once I reached Russia. Receiving good news, Clark had become engaged to Catharine Lyman a young lady from a wealthy Massachusetts family. The letter reached me almost nine months after it was written and thereafter mail became problematic and sparse.

It was at least a year later that I managed to obtain from a hotel several publications of the Boston herald . On the front page of the newspaper was an article on the wedding of Clarke Samuel Russell to a Miss Catherine Theresa Lyman of the Astor family. It contained a long list of wealthy guests, dignitaries, governors and VIPs, some of whose names I recognized. I whispered to myself, "Congratulations, you've made it."

It would be many years after the first World War before I would set eyes on Clark and his family in the guise of Simon's son, Gregory. Astonishingly, loyalty and the network remained.

James Samuel Russell is the descendant and successor of the Clark Samuel and Catherine Theresa Russell foundation, a powerful and influential society.

CHAPTER 16

Incident at
Guangzhou

L ying almost one hundred miles inland, Guangzhou located at the head of the Pearl River and perfectly situated to serve as one of the main commercial and trading centers performed as an entryway for foreign resourcefulness that they commonly called Canton. Some days ago, the Chinese constabularies had confiscated our refined opium, unaware that a paid informant alerted us of the raid. Obviously, it was far from successful even though forces were demolishing some stocks, enforcing was totally ineffective, bribing administrators was rampant and merchants learnt unloading the foreign ships at anchorage into smaller river boats avoided interference from officials.

We were in the progress of restocking our warehouse from the hidden supply when a runner appeared, alerting us the arrival of a British naval force some miles away and received a signal from the fleet that they would arriving at the Port within the hour. It was reported by the Chinese Commissioner Lin Zexo an estimated three million Chinese were habitually smoking opium, causing great concern by the government that started a campaign to enforce the prohibition of the Dream Dust. Notices of this proclamation was placed all over town and the harbor to decree how serious they were taking this ruling causing a great deal of nervousness to the importers.

Unassuming and always wanting to be one step ahead, I dispatched Somnang and Kong-kea south to a landmass divided by water from the mainland China named by the British as Hong Kong. An island that was being developed, heavily fortified and ripe for expansion. Making our way through the bustling market to the harbor waterfront we and many others watched with interest as the flotilla were docking. Lowering and securing their gangways, an officer disembarked from the largest man of war and approached us. Handing us a declaration to be placed on a public board for all to read it commanded a meeting to be convened the next morning between the officers of the fleet, the British East India Company and the independent opium merchants.

Attending along with nine other traders at the offices of BEIC, we were informed the Navies mission from the Admiralty were to defend and rectify Britain's standing policy by force, if necessary, that included lifting of the prohibition, seeking reparations in silver bullion and proclaim the legalization of the opium trade once again. Apparently, a civil war was underway in the north by the Manchu's Qing Dynasty and the Hakka led Taiping Heavenly Kingdom but should not concern us for the time being. Although there were questions from both the British East India Company and the merchants, the naval officers declared the meeting over. Disgruntled and irritated, we were escorted from the building where we continued to discuss the situation amongst ourselves when, from the corner of my eye I sighted a small column of Chinese Militia approaching. Calling a halt, the squad Captain approached and loudly demanded to know who was in charge when the naval officers appeared and several of them hastily left in the direction of the harbor to get help. The presence of the Chinese column was unusual and unnerving within the fortified walls of the foreign compound that scattered strolling bystanders away from the confrontation.

Whilst a heated conversation ensued between the two leaders, a large contingent of British soldiers arrived brandishing their rifles at the ready, awaiting further instructions. Upon the shouted command of the Chinese leader for his force to maneuver into the defense mode, lowering their pikes all hell broke loose as rifle shot after rifle shot rang out sending bodies to the ground but not without response from the disciplined apposing band hurling their lances with accuracy and drawing their swords. With great haste most of us rushed into the building but a stray bullet hit Kahmuu in the leg landing heavily on the ground as I dragged him to safety. Another pierced the face then out through the ear of a naval a captain who fell dead before he hit the surface. Screaming and shouting, more gunfire, suddenly ceasing as I examined Kahmuu's wound that thankfully was an in-out at the back of left leg. Looking at him face to face I instructed him to sit still while I fetched my medical bag and headed out the door to absolute mayhem but did not stop until I reached our own office warehouse. Gathering assorted tools, medications, potions and ointments I headed back as fast as I could, knowing that my attention would be needed by many souls.

After many hours, I was able to help just a few as most were deceased or perishing, at least I could ease their pain. Only one Chinese individual survived without anything serious but a few bumps and bruises dispensed from one of the Captains, who had to be restrained from killing him. I could see from the glare of the accosted that he wanted to do likewise until he was knocked unconscious by the butt of a Remington. All in all, twenty-nine of the militia, two officers and five soldiers were slain with eleven troops wounded but not severely. The senior officer commended me for my actions, intended to state so in his dispatch to the naval Admiralty and would highly recommend some form of award. Thanking him, I declared I was only doing what I could to save lives then asking him what they intended to do with the lone survivor, after all, he was only invoking their law, besides we were the assailants and fired the first shot. He, nor his subordinates supported my statement inasmuch they raised their weapons first and would be documented so. Authority had spoken and the captive would be enslaved until such time they decided his punishment

On strict instructions from the senior captain, the burial ceremony for the British servicemen would be attended by the Navy contingent only whilst the militia were wrapped in sail cloth and stored in a warehouse. Armed soldiers were strategically placed to enforce the ruling but most everyone knew to avoid any discord. Rising early, before sun up, I made my way to the stockyard in the vicinity of my storage when I noticed the empty warehouse and the bodies had gone. Looking in the distance I could see one of the frigates leaving the dock sailing out towards the sea. At that same moment I heard the sound of an alarm bell coming from the soldier's temporary barracks and made haste towards the commotion where bodies we scurrying here and there. Stopping one of the men I enquired what was happening and he replied the prisoner had escaped in the night wounding a compatriot in the process.

Turning away, my thoughts were asking, who would assist him, but nobody came to mind, at least not immediately. Gazing ahead of me was Baiyun mountain or White Cloud as we taipans called it, some four or five miles away and if I was to hazard a guess he would be heading there. Some thirteen hundred feet high, it wasn't a huge peak but plenty of hiding places I bet and the terrain was treacherous with lots of lose rocks and boulders. Very quickly, the search party had assembled, some two dozen men headed up by Captain Williams the officer who tried to kill the fugitive some days before. Abruptly, Hmong appeared and volunteered his services, not only because he spoke the escapee's language but knew the slopes having ventured them on many occasions. Like a flash, I knew it was Hmong who helped the young man escape, having spent considerable time in conversation with him. Be careful, I said, Bandits roam this region and Hmong replied they intend to return before dark and raiders are not likely attacking a well-armed troop during daylight hours. Off they marched at a rapid pace. Knowing what Hmong had done disturbed me but an explanation would have to wait until his safe return and in all honestly, I was pleased the solitary survivor fled as I would bet his life was forfeited anyway, being the only enemy witness . Taking the opportunity to speak with Captain Blake, the naval officer in charge, I questioned the disappearance of the militia bodies from the storage. "Buried at sea so there would be no evidence of them being here", he responded.

"Let's hope not a soul finds out, I replied, the Chinese have deep rooted rituals, belief in the afterlife and being buried in mother earth".

Blake scoffed, turning his back on me, remaining silent which was the gesture for me to leave.

As Hmong had promised the disheveled group returned before dusk with one of them being supported by two others and no sign of Captain Williams. Hmong explained they were hiking up a steep precipice of lose rock that the Captain was leading when he slipped causing a landslide of stones and gravel to the men below. This caused an injury as everyone fought to gain a foothold when they noticed that the Captain was missing and as much as they searched could not find him in time before the sunlight was rapidly fading. I tended the wounded ankle, some cuts and abrasions on others all awhile they talked amongst themselves as to the disappearance of their officer, wondering what had become of him. By the time everyone had settled down and I had finished with my treatment, cleaned up, I was ready to have a heart-to-heart conversation with Hmong. Walking together to my home, we made ourselves comfortable on my veranda and poured ourselves a stiff vodka each before my interrogation begun. Before I asked my question, 'Why', we heard a distant scream from the vicinity of the mountain, then another, followed by many that lasted a good twenty minutes before it stopped. We stared into the darkness of a cloud covered sky straining our ears for what seemed a few minutes, but nothing. Hmong looked me straight into my eyes, spoke very clearly, and decisively said that he could not disregard the probable execution of an innocent Asian having been in that situation himself. The far-off squeal started again, only fainter as it echoed from the slope and it continued for another fifteen minutes or so before ceasing abruptly. Again, our attention was drawn to the resounds of a voice in obvious pain, we stood, moving several paces forward, wondering where and what was happening. What seemed an eternity, we remained frozen to the spot, when it begun once more but with the sound of less despair, more like a whimper and for a mere few minutes only.

Hastily striding to the garrison that took almost half an hour, we were met by two armed guards demanding to know our business. After a brief explanation, one guard remained while the other took us to the room of the officer on watch.

After an explanation for raising him from slumber, he questioned both guards who heard nothing but as we enlightened the gloomy sergeant, our house was not too distant from the slope and considering they were missing a Captain, it should be investigated. Giving orders to gather another search party and just as we were leaving, the sergeant insisted I accompany them just in case they find the missing commander injured. Nodding, I could do nothing but comply with his directive when Hmong agreed to join the group. Heading back to the lodge to get a few hours' sleep, we feared the worst for Mister Williams especially with the fugitive on the loose.

Somewhat drowse from the lack of rest, we sat on the terrace waiting for the army unit to arrive and finished our tea as they came into view. Off we sauntered as the sun rose to our right and I could tell there was a sense of uneasiness amongst the men. As we approached the ridge, spreading out, the elevation increased and the climb intensified when Hmong pointed to a massive rock and indicate we should walk around it. I was bringing up the rear so was last to see the hideous shape pinned to a boulder and kept on walking as almost everyone else stood in a daze. The totally unrecognizable, naked body of a man was covered in dried blood from head to toe, infested with flies, cockroaches and other insects that made it difficult to examine With Hmong's assistance swatting the vermin away I scrutinized the corpse discovering countless cuts entirely over his body, probably from a knife. I have seen this before in my home country, a torture that the Chinese devised called death from a thousand cuts stated Hmong, a prolonged unimaginable and painful execution. Suddenly I heard a shout, the sergeant brushing past me and grabbing the wrist of the lifeless remains. "Look, he said, a tattoo of a turtle over an anchor which is identical to the one Captain Williams had".

Returning amongst a great deal of chatter and speculation, the conclusion was he was murdered by the fugitive and although many weeks were spent searching for him, not a solitary sign or clue was found. Due to the condition of the cadaver Williams, he was consumed by fire without ceremony.

CHAPTER 17

Opium Wars

I had a long history with opium or at least various forms and used it often in my medical practice to relieve or overcome pain but also numbing the senses in the cases of amputation. In recent years laudanum, a diluted solution of opium became popular for relief of minor ailments or headaches but morphine, a much more powerful narcotic was segregated at the turn of the century, used as a primary pain reliever by physicians. I had never contemplated the use of opium as a recreational drug, however, to know the appeal and effects I decided to try the common use of smoking the pipe. Consulting with Hmong, he guided me to a Taipan Opium den, a retreat frequented and serviced to foreign businessmen only. Taipan was a common term given to the overseas born merchants operating in China and notably wealthy. We were greeted by several short oriental ladies dressed in European menswear who offered alternative lose garments to change into for comfort purposes. I decided to do so to accommodate the full experience as did Hmong and was shown to a curtained cubicle to change. As I disrobed, my clothes, all of them were neatly folded by the hostess and placed in a basket, then helped me with the silk, wrap around vestment supported by a waistband, kneeling she placed my feet into a pair of open toed slippers. Smiling, I was gestured by hand to pass her where

Hmong was already waiting for me and seemingly knew his way around so I followed.

It was a passageway of sliding doors and the air reeked of overpowering flowers when we came to a stop and the scantily dressed very young girl in front of Hmong glided open the door and bid us to enter. It was a lavish room with mockup windows showing garden views and extravagant hanging silks, fresco art walls, excessive, scattered large pillows decorated the floors with the only piece of furniture being a French looking designed Chaise lounge. I decided the divan looked more comfortable as Hmong settled for the cushions. In walked two minors wearing thin muslin full robes that left nothing to the imagination and ornamental face masks. They were carrying trays displaying long clay pipes, an oil lamp, dishes with a composition that I assumed was opium and flask with cup that was probably local Baijiu, a fermented alcoholic drink made from grains.

Hmong had already put the pipe to his lips and exhaling rapidly whilst I had to be shown to hold the stem over the lantern, watching the aromatic cuttings vaporize before I could inhale. I have a sensitive palate so the first aftertaste was rather a bitter flavor although the aroma was delightful as I sucked more aggressively. It took quite a while before I sensed the tranquility and calmness, as I later learned I was given a mild dose, being my first time and did not have the intensity that Hmong was achieving.

The whole experience was at best enjoyable and although I did return a few times, it never really appealed to me, so I did not venture back to the den. However, I witnessed the obsession, how habit forming and dependent to the point of abuse that led to rack and ruin of many men that included Hmong. It infuriated me as he became quick tempered, experienced paranoia and totally preoccupied with returning to his fixation almost every other day. Kahmuu and I agreed to take action, deciding to abduct him after one of his sessions, place him aboard ship to take both of them to England and it was not too long before we were able to buy passage on the Sutherland, a frigate of the British East India Company. Everything went as planned as they set sail on a vessel with no opium aboard.

All the while, war was waging in the north, the flow of opium never ceased, although bandits were becoming a problem, the loss was minimal compared to the profits. With the constant residence of the British Empire in Guangzhou, we were safe, secure, sheltered and without any real concern. Making several trips to India, it was upon my last return and disembarking from ship that I was extremely delighted to see Hmong and Kahmuu standing on the dock. Without hesitation, I reached out to them both, grinning from ear to ear, giving them a bear type hug. Hmong stared at me and thanked me for saving his life, even though he hated me for the abduction for some time and he suffered with severe withdrawals, but found reconciliation of his old self and tranquility. Kahmuu joined in stating he suffered the most that emitted a roar of laughter from all three of us.

It was announced by the British Navy the wars were over with the fall of Taping with the Quing finally defeating the rebellion. After fourteen years it came with a heavy price, an estimated twenty-five million fatalities and unknown numbers maimed or wounded that left the country in an economic upheaval and once again, legalization of opium. Nearer to home, I could not be happier that Kmong's personal war was over with dependence on the dreaded poppy.

The world was changing dramatically and my visions told me it was not necessarily for the better. It was time to leave China.

CHAPTER 18

The Time of
Philosophical Change

I would have to say the nineteenth century was a time of great revolution and transformation more than all of the previous 1800 years that I walked in life. It was time to tally all my wealth scattered across many countries and how was I going to maintain access during my travels. It didn't prove to be that difficult, inventive luggage and garments solved most of the issues.

The English Queen Victoria reigning from 1837 commanded a vast empire whilst it was the development of industrial transformation. Most notable, the telegraph system, steam locomotive, the telephone, combustion engine, electric lightbulb, moving pictures, all kinds of motorized devices from the lawnmower to the vacuum cleaner. In the medical discipline, the stethoscope, anesthesia and the process of pasteurization and surgery enrichment. The development of firearms, the revolver, the multi barrel gun and dynamite. Even simple items like the safety pin and zipper. It was a remarkable period in literature also.

It was just before Christmas in 1864 and I had just read the book *On the Origin of Species* by Charles Darwin which strengthened my belief in change by evolution. As a matter of fact, I read the book several times and as I recall It was a few years after Queen Victoria's husband, Albert, who died of typhoid fever. Timely news and advanced communication were widespread which brought the world closer to every individual. It was having an alarming effect. I left Paris, spent seventeen years in London, England where the advancement of medicine was compelling and absorbing. During this time, I gave instruction to Clark Russell until his return to Philadelphia. Thereafter, I moved to Gothenburg, Sweden to study under Professor Eilert Adam Tscherning. for surgical instrument enhancement, especially the different alloys being tested.

1885 and the news from Russia was disturbing and I was somehow drawn to her. I had two options of travel to St. Petersburg, one, overland by rail and road, but conditions were not maintained, especially with harsh weather that made it risky and unsafe. It was also unhealthy and challenging to find suitable places to rest with quality often being unsuitable. Frequently, accommodation had no provisions and bandits would also take refuge in these lodgings, committing theft, abuse and often worse.3

CHAPTER 19

The Schooner
KRONAN

I t had to be by sea. My plan was to spend and much time as needed in
the dockside taverns, keeping my ears open for a possible prospect and
it did not take long Apparently, the first mate was looking for a position
as his captain could not afford to pay the crew or outstanding debts to the
shipyard for repairs. Approaching the first mate, I asked him to join me for
a brew of his choice which he accepted. Whilst nursing a tot of rum with a
beer chaser, introducing myself, I asked him about his ship and the whereabouts of his Captain. He replied, my name is Zigmund, first officer of the
KRONAN bragging that this schooner was one of the finest sailing vessels
in Sweden and under better circumstances not a finer captain or crew.

Smiling, I replied that I had serious need of such a vessel and would
be willing to discuss the prospects with the Captain including the intent
to pay the liabilities and secure income and bonus for the crew. He had
already swilled the rum, guzzled the beer, stood up and demanded me
to follow.

It was a short walk to the dockside where the schooner was secured by many ropes and an armed guard. After a brief discussion between the sentry and Zigmund, we were allowed to board the vessel. Captain Anders Larsson was looking down on us as we climbed the gangway, a stout but fit looking man with a ruddy face and long blond hair falling to his shoulders. Zigmund introduced us stating my Swedish was poor but understood I spoke several languages. Call me Anders, the Captain said, and would you prefer we communicate in Russian or German. I thought it prudent to state German and we continued in that tongue, which, they both spoke well.

I was led to the Captain's quarters, offered a seat and asked my business. I need passage to St. Petersburg, no questions asked. It would be a one-way passage and in return, I can release you of your indebtedness and propose payment to you and your crew in kronor coin or equivalent gold standard. Anders spoke, excuse us for a moment and with that they left me alone in the cabin. It was not long before they returned and sat down in front of me.

"We have a crew consisting of sixteen hands, including myself and first officer with an anticipated voyage of four days for the 1,000 kilometers sea distance, weather permitting and maintaining a speed of twelve knots. We have a safe anchorage at St. Petersburg, taking the final passage by rowboat where you will be accompanied by two mariners to your destination, presuming you know where you're going? For this service our compensation will be 20,000 kronor, non-negotiable." Before they could comment further, I responded immediately that I was in agreement. "That was a quick response," stated Zigmund. "Maybe we should have asked for more!" I laughed. Captain Anders added, "the fee is one hundred percent up front, after all you could fall overboard," and we all chuckled.

It was several day days before departure, the debt took a little longer to settle. Everyone was in good spirits, especially as I had paid up front. Nevertheless, It was a pleasant voyage, the weather was favorable and we arrived within sight of St. Petersburg just before dusk on the fourth day. Bidding my farewell and as promised two mariners took me ashore and to my safe house. After handing me my two large pieces of luggage, they quickly took their leave and was glad to see the dwelling still standing without any visible damage. Removing a brick from the gate post and retrieving the keys I opened the lock on the gate followed by the sturdy front door.

Slowly walking to the reception hall, as the house was rather dark, I reached up until I could feel the lantern hanging from a hook. Taking from my pocket some matches, (another 19th century invention) I opened up the glass frontage and lit the taper. Having light, I made my way to the main living room

Although a musky lavender smell and thanks to a revolutionary textile industry, everything was covered in a lightly oiled fabric that had gathered substantial dust that I quickly removed. I sat momentarily, taking in my surroundings then moved swiftly upstairs to the main bedroom. The large mural wall revealed a hidden door to a safe room containing personal possessions, gold and jewels, enough wealth for a prince. Smiling to myself, removing the bed coverings and making myself comfortable on the bed I drifted into sleep.

CHAPTER 20

The Fall of a
Monarchy

I did not waste any time in re-acquainting myself with the hierarchy of St. Petersburg and over twelve years made plans to infiltrate the upper society to be in the know of the governmental establishment of Russia It became abundantly clear the country was run by fools with other fools looking on and that the new Tsar, Nicholas was being misled as to the needs of the people. After several years I once again had favorable affluence and respect as a doctor when I was introduced to Anna Demidova, the daughter of a well to do merchant, Stepan Demidov. She had recently graduated from the Yaroslavl Institute with a teaching honor and likely to take employment as a tutor and lady in waiting with the Empress Alexandra Feodorovna. Anna was not a beautiful woman and shy hence a lack of suitors, but I knew to be more accepted in social circles I needed a wife. After almost two years of courtship, she finally accepted my proposal and we were married in September 1899.

I was treating the Grand Duke Michael Alexandrovitch with a difficult birthright disease of hemophilia when Queen Victoria died and he was requested to represent Russia at her funeral. I was to attend in order to treat him, if necessary but I was requested a favor and escort his mistress Natalia Sergevevna Wulfert which did not go down too well with my wife Anna.

It was a cold, foggy day walking at the state funeral on February 2nd 1901. A vast entourage of European Royalty gathered at St. George's Chapel, Windsor Castle that there was no room inside for the non-elite. Thousands were waiting outside but I had pre-arranged transport a mile or so away to take many of us back to the Hotel, whilst the memorial and tributes were taking place, I happened to share a coach with Natalia without a word being spoken as we were too busy trying to stay warm. The overall journey was arduous, arriving back in St. Petersburg by end March, 1901.

After three years and two miscarriages, Anna became pregnant again and with careful vigilance, managed to go full term. And so, I became a respectable husband and father to a boy, Ruben, who was born on July 29, the day before the Tsar's youngest son Alexei Nikolaevich, was delivered. Unfortunately like his uncle and many of the European nobles, Alexei was born with hemophilia. Even though Anna and I were virtually residents at the palace, we saw little of each other, however, Ruben and Alexei grew up together as very good friends, dressed similarly, cutting their hair the same and were often mistaken of each other's identity.

I was getting quite bored with my life but at least we were safe as the situation became worse all over Russia Turmoil within the government and the Tzar reached unbalanced proportions, most of which I learned in idle conversation with the Grand Duke Michael.

The situation became worse for Russia after trying various European maneuver's and accepting huge loans from France to rebuild its military strength, due to conflicts with Serbia, Albania, Greece, Turkey and Austria with the first and second Balkan wars raging over 7 years.

With the assassination of the Archduke Franz Ferdinand a general European war escalated that would result in the destruction of the monarchy. In August 1915 Nicholas took command of the army with the

Empress taking the responsibility of the government and Grigori Rasputin as her mentor.

It was then that Anna informed me of the intended relocation to Belarusia of the Tzar, his close family, advisors and necessary staff that included her as the lady-in-waiting to the Empress. Neither I or our son, Ruben was to be included. It would seem my services would no longer be required. Expressing my farewells, I disclosed my fear to Anna that I may never see her again and between the tears and laughter, she denounced my fears as nonsense. Then on her knees, gave a huge hug to Ruben, smothering him with kisses and for him to be a noble boy for his father. Then she was gone.

I did not see Ruben that evening, excusing himself to early isolation that I put down to the departure of his mother. When he didn't show for breakfast, I went to his room and found him sitting on his bed with his head in his hands. As I drew closer, I saw a cloth held to his face and what looked like blood dripping to the floor. Pulling his hands away, I could see he was having a severe nose bleed. With astonishment and disbelief, I was looking at Alexei. Whilst I tended to his hemorrhaging, he blurted out the plot instigated by his mother, the empress, his two elder sisters, and my Anna. It would not create any immediate suspicion as the boy was tutored by my wife and was soon to be segregated from the family under the care and protection of Rasputin. Giving Alexei a narcotic sedative, I supported his leaning head by a pillow which slowed down the flow of blood. Instructing him to rest and stay in the reclined position I advised him of my return later in the afternoon. I returned on several occasions, thankfully, he was sleeping and the bleeding had ceased.

That evening, I was expecting a guest, someone I trusted. Over the years I struck up a friendship with the British Consul Robert Preston spending many an evening discussing Russia's political fate. He warned me of peasant dissent, the food queues, prospective strikes and the probable deadly response from the government. In short, he advised me to strongly consider departing Russia, at least until the circumstances improved. He was right. What he did not know was that I had the crown prince and my son was with the Tzar. I decided to enlighten him and he was as stunned as I After much discussion, we decided to do nothing and wait for news from Belorussia.

The winter was particularly cold and very little news from the east. We kept to the house whilst I treated Alexei from time to time and he actually seemed quite happy, missing his nursemaid most of all. July, 1916, we celebrated Alexei's fourteenth birthday and he was getting used to living with me, which was a blessing but I couldn't help but wonder how Ruben was coping with his pretentious life. I have never understood how or why my dreams fluctuated or understood their meaning, but I was not having many for the past year.

Winter was upon us again and during the celebration of Christmas, Robert received word of Rasputin's assassination and in fighting between some of the monarchists and the Romanov family. It was early March, 1917 and the situation amongst the peasants was appalling. Lack of food supply was dreadful; starvation and death were everywhere. More news, the Emperor, his family and all their servants were abandoned in his train whilst on route Petrograd. His abdication followed shortly leaving the revolutionists in command of the country.

Meeting with Robert, we formulated an escape plan along with other nobles that he was supporting and the strategy was to take immediate effect.

BOOK 4

CHAPTER 01

1918 St. Petersburg

"I am afraid Simon, for us, for you," cried Catherine speaking in Russian. "It is good for us to be in St. Petersburg," I said in the same language, "And not in Moscow. The boy has been sick for some of the time suffering with hemophilia but he is strong and once we get him to London his Royal family will provide specialists to treat him just like his Great Grandmother Victoria."

"It is good he is getting used to his change of name to Ruben Frederick Stepan and you must avoid and deter him from mentioning anything to do with the Romanov family. I insist we speak English from here on. My friend and British Consul Robert Preston will be here shortly to take you and the boy to a British Warship where other Romanov's will be boarding including Duchess Xenia. For the time being all the passengers will have fictitious names."

"What of you?" asked Catherine.

"I will travel back east to meet up with loyalists to rescue the Tzar, if possible. The Bolshevik's have them under guard at the Imperial palace but we are led to believe they intend to move them further east soon," I said.

On arrival London the most important issue to address is Ruben's health. Once he is well enough to travel, passage for the both of you will be provided to New York, United States of America. We have friends who will provide for you and you will know them when they say to you in Russian". Catherine gave me a strange look which prompted me to repeat my statement.

Grigory Nikulin, my fellow conspirator entered the room and announced the arrival of Robert. We quickly grabbed the luggage and rapidly passed through the front door into a busy street where two vehicles awaited us. Robert and his driver were in the first car and I ushered Catherine and Ruben into the back seat whilst Grigory was loading the luggage into the second vehicle. They sped off as I waived and that would be the last, I would ever see of them.

Grigory was a revolutionist and an opportunist so I did not entrust him with the knowledge of who Catherine and Ruben were. Only close family friends of Robert Preston, the British Consul knew they were important and worth the risk. Besides I rewarded Grigory with significant cash knowing he would use it to help his own family in Moscow. Grigory and I parted ways, he for Moscow and I to Minsk. It was early July.

If I had known, or had one of my visions of his involvement with the Romanov's I would have put him to death. As it happened, I was to meet up with a strong group of loyalists to Nicholas II with a plan to rescue him and his family before the Bolsheviks moved them further east. It was the early days of a warm July when I arrived in Minsk now proclaimed capital of the Belarusian People's Republic but not for long, I feared. Devastated by war and foreign occupation the city laid in ruin consequently we were to meet in the Pinewood Forest northwest of the city on the Svislach River. It was late evening when I entered the camp and warm greetings from my comrades. After a late supper I learnt we were to meet our final group in the northeast of the city on the road to Moscow.

The sun had not yet arisen but the thirty-three of us were already en-route, traveling on horseback through the heavily wooded forest as quietly as possible. It took us but hours to reach our destination attracted by whispers of smoke and a small clearing. There, hanging from three separate trees were our brethren, naked, beaten, dismembered with grotesque facial expressions. They must have been taken by surprise as there was no physical evidence of a conflict. Not knowing if the offenders would return, we could not give our lifeless comrades a decent burial and made haste towards Moscow.

The weather continued to be warm with a refreshing breeze from the southwest when we reached Moscow heading straight for the palace but we were too late as it was abandoned and the Romanov family had already been relocated. We could only guess they must have anticipated an attempt to liberate them. Separating in pairs except I, we attempted to find information as to where the Bolsheviks would have taken them. It took me the best part of the two days to locate the family of Grigory Nikulin, but his wife Olga was alone with her five children. She recognized me and made tea whilst her children were running around in mild mischief. Several days before senior Party Member Yakov Yurovsky and two others Peter Ermakov and Stepan Vaganov came by all excited but all she could hear was something about special orders, the Romanovs and a place called Tobolsk. Grigory packed a few things, left some money and departed saying something about destiny.

It was late and Grigory's wife Olga offered the cot for the night which I gladly accepted as it was dangerous to travel at night in the city. She retired to her bedroom which she shared with her children. I slept deeply and just before the dawning light I had a very vivid vision that awoke me in a sweat and shaking erratically. I staggered to the small kitchen, grabbing a grubby towel, dipping it into the bucket well water and soaking my face. As I was fully dressed it took me only moments to depart as quickly as possible exiting the front door as the sun was rising.

We had agreed to regroup within forty-eight hours at the stables on the outskirts of the palace grounds to pool all the information we had gathered. As I arrived, many were there and some still sleeping. The last pairing arrived several hours after myself describing looting and atrocities all over the city. After resting, we sat around on any object available and started our discussions. Many had nothing to offer except for strong evidence of Lenin's location over the next few days and keen interest to attempt his assassination. I then stood and spoke clearly and precisely of the Romanov location and possible intent to murder them all. Silence filled the air whilst my statement sunk in. I then explained that my information came from one of the captive's wives. I further explained that the Romanov's personal jailers consisted of no more than ten men and we needed to proceed immediately as time was of the essence. Much discussion followed when it was suggested that we divide our group into two, one to the rescue and the other to the assassination attempt of Lenin. Although I voiced my opinion against the assassination, others thought it most unlikely that the Tzar and his family were in any serious danger. It was finally agreed I would take twelve men to Yekaterinburg and ten men would plan the elimination of Lenin.

On my insistence, we left immediately and calculated six, maybe seven days journey if we minimized our stops. Several of my force knew the location of Tobolsk but none of us had any familiarity of Ipatiev House or Yekaterinburg so we would have to obtain this information as we progressed nearer. Tobolsk was the only true information as the other came from my vision.

Other than a few small showers of rain the weather was good to us and we arrived in Tobolsk when a sniper took out one of my men. Luckily, we could see the small group some one hundred meters ahead aiming their weapons at us and our immediate reaction was to charge with our pistols drawn. On seeing our assault, they panicked and started their retreat but we were too fast and our accurate shooting quickly annihilated all five of them. After dismounting, two of them were still alive and after questioning and some violent persuasion, we were able to obtain very accurate directions and the force present at Ipatiev House. After putting a bullet in each of their heads we continued with the path given for many hours before reaching a thick forest of pine trees. It seemed prudent to walk from here with our horses in tow and cutting the undergrowth ahead of us. After a while we heard a man's voice singing and laughing ahead and stopped in our tracks momentarily. Moving slowly forward we suddenly came across two men, the singing, laughing and having a hard time standing man and the other on the ground seemingly having passed out. We grabbed our comical idiot but all he did was continue shouting we killed the Romanovs; we killed the Romanovs. I gave him a swift blow to the head and he sank to the ground in a heap. Looking around I noticed a footpath leading through the forest and bid two of my companions to follow me whilst the others remained with the inebriated prisoners.

It was a brisk twenty-minute walk when the forest ended to open pastures revealing a small town. As we approached, watchful, guns at ready I saw a broken gate hinged on a brick post with the name Ipatiev House. We approached the building with caution and the front door was clearly open and no sounds came from within. Entering the house, we separated and made a thorough search of the two floors but found nothing but strong indications of occupation with bedding and blankets lying on the floors. Suddenly I heard a loud shout to hasten to the basement and scurried down the stairs to my awaiting allies and stopped dead in my tracks. The acrid smell was still in the air, blood on the floor and spatters on the walls with holes and fractures made from gunshots. Searching the debris, we found a bloody bayonet, torn women's clothing and several gemstones. We ascertained from the scene that whatever happened here in the basement was at least a few days old and there was little else to do but gather up the small pieces of evidence and head back to our comrades. It was July 19.

Upon returning the two prisoners were awake and from their bloody features had already been brutalized. We were quickly informed the cap-tives were part of a burial detail after retrieving the bodies from a mine shaft and told that the deceased were the Romanovs. They described the mutilation of the bodies by others, in particular the burning of a boy and crushing his bones. They were questioned further as to the whereabouts of the others but all they knew was they left on horseback and told to get far away as possible due to the White army approaching and not more than a day or two away. These two were too stupid to take advise and instead decided to celebrate with cheap vodka. I then described the scene in the deserted town of Yekaterinburg and all I could see was angry and tearful faces. As I turned and walked into the woods All I could hear was outraged voices and screams as vengeance was taken. I stopped after a few minutes, knelt and bitterly wept for Anna and my Ruben and everything was silent except for the rustling leaves of the Koptyaki Forest.

CHAPTER 02

Early Years in New York 1918 through 1966

R ussia had always been of keen interest to Alexei who many generations before had been his ancestors, hence his name. His Grandfather, Ruben Frederick Stepan, a teller of tall tales from the motherland Russia, much of which seemed fiction or at least blown out of proportion. Nevertheless, Alexei listened to the stories hanging on every word even though they became repetitive as Ruben became older. Grandfather Ruben was almost nine years old when he and his Aunt Catherine arrived in New York during the winter months of 1918 after the end of the World War. They had travelled via London to seek medical help for Ruben, where treatment was given by the best Doctors fully paid and arranged by Simon. It was more than a year before the Specialists would allow further travel and the Trans-Atlantic voyage was indeed a pleasure with first class reservations. Accommodation had already been arranged in advance in what was the start of the Russian immigrant community, many of which were fugitives from the ongoing revolutions back home. As far as Ruben knew, except for his aunt, most of his family were deceased or where-abouts unknown.

In the summer of 1920, Aunt Catherine had opened IPATIEV, a linen, fabric and tailor store which by 1925 had three locations and employed forty-seven shopkeeper sales, tailors and machinists. Catherine maintained the bookkeeping records with early help from Ruben who was a natural mathematics student. She had many friends the closest being Vera Constantinova, Georgy Constantinovich and father Seraphim Slobodskoy. By 1932 with Catherine's failing health, Alexie's grandfather aged twenty-four was given control of the business albeit still under the watchful eyes of his beloved Aunt. He was already courting Alexie's yet to be Grandmother, Alexandra, who was one of the locations Supervisors (Catherine would only allow herself the title of Manager) and came from a good Russian immigrant family. They we married that same year.

Alexie's father was born in May, 1934 and named Frederick after his father. It was a complicated birth that resulted in the early health issues. A sister was born in 1936 and they called her Sophia Catherine but she died of polio complications before the age of four. A miscarriage and additional complications thereafter proved impossible to conceive more children. Frederick Ivan Stepan was groomed from early childhood to be educated in the American way, law, history, mathematics, sciences, and languages. Nevertheless, even with the depression years through the 1930's the 'rag trade' as it became named, survived by change to life expectancy of garments rather than style and an increase in home made dresses. Although tailored items decreased, the sale of cloth increased, paper design kits, the income of which maintained sufficient profits to afford keeping most of the staff at IPATIEV.

Grandfather Ruben knew that to survive, the business needed to grow and to grow you needed an edge, a niche in the market. In 1937 a notice in the newspaper appeared inviting all interested garment manu-facturers to attend a meeting at the Ministry of Defense, army headquar-ters the following day at 08.00 hours with the opportunity to produce uniforms. Ruben knew this was the opening his firm needed. He arrived at army Headquarters twenty minutes early and observed the notice directing interested parties to Hall Number 12. On entering there were already seven other representatives two of which he recognized. On an oblong table there was a sign in register and a box containing packages consisting of lower ranking and junior officer uniform patterns, sizes and quantities to be produced per week with several samples of woolen cloth attached, olive drab light shade wool serge for winter and cotton khaki for summer. Ruben signed in and took a package from the box.

It did not take long for the hall to fill and at 8am sharp a group of soldiers appeared led by elderly, ruddy face officer with a silver handlebar moustache. He raised himself onto a platform and requested attention. There were no chairs to sit upon and silence ensued as the audience waited for the officer to speak.

"You have been invited by open invitation to offer a quotation to manufacture uniforms for the Armed Services at a fixed price that will continue without increase for three years," he said." All the details are in the packages you should have collected from the box on the table.

We expect these proposals within three days from today in large plain envelopes. These envelopes will be sealed by a member of my staff and placed under lock and key. No proposal will be accepted thereafter, he continued. Those who chose to bid on this service shall return one week from today when I will open all the envelopes and document their findings. That is all," he said.

Ruben left the army premises with a wry grin. That same day he would obtain the pricing of the previous contract holders and a sample uniform to study the stitching and quality. It so happened Ruben had purchased the previous contract holder's business and part of the buy-out agreement was a non-disclosure until after the army had made the award.

After the opening of the proposals and Ruben's bid proved to be the winning offer, the terms and requirements were negotiated. Ruben was relieved that his competitor purchase proved to be a blessing. He knew this move would not please his Aunt Catherine but it was never his intention to make any changes to IPATIEV. He would rename his acquisition The Modern Uniform & Garment Company which within a year expanded from 60 to over 200 employees and by the early months of 1939 to 6 locations and 1000 employees. Frederick started school in that same year. It was also the start of World War Two in Europe

In 1941 Ruben's Aunt Catherine died of various complications but the death certificate stated pneumonia. Her wishes that the IPATIEV stores would become a cooperative with shares owned by the employees was so arranged by Ruben. Years of service and position depicted the number of shares distributed.

The Modern Uniform & Garment Company profits for the next five years were beyond Ruben's wildest dreams with new factories in Chicago, Pittsburg, Baltimore and Boston. The future was also a major concern to Ruben when in 1944 he was approached by the newly established World Bank in Washington DC with a proposal. They represented a large diamond mine consortium in South Africa looking for investment opportunities and even though Ruben had not contemplated selling, an offer would be interesting to review. If nothing else he was curious to establish a market value for the company.

After numerous meetings, legal counseling and family consultation, a purchase agreement was finalized which included a non-negotiable board position for Ruben to a period of one year. During which time he would gradually hand over the reins to the new owners elected President. It would be one year and eight months before Ruben said his farewells to the Modern Uniform & Garment Company.

Frederick was thirteen at the time, a pupil top of his class and an excellent tennis player.

Pretoria Diamond Mines largest shareholder was domicile in Australia with roots in Singapore and Hong Kong. Instructions came from there to purchase the Modern Uniform & Garment Company. Ruben was a wealthy man, the sum of which nobody knew except his close lawyer and counsel. Not even his wife Alexandra had a clue, not that she cared as she was allowed to purchase anything she wanted without the worry of the expense. It was obvious to the community as to his wealth and many of them approached Ruben through his family members the possibilities of a loan or business investment opportunities. Initially surprised but after discussions with Paul Merritt, his legal counsel the idea of developing a Loan Company appealed to him.

Manhattan Credit Union was born in 1948 with the intent to provide individual loans some of which were established on the payday plan. The first customers came from within the Russian Community, each one justified on a case-by-case basis, many of which were to expand or modernize their businesses. Repayment plans depended on period and sums provided with others rewarding in a profit sharing or even shareholding scheme. Ten years later, the Manhattan Credit union was one of the top five lending institutions in America. Ironically enough, Modern Uniform & Garment Company became the largest supplier of uniforms not only to the military but Medical Industry, Shipbuilding and Labor Unions.

In 1957 at the age of twenty-three, Frederick graduated from Harvard University with BA degrees in both business Law and Applied Mathematics. His ambition was to enter the legal profession with a well-known practice but his father had his own ideas as to his son's future. The Manhattan Credit Union had grown so rapidly and successfully that managing the day-to-day affairs were now left to Ruben's Loan officers and Accounting Management. He needed another set of eyes, to report legal and other problematic issues but most of all someone close to manage audits. Who could be closer than his own son? Frederick was not attracted to his father's wishes but the more he painted the rosy picture of his future, he finally caved in.

For the first three years Frederick was assigned to various departments at pretty much ground level but it was clearly understood by each management head he was to be groomed and mentored. Frederick was a mighty quick learner, showed leadership and in general well liked. He spent the fourth year in the legal department when he met Kathleen, the daughter of Paul Merritt, his father's legal counsel. Kathleen's great Grandparents were from County Cork, Ireland and later many a joke was told of an Irish Russian alliance! Nationality aside, Kathleen was a tall, beautiful curly redhead, green eyes, broad thick lips that showed prominent dimples when she smiled. They met at one of the many evening dinners his mother and father hosted for which they never needed an excuse. The events also proved to be popular due to the lavish and extensive menu, not counting the fine wines. Paul Merritt had been divorced for some years and his ex-wife and daughter lived in Chicago consequently she and Frederick never met. She graduated in Biology from Brown University, Rhode Island and this dinner was the opportunity to present her to society, so to speak. The year was 1961, Frederick was twenty-seven and Kathleen was twenty-five. After a three-year courtship they were married at City Hall much to the displeasure of Kathleen's family, many of whom were devout Catholics. After two years there was also concern and much discussion when no children were produced but, in the spring of 1966, Kathleen put their fears to rest announcing she was with child and due sometime in October. Alexei was born at 11.21 pm on October 31st.

CHAPTER 3

ALEXEI –
Growing Years

A lexei Stepan in his early years was raised in Greenwich Village. It was the young and imaginative center of art and music, literature and modern politics, inventions and ideas, of protests against the Vietnam War. Novelists, poets, songwriters, Dylan, Ginsberg, Dali and Andy Warhol's Happening, Unlike his grandparents who lived for many years in the tight Russian community of Hamilton Heights before moving into their gilded mansion in Manhattan. Alexei did not know of any persons as happy and so well balanced as his parents. There were no other siblings and when asked of his father why there were no brothers or sisters, he responded with a wry grin and said it wasn't for the want of a great deal of trying but had no real explanation why Alexei ended up as the only child. Now, this was not without its benefits. He grew up loving and being loved by both sides of the family. In fact, he was spoiled. He later learned his mother had no intention of having any more children.

Together, his parents were his greatest influence. Education was the future they always told him and they exposed him to the arts, music, sciences, mathematics, history, nature and food. family gatherings were always full of stories, music, beer, wine and vodka. On Alexei's sixteenth birthday his father gave him the gift of a Kodak Retina 35mm Camera and a photography course at the New York Institute of Photography. Much to the regret of his father this became not just an interest but a passion that proved to be more than a temporary hobby.

Always within the top five in his class at high school, Alexei's achievements made his parents proud and led to his acceptance to Columbia University, Manhattan, New York where he studied and majored with the class in sociology. His Bachelor Degree with Honors was earned with his thesis between materialistic and a spiritualistic person.

Alexei had his fair share of lady friends and dates but none shared his mixture of interests or conversation. In essence his attraction to the opposite sex was nowhere near as aggressive than that of his co-students but he was satisfied with the relationships and believed there was plenty of time to pursue when the time was right. Although Grandfather and Alexei's father, Frederick often spoke Russian between themselves, English remained the common language in the family.

Nevertheless, by the time he started high school Alexei chose to study the Russian language albeit arduous and difficult. The major problem was finding someone he could practice the East Slavic language with especially as his own family had little or no time on his schedule.

Many years later after leaving school, having studied photography and already working at the Globe, he was fortunate to meet Mikhail at his local coffee shop, the Java House. Alexei was staring out of the window watching the passersby scurrying in the rain when he heard the Russian language being spoken. Turning around swiftly he saw a tall young man with chisel features, cropped hair and sporting a bushy goatee searching for a seat and talking on one of those new brick like cell phones. Alexei spoke to him in his juvenile Russian offering him a seat at his table. His smile showed the dimples clearly, disconnecting the phone and thanked

Alexei in English whilst removing his coat when Alexei responded with, "Was my Russian that bad?"

"No," he said, "But I could tell it was not your mother tongue." After introductions and brief explanation of our commonality, we drank our coffee, continued with conversation then ordered another coffee. This was the birth of what turned out to be a lasting friendship.

Mikhail was well educated, employed as a linguist, spoke excellent English and was a Russian History major at Moscow University. It was with utter excitement for Alexei to able to ask untold questions during their discussions and absorb the knowledge received of his ancestral homeland that he never read in books. Specifically, his particular interest was the political strife and poverty at the turn of the 20th century leading up to the revolutions and the end of the Romanov regime in 1918. Mikhail had studied and wrote a thesis of the life of Lenin, whom he admired, hated at the same time and often spoke how history might have been different if Lenin had not survived the assassination attempt shortly after the demise of the Romanov family.

As the discussions progressed which for the most part Alexei insisted be in Russian, he became more determined to investigate his family history and knew it would have to start with his grandfather. He had been told practically everything was lost during the tumultuous civil and political unrest during the early twentieth century, however, there are many questions to be asked and somehow, he knew answers would not come easy.

Grandfather Rueben, now widowed for some years, was living with Alexei's parents in a very comfortable and practical designed suite, surrounded by all his precious memorabilia. Unfortunately, the family was seeing signs of dementia which was deteriorating at a rapid pace. Alexei would visit several times a week, sometimes more when he dined there but the conversations were becoming strange during their get-togethers and always in Russian. It had reached a point when Grandfather no longer recognized his grandson and would ask his name? He would chatter on about living in a palace and playing with his cousin as a boy. They would play games with his sisters and his father's close members of staff as they looked extraordinary alike, so they dressed alike. When Alexei questioned his grandfather further, he would remain quiet, the beckoning Alexei to get closer he would whisper that he was not allowed to talk about it, being a secret and putting his forefinger to his lips. Other times he would speak of his favorite horse, his father Nicholas and adorable Uncle Simon and cousin Maxim. Alexei would entertain his stories not knowing what to believe until he would speak no more and just smiled. Although bewildered by all of this, he kept this to myself until at least I could make more sense of it.

Grandfather died peacefully in his sleep at the age of eighty-two. It was a grand funeral with hundreds of mourners including local dignitaries and a distant relative of the Romanov family.

CHAPTER 4

Country & Western

Alexei, at twenty-four' years of age had been employed at the Globe newspaper for just six months when he was temporarily assigned to the Entertainment section and photo support covering Country & Western life in New York. He was amazed to discover how much activity existed in Bars and Clubs all over the city. You would never guess it, but in New York City there are quite a number of horseback riding, country music singing, whiskey and rye drinking, line dancing folks in town. Where do all these foot stomping folks meet? At the country bars, of course! Texas 2 Step, 25 W. 51st St., Dakota Slims 153 1st Ave., Ram Rods 793 9th Ave., Red River Ranch, 25 W. 31st St., 4th Floor. Gil's Honky Tonk, 1154 1st Ave., and a few more but less known. While they are scattered around the city, the country bars are all worth a visit – you might even find a cowgirl or cowboy to dance with. While Texas 2 Step is all about dancing women, Ram Rods is made for dancing men. Apparently known around town as one of the best gay bars in the city, Ram Rods is another place you can go to simply have some fun. Bringing a little bit of the South to the Big Apple, the saloon is decked out with a Wild West theme, including wood plank dance floors and steer antlers above the bar. With bartending dancing cowboys and drink specials almost every night, how can you go wrong?

Courtney, one of the Globe's shining reporters had a personal interest in this subject as she was dating a "Cowboy Pretender," so to speak. Darren was our guide and was relishing the part. A formidable six-foot 3-inch ex university football player, Darren was dressed in tight fitting blue jeans, gold tipped black boots and belt buckle to match. His white short-sleeve designer shirt barely covered his arm muscles and his chest hairs very visible showing above the second button down from the neck. His black hat with a coin covered hatband only made him look even taller and was every inch the part.

Courtney made it very clear to Alexei to take random photos and she would choose the appropriate prints to go with the article. In other words, whilst we traveled to the various locations together, I was on my own. Five clubs were chosen to visit over seven days the rotation of which was left up to Darren.

The week started quietly enough, visiting Honky Tonk, Dakota Slims then a rousing night at Texas 2 Step. A night off then planned visit to Ram Rods and finally Red River Ranch. Darren had organized this schedule based on the nights of events and incentives. It was during the visit to Ram Rods that a fight ensued and Darren was right in the mix of things trying to defend a young man being abused by a much larger man. Alexei kept snapping away taking as many pictures as he could when the larger man broke a bottle and aggressively punctured Darren's face causing blood to spurt everywhere. Several security personnel arrived at the scene and subdued the man and Alexei later learned named Patrick Crowley. Front page news followed by Alexei's own deposition, then several weeks in Court put Patrick Crowley away for fifteen years and Alexei could never forget the glaring eyed twisted mouth look he was given as he was taken away.

Sitting in the dining room of the Sonesta, he drifted to the events of lunch and memories of his past flooded back to him and in particular and because of the present catastrophe, the Crowley incident.

CHAPTER 5

Patrick John Crowley

W ithout any indication, his father had left his mother within a few days of his sister's birth and Patrick was six years old. Confused and angry he had little recollection of his father, having spent most of his time at the local tavern, then taking an offshore job in a country he couldn't pronounce and never seen or heard from since. His mother was working two jobs to make ends meet when Uncle Martin came to stay. Uncle Martin also worked offshore, hence the introduction of my father to my mother years before when both were on leave/rotation. Uncle Martin's arrival was a welcome relief to my mother as she could rely on an adult relative to supervise her children and not have to pay the local teenager to babysit. Uncle Martin was a joy to a lonely boy and he hung on every word of the stories of travel and faraway places. Although Patrick could not recollect the exact details of the first time, he was twelve years old and remembered it was a very hot and humid evening. Uncle Martin was dressed in boxer shorts reading a magazine when Patrick was initiated into touching his genitals and his hands became all sticky. Practically every night after the first event, the action became routine for several months. Seeing him spurt his juices made him giggle and Patrick looked forward to each evening after his mother left for work at the diner. This was our secret, a secret among men, Martin had said.

A year had passed and one day Patrick came home from school to discover Uncle Martin was absent. His mother informed him that he went for an interview and would be a little late. It was the first time he showed his bad temper for reasons he was not sure of. His mother calmed him down with reassurance of Uncle Martin's imminent arrival. She took a risk, leaving Crowley alone for what she knew would be a few hours. Young Jessica was already sleeping and unlikely awake before early morning. The waiting time seemed like forever and out of curiosity Crowley opened Uncle Martin's bedroom door, peeking in before entering. Other than framed family photos and some nick-knacks his mother had placed around, little evidence showed his Uncle Martin was sleeping there. He noticed some keys, change, and a man's bracelet on the bedside table eying the contents as he sat on the bed. The table drawer was slightly ajar and Crowley opened it full. Under a couple of T-shirts, a small magazine with a naked man on the cover caught his eye. Flipping through the glossy publication, picture after picture displayed activity between young men that he could not quite understand. He quickly put the magazine back in the drawer and went back to the living room

Within the next two hours Crowley ventured back to that drawer several times to gaze upon the pictures that gradually but firmly imprinted in his mind. It was during the last session that he heard the motorbike and knew his Uncle Martin had arrived. In a panic he threw the magazine in the drawer and closed it firmly. He quickly sat down in his favorite armchair and turned the tv on just as Uncle Martin came through the front door. With his usual smile he announced his arrival and Crowley jumped up to give him a huge hug. I need a shower, he said and proceeded to his bedroom closing the door behind him. Crowley started to watch the action show on TV but his mind was elsewhere. He continued to watch the program for approximately twenty minutes when Uncle Martin appeared.

He was dressed in long lounge pants and T-shirt and proceeded into the kitchen where he took a beer from the refrigerator.

Martin threw himself on the sofa. Took a long swig of his beer and stared momentarily at Patrick. From behind his back, he produced the magazine from his drawer then calmly spoke. "Now Nephew, seems you were looking through my stuff and in particular this magazine? Now don't lie, I know when my things are moved. No matter, it's time we go to the next step." Martin stood up and approached Patrick in the armchair. Dropping his lounge pants, he said, "Now let's begin."

For nearly two years it was a one-way gratification relationship but Crowley didn't mind. He loved his Uncle Martin and he made him feel special. The problems started when Uncle Martin was spending more time offshore and Crowley decided he needed another playmate. Justin had been his friend for many years but it had been only a couple of months now that he felt it could be much more. The opportunity arose during a sleepover and Justin initially turned out to be a willing play partner. During fondling and play that evening Crowley experienced his first climax. He was thrilled and eagerly wanted to play the other games his uncle had taught him. Justin's interest stopped short of venturing further and rebuffed Patrick to participate in other sexual activities. Rejection ignited Crowley's temper in such an uncontrolled manor that he was unaware of the violence that took place until he was restrained by his mother. He was still shaking when the ambulance arrived, men in uniform, and Justin's angry parents. From there on reform school, his mother passing after two years suffering with cancer, Uncle Martin's untimely accidental death, scrapes with the law and prison time developed his character in becoming a narcissist, sadistic homosexual predator.

His bar room brawl had disfigured Darren but pictures taken of the event was the most damaging evidence. His criminal record and as the Judge had described his actions demonstrating a "depraved indifference to human life," and being Crowley's third felony, he was given a fifteen years sentence.

Sing-Sing Correctional Facility: Ossining, New York. This notorious prison hosts a number of violent criminals, nearly a third of whom serve time for murder. Whilst in prison Crowley met all kinds of lowlife and in the latter years met a number of ex-military men, soldiers of fortune and murderers. It was their connections on the outside he was interested in, particularly an introduction to a sadistic killer for hire. Parole Board 9 years and 2 weeks into sentence. Parole granted. Waiting to finish the necessary paperwork and Warden farewell, Crowley pondered on the wasted years in Sing, catching syphilis twice, and the burning hatred of the man who put him there, Stepan. Revenge was going to be sweet and he wanted Stepan to suffer a slow, cruel fate. As he walked through the outer gates a free man, a demonic grin on his face and details imbedded in his mind of the murder for hire contact a shiver of sheer pleasure overwhelmed his whole body. Be patient he told himself. First stop, his sister's house, then calls to make an appointment with his parole officer.

After a phone call from her brother in prison with the news of his parole, Crowley's younger sister Jessica agreed that he could stay with her a while in Queens until a suitable job and lodgings could be found. She was afraid to say no and hoped the duration of stay would be relevantly short. Patrick's bombastic arrival, cursing his travel time, ignoring his sister's embrace, threw the small dog from the chair, sat down in said chair and demanded an alcoholic drink. Jessica's first reaction was pick up her loving pet and hold her close to her chest for reassurance then quickly directed herself to the kitchen collecting a bottle of Tennessee whisky and a glass. Placing her pug Bonnie in her basket, Jessica returned to the living room. She stared at her brother as he poured and large quantity in the glass and aggressively drank the contents in one swig. A smug look on Patrick's face and eyes closed as he felt the effect of his first freedom drink. Opening his eyes, he stared at his sister for a moment before stating his demands. "I mean you no harm Jessica and all I require are two things. One, any calls from my parole officer or any other police officials as to my whereabouts, I am living here and seeking employment. Secondly, within 30 days from now I need you to loan me $10,000.00 cash. I don't know, nor do I care where you get the funds but I suspect you could obtain a loan on this property if need be. After all mother left you this house and her savings whereas left me nothing. I will require another $10,000.00 within 6 to 8 weeks from now." Patrick poured himself another drink.

For the next few weeks Patrick behaved like a model citizen, obtained menial employment at a local car wash and reminded his sister on a daily basis of the loan commitment. Day 28 passed and Patrick was getting impatient and it showed. It was the following day that Jessica produced the $10,000.00 cash and handed it to her brother. As he held the money in 10 wrapped $100-dollar bill denominations, his wry grin sent a shudder down Jessica's spine. "Hello, I am calling regarding personal training and you came highly recommended by thirteenth brigade. Yes, I will hold."

Patrick replaced the public phone to the wall unit having memorized the date, time and place to meet his contact. Just a couple of days before the wheels of motions are in place, he chuckled to himself.

It was just before 10pm when Patrick entered the Belfast Irish Tavern and approached the rather dim-lit bar. Only one rather elderly, overweight person sitting at the bar with a fresh glass of beer and what looked like a shot of whisky on the side. The bartender looked at Patrick and requested his choice of refreshment. "A Guinness and where can I find Mack," replied Patrick. The bartender frowned as he slowly poured the Guinness and replied he didn't know any Mack. This momentarily confused Patrick when the elderly customer without looking quietly said Mack is sitting in the far corner. Patrick paid for Guinness then proceeded to the far corner. It was quite dark as the light bulb above this table did not function and without a word, Patrick sat down opposite a heavy-set person wearing a black baseball cap and thick rimmed tinted glasses. After a moment Patrick spoke. As instructed, here is the Guinness you requested and the envelope containing instructions and $10,000.00 cash retainer.

Without looking up the stranger opened the envelope, placed the cash in his jacket inside pocket whilst simultaneously reading the instructions of torture and dismemberment on the photographed person attached. A note was presented by the gloved hand to Patrick and without a word being said or even a sip of the Guinness, the stranger stood up and abruptly left the bar. The note was typed written where and when to meet after the deed was done and evidence of such deed produced whereupon the second installment of $10,000.00 would be due. Exiting the Pub door, the stranger pulled his coat collar up over his neck briefly looking at his pimply plump reflection in the adjacent shop window. Grinning, he disappearing around the corner to where his car was parked.

Starting the engine to obtain some warmth, he took the phone installed in the glove compartment and pressed one button. After a few moments a man's voice answered, "Speak," he said.

"The trap has been set," Tony stated, then the line was disconnected.

After ending the call, the man took another gulp of vodka martini, staring out at the Atlantic Ocean as the sun started to set behind him.

CHAPTER 6

Jessica

It was a cool early morning as Jessica walked Bonnie towards the dog park and the Pug was pulling the leash hard as his instinct was telling him they were close. A rather scruffy bearded jogger was approaching wearing the typical running attire, bobble hat and sunglasses. As she drew closer the jogger stopped immediately in front of her holding out a paper bag. Jessica froze not understanding the situation presenting itself. The Jogger spoke clearly and softly in what appeared to be an accent. Jessica, this belongs to you and your life will not be complicated further. After taking the brown bag the Jogger continued on his way. It was a few moments and with Bonnie tugging hard at the leash before she looked in the bag full of money. As she entered the park, she looked back to see the Jogger but he had already vanished. Bonnie was already relieving herself as Jessica sat down at the park bench and after looking around, seeing no one else in the park she opened the brown bag and counted 20 wrapped bundles of $100 bills and calculated it was $20,000 in total, the exact quantity she had given her brother. Even more confusing was that Patrick had not been home for three days.

That evening, Jessica answered the front door bell when two plain clothed police officers introduced themselves and requesting if they may enter. After sitting comfortably, she was informed that her brother Patrick had been retrieved from the Hudson River that morning and would she mind answering a few questions. They enquired as to Patrick's whereabouts, acquaintances etc., but Jessica knew nothing, explaining her brother kept very much to himself and other than working at the car wash she was aware of little else. The officers thanked her for her time, expressed condolences but would not expand on the circumstances surrounding Patrick's death other than stating the investigation was still ongoing.

After their departure, Jessica sat in her chair holding Bonnie closely trying to make sense of it all. She opened the Daily Globe newspaper and read the headlines of the assassination at the Sonesta Hotel. Never seems to be any good news these days, she thought. However, she felt a huge burden had been lifted, she did not need to be afraid anymore and notions ran though her head of a needed change in her life.

CHAPTER 7

Alexei 1995

I t was the early days of February 1995, winter time in New York City. Nursing an annoying hangover, Alexei poured his second cup of office percolated coffee whilst cursing under his breath. God this coffee tastes like, like, I don't know what it tastes like but it sure wasn't anything like decent coffee or was it the whisky lining in his mouth confusing the taste of anything else. Happy hour was getting the better of him especially when it involved John Walker, his Editor. It is ironic that John's favorite drink of choice happened to be Johnny Walker Black Label Whisky with a splash of soda water and a small splash at that. These early evening events were happening on a regular basis since John's divorce some four months back and like a typical lamb to the slaughter, Alexei followed. Fortunately, he was not consuming the same quantity as John and needed to stay somewhat in control to get John safely home. It never ceases to amaze him that John always managed to get to the newspaper office early the following day and unlike himself seemingly no visible effect from the previous evening.

The phone rang sending a sharp pain to his head. After hesitating for a moment, he slowly picked up Mr. Bell and in a dull low-pitched voice said 'hello'. "Alex MI AMIGO," the caller said, I have some information for you but will cost you lunch. Does it have to be lunch today; Alexei asks? Not exactly in good form Tony. Come on Alex, you got to eat and besides it's been a while since you last paid."

Alex full name was Alexei Lucius Stepan but for obvious reasons Tony shortened his first name to Alex! "Meet me at Casa Puebla around eleven thirty, I know it is early but I am hungry," then immediately hung up.

Alexei stared at the phone momentarily and mumbled a few curse words under his breath. No sooner had he replaced the phone when it rang again causing Alexie to jump slightly. This time he knew who the caller was, his editor John. "Good morning, Alexei and how is your day going so far?" And before Alexei could respond John continued, "meet me in conference room 3 in say 30, no, make it 45 minutes as my gut is telling me I need to make a port of call". He also abruptly hung up.

What a start to the day he thought.

Close to 10am and feeling somewhat better Alexei was staring out of the window of conference room 3 on the 17th floor when John entered the room holding several good size portfolios. Placing them on the large ornate table he opened the top file and displayed the photos within. Placing 3 color and 1 black and white photos in a row, John took a deep breath before commencing his well-rehearsed speech. What we have here are four persons of interest that will be guests at the Environmental Gala Ball this evening. Behind each picture are details as we have it, name, status or rank and personal history. At that moment in walked Marie Stapleton, reporter and political analyst for the Globe. She sat next to me, touched my sleeve and smiled. John did not even pause and continued with the statement "As I was saying, these are persons of interest. Study the files and memorize as much as possible, find out their purpose at the conference, see who they talk to, what they talk about, ask personal questions, where they buy their clothes, favorite foods, where they take a vacation, anything of note we can add to these files. In particular this rather anonymous gentleman, pointing to the first very poor black and white photo."

"The name on the attendance list is Anton Kniaz VOLKOV and all the information we have is he is a high-ranking international advisor to the Russian Minister of External Affairs. This black & white photo is the only picture we have and from an unconfirmed source we are led to believe Mr. Volkov holds a Party Member title of General with the Ministry of Information

Nikolay POPOV, Russian Minister of Finance is depicted here in photo number 2, John pointing his finger. James Samuel Russell, here in photo number 3, American Billionaire several times over with family history traceable back to the early 1600's much of which involved major international trade including a family history of smuggling".

"The Chai Brothers, Somnang and Kong-kea here in photo 4 manage their empire from Singapore with holdings through hundreds of corporations throughout Asia with a particular stronghold in China. Although unproven there are a lot of rumors of drug trafficking".

Taking another deep breath John blurted out his question. "What have these guys in common with the Environmental Conference?" Staring at Alexei, then at Marie, He screamed at the top of his voice, "Nothing! Nothing at all. Or, is it something? All the distinguished guests from around the world are obvious fits for such a conference but not these four. That my trusting sleuths is your assignment."

With that he sat down and mumbled something to do with needing a drink. "Lunch anyone John said staring right at Alexei. Sorry John, I have lunch with a news source" and Marie had already picked up her copy of the files and disappeared through the conference room doors. Alexei collected his files and departed as quickly possible through the same doors before they closed behind him.

Shit, Alexei said knowing he was running late for lunch

Like anywhere in mid-town New York, getting a taxi this time of day was a major problem so Alexei took the metro to 65th and 3rd and by the time he arrived it started to rain heavily. As he entered Casa Puebla It was surprising to see they were already quite busy for 11.45 am. Although 15 minutes late Tony was already sitting at his usual table nursing what looked like the remnants of a large margarita. Tony was in his early 40's but you wouldn't know it by his round plump and pimply face and a small but very visible scar over his right eyebrow. His floppy ginger blonde hair added the touch of his boyish looks. Only when he opened his mouth and showed his crooked teeth did his appearance change. Tony boasted of a Mexican father and a Scottish mother and he was proud of both heritages.

Tony Alvarez is a New Jersey detective that Alexie had known since his early days as a student photographer. Tony was moonlighting as security at the college and introduced himself during one lunch break. In many ways Tony had been responsible for Alexei's career advancement. First through introductions for weddings until Alexei attended Columbia University then Tony recommended him to the Daily Globe here in New York for what was intended to be a temporary appointment. Tony was not only a lucrative supply of information but he was a real friend and supporter.

"As I live and breathe Alexei Stepan, you look like shit" Tony grinned as he licked the salt from his glass, waiting for Alexei to be seated then immediately blurted out "Crowley was released from jail 2 weeks ago, apparently for good behavior and a sympathetic review board". Alexei made a blank stare whilst slowly seating and feeling numb.

Tony paused for a moment and he noticed a concerned look on Alexei's face. "Look, he said, Crowley is just out of prison and I think it hardly likely his first intention is to come after you. He's already registered with his Parole Office and given his sister's address in Queens as his temporary place of residence".

Without saying, a plan was already in motion to catch up with Mr. Crowley and ensure no harm comes to Alex.

Nacho chips and salsa arrived and Tony ordered another margarita. "Come on Alex, punching him lightly on the arm, relax, let's eat and enjoy the moment". With that statement he called the waiter being anxious to order.

Bummer, Alexei thought, a hangover and now the bitter news of Crowley.

Considering the unwelcome report, lunch was quite enjoyable and actually eased some of the dull throbbing in his head. Unlike Tony, he avoided the margarita's especially as he needed to be at the Royal Sonesta Hotel that same day by 5pm with all his faculties intact. On behalf of the Globe, he was to attend the Gala Ball prior to the 11th World Environmental Conference starting the next day.

Standing under the restaurant awning Tony and Alexei parted company slightly after 2pm. The rain continued to fall with the same intensity, if not more so than upon as his arrival. An unmarked Police car awaited Tony and although a ride was offered to Alexei, he declined, wanting to walk even though it meant getting wet. Besides his apartment was only 4 blocks away.

Upon arrival at his apartment and still concerned over the news of Crowley, Alexei needed to direct his attention to the present project on the Environmental Conference and for the moment and leave Crowley to Tony. He spread the files out on the kitchen table changed into sweat pants and T-Shirt to be comfortable and started to read his files one by one. After completing the first pass he pulled some highlighters from his desk drawer and started over again.

An interesting group of people indeed. Plenty of information in the files on Russell and Popov but nothing that would indicate good reasons to attend the Conference. Even less for the Asians or the mysterious Russian. Alexei scanned the poor black and white photo of Volkov then did a search on the vast internet. To his surprise a picture appeared on his screen showing a large group of men standing on a balcony and Stalin front and center. He recognized Molotov was to his right then realized the Volkov photo was immediately left of Molotov. Looking at the caption below it was dated 1947 Moscow military Parade. Using a hand magnifying glass, he took a closer look at the photo on the computer screen, in particular Mr. Volkov. It was difficult to tell but if Alexei had to guess, the man did not look much older than thirty which would make him in his eighties today. Curious, he thought.

Alexei looked at his watch and it was already 3.20 pm. Damn, he said I had better get ready or I will be late for the second time today.

By 4.15 pm with cameras in hand (always carried a spare), press pass and other credentials, Alexei left his apartment adjacent to Hunter College, hailed a cab for the 30 to 40-minute ride it would take to the Royal Sonesta Hotel. Even though it stopped raining, this is New York where traffic was impossible to figure out and he could have walked the 20 blocks but not without getting his shoes nor lower part of his trousers wet and dirty. He arrived at the Sonesta in good time at 4.42 pm.

CHAPTER 8

The Convention

Marie was already there dressed in a tightly fitting red skirt and white blouse showing just enough cleavage to attract attention. A natural blond with pleasant features that included green eyes, broad mouth and voluptuous lips made her a target for most men. At 28, once engaged, mile high ego, she was very much in control of herself with convincing confidence to obtain the right story. She gave me a brief wave, sipping her champagne and engaging in a conversation with none other than James Samuel Russell, our American Billionaire.

"They make a nice couple do they not"? Spoken softly, almost a whisper and as I turned came face to face with Anton Kniaz VOLKOV, standing erect the mysterious Russian who didn't look a day older than 65, 70'S tops. "Pardon my intrusion", he continued, then introduced himself. I followed by giving my name and position at the Globe. "Interesting, he said. You have a Slavic name young man. Yes, I do Mr. Volkov and before he could speak further, call me Anton if I may call you Alexei? Of course, Alexei responded somewhat baffled by this experience. Do you still have family in Russia"? Anton enquired to which Alexei gave a brief summary of his grandfather's arrival with his aunt, some history since and ended by saying he knew not of any existing relatives back in Russia.

"It was a sad time during those years your grandfather migrated to the United States of America Anton said in a low tone and do you know how he managed his escape? Escape, Alexei exclaimed in a voice that turned people's heads in close proximity. Why yes young man, one couldn't leave without the right connections or legal authorization back then. Alexei frowned then answered slowly, I never questioned my grandfather or wondered under what circumstances he and his aunt departed, after all he was only nine years old".

It was about that time when Alexei noticed the Chai Brothers and another gentleman approaching and recognized them all as they came closer. Anton smiled and proceeded to hug, then kiss on both checks of the Russian Nikolay Popov followed by the same ritual with the Asians. Alexei started to withdraw when Anton grasped his arm and quickly introduced him to Popov, Somnang and Kong-kea. Somnag took Alexei's hand with both his hands expressing a delight in making his acquaintance and to call him by his first name. It became abundantly clear they all knew each other. Alexei looked around but could see no sign of Marie and come to that nor James Russell. Small talk ensued that included disclosure of his grandfather's departure from his homeland which seemed to intrigue Popov and Anton. Perhaps we may offer assistance, stated Anton, we have access to many personnel files, looking at Popov. At the time it all seemed overwhelming.

Alex had not noticed the waitress approaching, nor the disclosure of a handgun and as one of the Chai brothers stepped in front of him, he heard two shots fired and Somnang collapsed to the floor. At this point the shooter became visible just as Kong-kea, tackled the woman to the ground and instinct kicked in. Alexei started focusing whilst clicking away with his camera taking picture after picture of the ensuing scuffle until the perpetrator was fully subdued. His last few shots were close ups of the woman with her face growling and screaming in Russian before Popov slammed her head to the ground rendering her unconscious.

Alexei quickly turned to view Somnang Chai bleeding profusely, running his left hand through his hair turning his dark to silver streaks to red and reaching up with his right hand for a brief moment. Suddenly there was no movement when Kong-kea appeared placing his fingers on Somnang's neck searching for life but from the look on Kong-kea's face was one of despair and as he stood his features changed dramatically to clear anger in his face when he started shaking. Anton grasped him in an embrace from behind and held on tightly as Kong-kea starting crying profusely. The woman on the floor was now lying on her face with her handcuffed arms behind her back but still unconscious whilst mayhem and confusion still ensued with the guests.

Out of respect Alexei did not take any pictures of the deceased even though and suddenly Marie was at his side insisting he take more photos. He pulled away violently but she followed until she was in his face and proceeded to inform him of the job responsibility and she was not going to suffer the consequences of not making front page. With a stern look he immediately informed her of the pictures that were taken and furthermore demanded to know where the hell she was when this assassination took place.

Suddenly Kong-kea was by Alexei's side with tears still running down his cheeks showing concern as to his wellbeing while Marie quickly departed and approaching guests enquiring who had witnessed the murder. She was desperate to get her story and didn't even think to question Alexei.

Alexei thanked Kong-kea and other than shock he was quite alright. Anton asked if he saw the whole incident and after brief reflection replied he did not see the shooting but within a few seconds captured the assailant on camera. At that point Alexei decided to sit. I wonder why there was concern for me, he pondered.

Abruptly, Police arrived in large numbers cordoning off the exits when a plain clothes officer in a loud voice commanded attention. Speaking very clearly, he requested everyone take a seat in the adjoining dinner hall where brief interviews would take place before releasing everyone to go their separate ways and in conclusions the Gala was postponed. Another plain clothes office then announced that all Hotel employees and associated personnel to remain in the Ballroom.

During the course of this announcement the assailant, still unconscious, was lifted from the floor by two Police officers and escorted from the room dragging her feet on the floor. At the same time medical personnel were kneeling beside the lifeless body of Somnang Chai, notes and photographs were being taken.

"Well fancy seeing you here", Alexei heard in a very familiar voice. He looked up and saw his dear friend Tony Alvarez, his floppy hair all over the place having just removed his hat. "A fine mess this is on such a prestigious event Tony continued. Did you know the deceased"? He asked. Alexei replied in a soft low voice that he had only just met Somnang that evening but Tony didn't catch it and asked Alex to repeat the response. "Somnang, he exclaimed, Somnang! You were on first name basis and you just met him tonight? Yes, it was how I was introduced, Alexei cried out angrily. Tell me more my young friend as Tony was giving him the eagle eye. There's not much to tell he continued", then explained the whole scenario of meeting and the conversation leading up to shooting.

Alexei continued further explaining his purpose at the Gala and that he accompanied a reporter to cover the event. "Did you take pictures Alex? Of course, you did and I want to see them" Tony said in a rather sarcastic tone.

Alexei had already removed the film from his camera, placed into a lead lined package to send to his Editor knowing the authorities would probably confiscate them as evidence.

"I suppose you already sent them to the Globe? Alexei nodded rather sheepishly. No matter, until we gather more information, the identity of the shooter we'll let you know if you can use them said Tony, meanwhile take a seat in the dining area with the others". Alexei discretely hid the envelope in the Men's Bathroom then called the Globe for a pickup.

CHAPTER 9

The Call

"Somnang is dead but not one hundred percent sure he was the intended target Alvarez stated on the phone but suspect the Tan's may very well be involved. The shootist was a madam Russian and judging from her tattoo décor was part of the Organization, as it was called with close ties to the Chinese criminal coalition".

"The Tan's have been a thorn in my side for too long now and maybe it's time to implement the final chapter that's been in place for some time now, the man said on the other end of the line? I am assuming our young friend was not involved and keep me appraised of any new information that comes to light", then the call ended.

Tony took a deep sigh before walking back to the Hotel Ballroom.

I terminated the call on my restricted flip phone, pausing for a moment. Hmong and Kahmuu will be sad to hear of Somnang's demise and I would not be happy to be the one to tell them. Picking up my cafezinho and tasting the pleasure of a great dark roast coffee I stared at the ocean just after dusk from one of my many homes, this one from the small town of Buzios on the Brazilian coast and one of my favorites. Simon, I said to myself, first thing in the morning changes will be made.

CHAPTER 10

Wang Li Tan

I t was 1987 and the explosive beginning of the internet. Fortunately, my advisors were enthusiastic and perceptive to see the advantages of such a system with powerful long-term attributes for a global organization such as ours.

Eliminating paper files, creating databases vastly improved our operations and capability a thousand-fold, allowing the speed of communication, results and rewards to be extremely fruitful.

For many centuries I had grown to understand how crucial it was to know and know well my competition, my enemies both without and within. In many cases there was room for them to exist but once in a while someone ruthless, someone evil comes along who also wants a piece of my business family, my Empire.

Much to the distaste of the Chai family, the Tan's had for over 120 years dominated illegal activities in south east China, spreading to Hong Kong, Singapore, Manila, Bangkok and Jakarta. In 1937 with the immediate threat of invasion by the Japanese. the heads of the family decided to move from Manchuria, China to San Francisco, USA.

For many decades we had been gathering data on all the Tan's rivals, foes and enemies with the intent to approach them for allegiances, alliances and constant information. This strategy proved to be vital.

I was kept aware of their undertakings and pursuits, even more so when they eliminated a whole Chinese American family in my employ. A masked gang entered their home assassinating all in a brutal manor. An informant led us to one of the attackers who was captured, tortured until we abstracted the grim plan in the making that came from the topmost leader of the oriental gang.

A large database was developed with profiles of all known Tan family, friends, employees and connections. It took several years to complete with over 1500 names of every man, women and child connected to the Tan's.

To complicate matters during our investigations, we discovered that for many generations the Tan family decreed that all boys and girls of gang member parents and reaching the age of twelve had to attend one of two special schools separated by male and female.

The curriculum varied according to the individual skills but both had compulsory subjects in two categories that included,

(1) physical aspects

Marshal art disciplines, weaponry, explosives, obstacle courses, long distance endurance, survivor skills, disguises, camouflage, scouting techniques and observation.

And (2) controls and learning;

Espionage, deception, medical training, body nerve points, poisons and potions.

These schools, Tutors and Students would also have to be dealt with. That's right I told myself, a massive eradication on a scale never attempted and for the moment, I was the only one who knew.

The most notable and principal head of the family was Mrs. Wang Li Tan. Merciless, cruel and cold-blooded, Wang Li controlled her realm with an iron fist occasionally taking part in the physical execution of anyone she thought a threat and organizing her business through fear. She was a narcissist, had a huge ego and vain, which might prove to be extremely useful.

Wang Li sat in her garden after receiving a full body massage from her personal talented therapist. He could bring her to orgasm in so many ways without intercourse or the need to receive satisfaction himself and she liked it that way. She had long avoided sexual activity that required grinding action, personal sweat, intimacy and familiarity.

Sipping her spiced ice tea, she recalled her past relationships but none were as memorable as the indiscretion of having an older and foreign lover

She cast her mind back forty-four years to her 16th birthday.

She had been told since she turned thirteen of being very beautiful with a seductive smile and having already lost her virginity in her fourteenth year to the charms of her young uncle. On this day she was introduced to many guests but one in particular attracted her attention. A striking, well-tanned hansom man, with shimmering dark wavy hair, tastefully dressed and an attractive smile.

She thought deeply to recall his name and after a while Simon came to mind.

Numerous opportunities to deal with the Tan's were reviewed and dismissed until the occasion of Mrs. Tan's 60th birthday and a planned celebration on May 28th,, which was a Friday.

What I had in mind required meticulous planning, critical timing and the art of complete surprise. I also needed the courage of my talented friend, Alexander Nomis to go through with it. It was Alexander's wife who was raped and murdered in Rome by a gang in the employ of the Tan's. Constant surveillance and observing movement of the family allowed us to note a pattern in their activities and determine when we would strike.

Emperor's Table was a Restaurant owned by the late Andrew Chen, who's family were slaughtered by the Tans, though yet unproven by the authorities. George Tan, the second eldest son of Wang Li Tan and a Lawyer produced a bill of sale document as the new owners of Emperor's

Table and intended to rename the restaurant as the Tan Dynasty on Wang Li's birthday.

The Emperor's Table would be closed to the public that day and dining guests would be immediate family and selected friends.

The planning was set in motion by our Singapore Organization by the very shrewd Chai Brothers and his family, calculating the strategy with infinite detail. All of which needed my seal of approval.

Very few people knew my real identity and that included many leaders in our own Organization. Amongst my other achievements, after the incident in Rome, I befriended Alexander Nomis, a Swiss/Russian born International Chef.

I had planned well ahead, that he was to be in San Francisco at a seminar and his presence would be brought to Wang Li's attention. Alexander was approached and offered a large sum of money if he would manage the kitchen on her birthday and feature a quality Menu consisting of a mix of fine Chinese, French and Shellfish dishes.

So, the day arrived and everything and everybody was in place. Alexander was to seat at the table with Wang Li's close family after preparation and before serving the many serving plates and bowls. He made himself comfortable and drank only water as he watched with glee the gathering consuming his contaminated cuisine.

Smiling, he watched as the family fell into an unconscious state, some tumbled to the floor whilst the rest lay slumped in their chairs. Wang Li staired about her in disbelief then focused on her grinning guest with hatred in her eyes. He smiled, looking right back at her and waited for her to speak. "This is for my wife". Alexander growled.

"Am I to assume you are responsible for this atrocity? Do you not know who I am and what I am capable of, she said, angrily, wincing in pain"?

"Indeed, I do", rising from his chair and smiling back at her.

At the same moment two masked men, dressed in black appeared carrying a cadaver, dressed as Alexander. Placing the 25-caliber gun in her hand, she had no power to resist as one of the masked men fired four shots into the face of the corpse, then she passed out. Alexander made sure she had enough fish venom in her system, but not fatal. She would die an agonizingly, slow death before any medical treatment could be administered.

A prominent newspaper account, written by a journalist in the employ of Simon's organization would chronicle the story as a catastrophe of the worst kind that resulted from raw fish. The food poisoning testimony would also be described as scandalous to happen in this prominent city and on such a grand scale.

Below the main headline was a photo of Wang Li, who would have been charged with murder of Alexander Nomis, the prominent International Chef, if she had survived.

CHAPTER 11

The Asian Realm

For close on 1000 years, until the 15th. century The Chai family, had been operating ostensibly legitimate business ventures in Laos, close to the Chinese border and sometimes under warlord dominance. Early copper and jade trading, mining interests, tools, weapons, crops such as rice and fruit were the main markets for the Chai's, first domestically then spreading to exports and buying other goods in return.

However, the more lucrative illegal endeavors were vastly more profitable, including the commercially rewarding Opium trade that exploded when introduced globally. It was originally small as the demand was mainly for medicinal and healing purposes but the recreational allure grew in China and the western nations, especially amongst the wealthy.

In the beginning of the 19th century the British Empire were seemingly dominating the overall trade to China in exchange for tea, silks, porcelain to name a few but it did not go unnoticed by the Philadelphia pioneering Americans, other Europeans or even the Simon empire and the Chai family.

Departing from Guangzhou at the start of the Opium Wars Somnang and Kong-kea established themselves in Hong Kong. Although lacking for a number of years many comforts due to the limited population of mainly fishermen, construction improved as the number of mainland Chinese residents increased considerably. In the beginning it was mostly men but the abundance of women increased dramatically over ten years that their numbers grew to almost double their male companions. This not only brought a feminine touch to the island but also wives and children.

Even though they had partners and children back in Kuang Si Falls it was not common for men 3in their country to be without a companion for so long It didn't take very long for Kong-kea to find a mate, as he referred her to; one the other hand Somnang was very selective and fastidious so he took his time and didn't find his confidant until Kong-kea's wife was six months with child. Living in the same house, it was just as well that both women became good friends and shared their duties and responsibilities.

Their business was successful and that was not the only thing that was booming as their families increased in numbers so a decision was made to build an adjacent house on the same property. Getting labor and the ideal skill set needed the help from the local pool controlled by Chinese agents found gathered at a local watering hole. By the time Kong-kea and Somnang arrived at the premises, considerable numbers had already been engaged, seemingly there was a construction boom and the agents were taking advantage of the demand, especially from the Americans.

They ended up discussing terms with a prominent Gong with control over skilled artisans and craftsmen that they needed, however the negotiations were agonizingly tough that ended up being more expensive than they had expected. Once concluded with a finding fee up front, works would start in two days after the agent had inspected the materials and tools being supplied by the twins.

Fabrication started on time but the progress was a little slower than expected until further discussions with the agent provided a promise to improve the production, at an additional cost, of course.

Due to the sturdy design, continuous inspection by Somnang, the accomplishment was still inefficient until the foundation was complete and approved. Erection of the second-floor structure went a lot faster and without interruption and what helped was the daily service of lemon water provided by the ladies of Mei Lin, Somnang's concubine. Mei Lin would accompany her servants when the refreshments were distributed and more often than not the Gong representative Wong Chen would purposely stand in her way and try to engage in shameless conversation, avoiding response she would glide by.

They had reached the third level and the womenfolk were dispensing the late morning beverages when Wong cornered Mei Lin only this time, he chose to fondle her and although she tried to ignore him, he seemed unrelenting and would not let her pass. What he did not know was that her benefactor had taught her some defensive tactics, grabbing his wrist and turning him, she elbowed him away, losing his footing and fell to the ground. Immediately, a small gathering encircled the body as Mei Lin stood motionless, lifting her hand to her heart.

Although the third floor was no more than twenty-five feet high, Wong had landed with his back directly onto a wood beam that snapped his spine like a twig, causing immediate fatality.

Mei Lin was in shock and work came to a standstill, meanwhile a messenger was sent to summon Somnang and Kong-kea to the scene as the body was covered by a painter's cloth.

Following the commotion, finger pointing to Mei Lin by the workers as to the blame, but nobody actually saw what happened, however she confided in Somnang telling him the whole truth and events leading up to the incident. His instruction was to say nothing to anyone and confine herself to her quarters until he thought the situation out before deciding their next action.

No work was achieved that day, nor the following when in the afternoon they had a surprised visitor, Cornelius Percival Ambrose, legal advisor to the British East India Company and to the spouse of Wong Chen. He produced a written letter retaining his services to ascertain the circumstances behind the fall with the intention of seeking compensation from the property owner or owners. He left abruptly stating we would be hearing further from his office as to the next measures to be undertaken.

It was decided by both Somnang and Kong-kea no further work would be assumed on the project until they convey the events to Simon, seeking his advice, assistance and asking him for his recommendation. Details of the tragedy would be conveyed by Kong-kea's hand as soon as they were able to obtain passage on the one-hundred-mile journey up river by sampan.

Nothing immediate was forthcoming from Mr. Ambrose but he was seen speaking with a small group of contract workers from the building site and anticipated hearing from him shortly In the meanwhile, Kong-kea had returned with a Mr. Andrew Duncan Brown with precise instructions, settle for a reasonable sum without any recourse to Mei Lin. Mr. Brown, a highly educated Scotsman from Edinburgh, a formidable barrister and a specialist in litigation was relishing this contest, having some knowledge of Mr. Ambrose.

Notice to appear before a public court was issued and naval Magistrate appointed when Mr. Brown started to prepare his defense, starting with the observation and movements of both Mr. Ambrose and the Wong Chen's widow. Andrew Brown was independently busy, questioning colleagues and associates of Ambrose which bewildered the twins as to the direction of his investigation.

The day arrived and it was always Mr. Brown's intention to resolve the matter amicably, after all the accident occurred on the Chai's property and there would be no deniability on their part, it was just a question of how much. This was made clear in Andrew Brown's opening remarks with Ambrose's retort of a suffering widow, her children and a hint that the accident may not have been a misfortune at all.

The defense called only one witness, Mr. Cornelius Percival Ambrose

Both the Magistrate and Ambrose were taken aback by the summons but was allowed and complied with. Once seated and processed oath taken. Brown wasted no time in attacking Ambrose's character asking what fee he had been paid by the widow and how long had he known her. His stammered response of not very long and services undertaken voluntarily without payment led to the what Brown referred to as the death, kill.

"Be careful how your answer your next question and we have witnesses, but how long have you had a relationship with the widow inciting personal interests". Sitting very uncomfortable, Ambrose was momentarily lost for words, then requested a formal meeting between councils and the magistrate.

A sum was agreed in private chambers, satisfactory at least with Andrew Brown that left a rather disgruntled prosecutor unhappy, not for the sum, but the fact he was outsmarted, by a Scotsman no less.

That evening the relief and the triumph was celebrated through a family feast with Andrew Brown as the guest of honor and redeemer, for if not without him and his shrewdness they may have paid a higher price and loss of respectability.

During the table conversation, the issue of moving forward with the construction was raised and Mei Lin was in favor of not continuing but there remained the problem of overcrowding . I think I have the answer to that question spoke Brown. Before he could continue further the celebration was interrupted by a serving girl screaming that the foundations next door was in flames. Rising from the table they all went out to look and sure enough a destructive blaze was roaring in the wind as they stood in awe, Instructing the staff to keep an eye on the inferno and stop from spreading, they all returned to their meal, giggling when Mei Lin announced that was one problem solved.

Like he was saying before the bonfire, the accommodation could be solved, however there was a downside, said Andrew, "Somnang and his family will have to move. I have a letter of introduction to Stamford Raffles of the BEIC in Singapore and under the circumstances Simon feels it prudent and advantageous to take this potential prospect".

After much discussion, some loud, Somnang graciously accepted the appointment as the fire continued to rage and they all kept drinking and enjoying pleasant banter.

By late morning as Somnang, Kong-kea and Andrew were staring at the burnt cinders and a cleanup crew were scooping up the ashes, it was a clear message that the intended departure to Singapore be made swiftly and they all nodded in agreement.

Andrew conveyed that Simon had already written to Ruffles in anticipation of acceptance to the posting and to prepare suitable lodgings for Somnang with a large family.

Andrew had already departed for Guangzhou when Somnang, family and several selected servants boarded the Clipper. With melancholy faces, tears from both Kong-kea's family and Somnang with considerable waving as the vessel sailed into the distance.

So, the legacy of Hong Kong and Singapore Thrived for the next one hundred years.

CHAPTER 12

Melbourne to Buzios, part 2

H e awoke with eyes wide open and raised his body from the bed. He had a slight sweat which for him was normal and all he could hear was the slight drone of the Boeing 747 engines muffled by the sound resistant walls then I uttered 'lights, dim' and immediately the room became clearer but not bright.

Slipping his feet into the sheepskin slippers he stood up and stretched out his arms followed by some customary body movements. Removing the damp pajamas and putting on a toweling robe he walked to the bathroom to relief his bowels that included a large fart. After cleansing his hands and face, proceeded to the opening of the living area and continued walking until reaching the business center. The map showed the current position, speed and arrival time and Simon calculated he had slept just over 6 hours. Sitting at the desk he pressed the intercom and Mario in the kitchen responded. "Mushroom and chili omelet please Mario, English Breakfast Tea with lemon and iced water he continued", then hung up. The Service staff worked in pairs hence someone always on duty and that included flight and maintenance crews. Simon could tell most of them apart by their various accents. In the kitchen Mario was from Milan, Italy and Li Na a third-generation Chinese chef from Singapore and between them his meals were extremely varied and first class. They each had a support hand making a total of fourteen all male personnel on board, 2 Italians, two Singaporean's, 6 Latin American Crew and four Security guards, all from Laos.

It was not long before Mario arrived from the service elevator and he wheeled in the trolley and laid the table adjacent to the desk. In addition to the order there was a selection of breads, fruits, sauces and a flowered centerpiece. Mario took pride in his presentations. Pouring the freshly brewed tea, footsteps were heard from the stairs and Khammu, Simon's security lead appeared. Wearing a tightly fitting white T-shirt, dark slacks and tennis shoes, he looked every bit the part of a bodyguard, which in essence, he was. If it wasn't for the scar on his fore-head he looked every bit alike his twin brother Hmong.

Mario finished laying the table and departed before Khammu spoke. "Other than some possible bad weather an hour before reaching Santiago should be smooth all the way, he said. Security will be in position on arrival and I shall confirm everything else is in place just before we depart for Rio de Janeiro with the new Brazilian flight crew. Sounds like your usual proficiency, Simon said as a broad grin appeared on his face. We'll review the Buzios defense plan when we depart Santiago" as he started Breakfast and was alone again.

Mario's assistant Giorgio had collected the Breakfast dishes and Simon requested more water. Meanwhile he opened the briefcase and started to review dispatches on the large screen computer copied on CD-ROM's. The disks were already prioritized and read those" for your eyes only" first. Spending many hours recording notes when suddenly the cockpit announced to expect some turbulence and strap into the take-off and landing seat. Switching all the electronics off Simon moved to the chair facing the forward position and locked in the seat belt.

The bumpy ride lasted no more than 20 minutes but Simon remained seated in case of another warning and after another 20 minutes moved back to the desk and noticed the flight screen showed any early arrival time Santiago in approximately 1 hour and forty minutes. Pushing the intercom, Li Na answered, "Coffee Sir? Grinning, Simon and replied yes, and any nice pastries to be had he inquired? Naturally Li Na responded".

Landing in Santiago the Security dealt with local Immigration and Customs. Making a brief personal appearance to the senior Customs Office at the bridge gate, showing his passport, endorsed, then straight to the VIP exit and awaiting armored Jeep along with two escort vehicles.

The drive was almost 30 minutes to the Hotel and Simon remained in the Jeep whilst his team entered to check the meeting room and other safety measures. The Gentlemen from Valparaiso would not be there as they were waiting in another Hotel meeting room not suspecting a change in venue. One escort vehicle sped off to collect them only 10 minutes away.

Refreshments were organized whilst the camera setup and audio system were checked and ready. The room en-suite on the top floor was fully prepared with four screens showing different angles of the meeting room with two separate tables 4 meters apart each with an individual chair. Both Table and chairs were each on top of a three by three-meter rug.

The two men we awaited were part of an acquisition group in Latin America and had been instructed to appear to review a report on recent purchases and local partner agreements.

Both men on arrival were visibly irritated by the change of venue and were immediately ushered to the meeting room and showed their seats. Simon could tell by the looks on their faces a state of confusion was obvious.

They looked around and saw seated two large Oriental men, one at each wall on either side of them and a similar large man of alike race standing some three meters in front of them. Looking at the computer screen, Simon switched on the audio button and spoke. "I suppose you are both wondering about the theatrics the Board have created and the known reason you are here? It is not to commend you as indicated before your travel but to obtain answers to some disturbing evidence of your actions". Simon paused for fifteen seconds to observe their facial expressions and body movement as they saw him on the screen for the very first time. They were speechless and Simon continued.

For the next twenty minutes Simon described in detail how they forged documents to reflect seven hundred and seventy-five million US Dollars spend when only five hundred and seventy-five had been expended on acquisitions. "Finally, he said, some of the business partners you have chosen in these ventures are dubious at best and do not fit the caliber of our world organization excellence. Normally, he continued, I would not get personally involved but wanted to see for myself the faces of treachery and deceit. You were both rewarded well, are millionaires in your own right but you were driven by power and greed. As he took a few moments to look at their fear and hatred in their faces then said "I am done"

As soon as Simon's last words were spoken, Hmong who was standing in front of the seated fraudsters moved swiftly forward removing his pistol from his shoulder holster shooting them both in the neck with poisonous darts with extreme accuracy. The Security men sitting by the walls moved with similar speed towards the now lifeless corpses, removing them from their seats, pushing the tables away and placing the bodies on the ends of the rugs than rolling them up inside. Lifting the carpets over their shoulder they briskly walked out of the meeting room.

It didn't take but a few hours to dismantle the equipment, the Hotel Management were paid well and the bodies would be disposed of in an airplane accident. Already plans were in the works to change their misdeeds.

In the air once again for the 4-hour flight to Rio de Janeiro, spending the time reading more business news and enjoying good expresso with on-board made apple doughnuts. Arriving in the VIP hanger Galeao International Airport, officials were waiting to process our passports. The whole procedure took no more than 15 minutes and the security team escorted Simon into the first of two black Lincoln estate vehicles for the two-and-a-half-hour journey to Armacao Dos Buzios. Simon slumbered some of the way and arrived at the 15-bedroom, 11-bathroom retreat in good time. The house servants had arrived a week earlier to clean and stock the Mansion as it had not any visitors for some years. Some House guests had arrived from the USA who were Financial Advisers and Planning Committee for the Americas with meetings set in place starting the next day. The evening schedule was to bath in the sunken pool with a young petite masseuse and soak further in the delightful pleasures of the flesh.

Simon awoke feeling absolutely fresh, alert and his companion was gone. Even though, his body odor smelt strongly of her and needed to shower. Decided otherwise, slipped on his robe, returned to the bedroom where a table was prepared for Breakfast and his Chef was standing by. "What would be your pleasure this morning, he said? With a grin, Simon looked directly at his face and replied, three eggs over easy, mushrooms, new potatoes, a fresh fruit plate and a crème de Papaya. To drink? He asked. Tea with lemon and plenty of iced water".

As he departed, Simon sat at the table and observed a folder had been left. On opening there was a photograph of a young man and the name that appeared at the bottom was Alexei Stepan.

CHAPTER 13

What was given to Me

Sitting under the spacious pavilion, sipping a vodka martini, staring out at the immense Atlantic Ocean I pondered on the vast number of decisions I had made. Had I the right to decide so many people's fates, controlling their destinies, the taking of life, sometimes in the most gruesome of ways to obtain answers. It has been incomprehensible and amazing how I manage to control all my thoughts, maintain the knowledge and sustain this complicated life.

All through time, in the name of Religion and Government man has molded history by his actions and for the most part through power, greed, possession, dominance, control, desire, selfishness, egotism, vanity, arrogance, narcissism or just plain evil.

Those who tried to make a difference through righteousness, kindness, honesty, ethics, morals, integrity were few and often suffered the fate at the hands of the corrupt, perverted and fraudulent because they were afraid of virtues they did not understand.

I have had many names, identities, sired numerous blood lines and owner of vast organizations worldwide but I sat at the head of none. Some of the recognized Principal Presidents were controlled by generations of families while others were appointed by committee. Once in place, only then were they introduced to certain secrets and a personal Secretary not of their choosing. They represented an independent organization, a watchdog corporation, who, in turn reported to an information institute that issued daily reports through a satellite system.

Everything was functioning as perfect as I could expect it, surrounded by intelligent, loyal operatives and in many ways, needed little attention from me.

The nightmares persisted and the true fact is, I was weary, being unsure of my path forward.

The sound of footsteps quickly cleared my scattered thoughts and I turned to greet my guest.

Hello Alexei, We have never met, but you know who I am. My name is Simon and I have been observing you and your family longer than you know. Shaking my hand firmly, "it is truly an honor to meet you", sir, he replied.

"Please, sit", I said solemnly.

"Do you believe in miracles, unexplained phenomena"? I continued.

"I really do not know replied Alexei; I've never given the subject any real thought".

Pausing for a moment, I then spoke firmly and slowly," Listen to me carefully as what I am about to tell you will transform your perception of life for evermore".

Into the mild evening, savoring on fruits of the sea and consuming much of my favorite wine, Alexei had countless questions, and I answers or explanations best given, yet, I could see disbelief in his eyes, nonetheless, he remained exhilarated and attentive.

I asked myself; Is he to be the one? Do I have the right? Can you guide me Yethuda?

For many more unrelenting hours through the stargazed night the unconditional bond of friendship was founded and I was fully aware, Alexei felt the same.

With the daylight hours approaching I finally grasped the courage to ask the young man before me; "Tell me Alexei, do you trust me"? A shiver passed through my spine and thoughts raced back in time, remembering so long ago that day on the hill,

As I was touched, I touch thee.

A new beginning, or is it?